W9-ARB-514

Havana Run

Also By Lee Standiford

FICTION

Spill

Done Deal

Raw Deal

Deal to Die For

Deal on Ice

Presidential Deal

Black Mountain

Deal with the Dead

Bone Key

NON-FICTION

Last Train to Paradise

G. P. Putnam's Sons

New York

Havana Run

Les Standiford

This is a work of fiction. Names, characters, places, and incidents either are the product of the author's imagination or are used fictitiously, and any resemblance to actual persons, living or dead, business establishments, events, or locales is entirely coincidental.

G. P. Putnam's Sons
Publishers Since 1838
a member of
Penguin Group (USA) Inc.
375 Hudson Street
New York, NY 10014

Published simultaneously in Canada

Library of Congress Cataloging-in-Publication Data

Standiford, Les.
Havana run / Les Standiford.
p. cm.
ISBN 0-399-15059-5
1. Deal, John (Fictitious character)—Fiction.
2. Havana (Cuba)—Fiction. 3. Contractors—Fiction.
4. Florida—Fiction. I. Title.
PS3569.T331528H3 2003 2002037021
813'.54—dc21

Printed in the United States of America
10 9 8 7 6 5 4 3 2 1

This book is printed on acid-free paper. ♾

Book design by Amanda Dewey

Acknowledgments

Many thanks are due a number of individuals who were of great assistance in the preparation of this manuscript, including:

Tom Miller, who not only made my travels in Cuba possible but kept me on course as well;

Mitchell Kaplan, travel companion par excellence;

Antolin Cavbonell, who told me where to look;

Captain Joseph Feheley of the United States Air Force;

Captain Scott Hardeman of the Conch Naval Reserve;

Chief of Police of the City of Miami Beach, Ray Martinez;

Surveillance Expert Jim Milford of IPSA International;

Rhoda Kurzweil and William Beesting, my eagle-eyed readers;

Claudia Lightfoot, whose *Cuba: A Companion* is a treasure trove.

And as usual, my special thanks and my love to Kimberly, Jeremy, Hannah and Zander. Your understanding and your support mean everything.

This book is dedicated to the people of Cuba.
May the country one day be yours.

And to Ferdie Pachero, fine physician,
fight doctor, writer, friend.

No one dies for nothing.

ERNEST HEMINGWAY

1.

Near Havana, Cuba

Midnight in Havana, the glow of the ancient city's lights curving above the distant horizon like some pale, enormous moon. Not as grand a glow as might have been cast in the days before the revolution, perhaps, but burning bright enough, even at this late hour. Beneath that curving halo to the east lay the still-busy streets of the Old City, sunburned Euro-tourists jostling from bar to bar along the cobblestones, past the sweet-smiling hookers and the rum- and cigar-hustling touts, all of them converged in a place you might mistake for some new-world Florence—when the lights were low, that is.

Saturday night in Habana Vieja, the old man thought, a person might have a couple of *mojitos* and forget the revolution had ever come.

Here, on the outskirts of Miramar, the fortunate suburb that had somehow managed to survive through everything, all was relatively dark and still, except for the idle clanking of halyards in the nearby marina and some faint *son* music drifting from the *paladar* on the far side of the harbor.

Was it a sinking moon or rising? the old man found himself wondering as he glanced at his watch, a good omen for his voyage or bad? In any case, his last view of the city, and who knew for how long.

"It is a good night," the Cuban beside him said, as a listless breeze picked up, then fell away again. It was late summer, hurricane season in fact, but the air lay heavy and the seas were calm.

The old man shook his head. "It's never a good night to leave Havana."

It brought a pause. "True," the Cuban said finally. "But the winds are in your favor. And you will be back."

"So you say," the old man told him. He wished they could stroll along the harbor's edge to the restaurant where colorful lanterns winked, join the late-night revelers for whatever catch might be on the menu and one or three icy Hatueys while the mournful music played.

"I am sorry," the Cuban said.

"It's not your fault." The old man shrugged and bent to pick up the valise he'd brought with him from the car that sat nearby. "One day El Presidente is your friend, the next day he's not."

He paused and glanced again at the car. "I've had a good run here," he said. "I'm surprised it's lasted this long, tell you the truth."

"The changes are coming to our country," the Cuban said.

"Everyone knows it, even El Presidente himself. He grows older, his fears cloud his reason. The faces of his friends appear as enemies . . ."

"Hell, he's right not to trust me," the old man said. "Nothing wrong with his judgment at all."

The Cuban laughed softly and reached out a hand. "We will meet again, my friend."

"I sure as hell hope so."

The Cuban pointed toward the nearby dock, one used ordinarily for equipment storage, the last slip in a distant corner of the harbor, where a lone cabin cruiser was tied, bobbing in the gentle swells. The boat would have slipped in just after dark, attracting little attention in this marina where even Americans might dock, if they were content not to make a show of themselves.

"The crew is Bahamian," the Cuban said at his side. "They know the out-island passages there well. We have worked with these men before, all of them. They are to be trusted. In any case, Rogelio will be with you."

The old man nodded, glancing at the broad-shouldered silhouette looming near the front of the car. He'd seen what Rogelio could do to Russian-trained mercenaries and a few of El Presidente's handpicked thugs. A crew of Bahamian boatmen hardly seemed a threat. Besides, they were being well paid for his safe passage to their country. He had little fear for his safety.

"You will be safe in Andros for as long as you wish," the Cuban said. "No one else here knows where you are going. And arrangements are in place for your transfer to Madrid. Or to Buenos Aires, if you prefer. Whenever you are ready . . ."

"How about Key West?" the old man asked. "A room at the Casa Marina and my old table at Sloppy's."

It brought another laugh from the Cuban, but there was a nervous hitch in the sound. Far less chance of such a visit than a stroll along the bay to a *paladar.* Not in this life, anyway.

"Hell, don't mind me," he said, clapping the Cuban on the shoulder. "Why don't we just get saddled up?"

The Cuban turned and gestured to Rogelio, who moved to a rear door of the car, one of the ubiquitous Fiats that were gradually replacing the equally ubiquitous Russian Ladas on the island, though this Fiat was an uncharacteristically larger model. The door swung open and the young woman stepped out and came to embrace him, bringing with her the scent of lime and hyacinth, and a flood of memories that weakened him at his knees.

"I will miss you so," she said, wrapping her arms tightly about his neck.

"You'll come and visit," he told her, returning her tight embrace.

She didn't bother to reply. After a moment, she released her hold and stood back to regard him in silence.

"You're every bit as beautiful as your mother," he told her.

"I wish she could be here," she told him.

He felt another jolt at the back of his knees. He would have to move soon, or Rogelio would be carrying him down the dock. "Probably just as well she isn't," he said.

"You will return," she said, reaching to touch his hand.

"People keep saying that," he said. He would not have chosen to come to Cuba those many years before, all things being equal. But he had come to love it, despite the impossible politics, despite the many hardships. It was the most beautiful place he knew. And he had come to love those who lived here, as well.

He paused, fighting to keep the quaver from his voice. "You take care, now. I'd tell you to stay out of trouble, but that would be a waste of breath." She and the Cuban and the others who were with them had a cause, and those who believed in a cause were destined for trouble. As for himself, he was too old for causes, but he had come to love some of those who had them, and that was why he would have to leave.

She smiled, and he raised his hand to brush her cheek, then turned and started down the dock toward the boat. He heard the car door close behind him and Rogelio's heavy tread following along the boards of the dock. He heard the car motor start, die, then grind uncertainly to life again. He fought the urge to turn and wave . . . dark after all, he could get away with it, who the hell would even see . . .

. . . and that is when the first shot exploded, and he felt the splatter of wetness hot and sharp across the back of his neck.

He spun about as the shot echoed, to see Rogelio tottering at the edge of the dock, one hand thrown to his bloody face, another waving in the air, clutching for support. He lunged for the big man as another shot rang out, and another, two heavy thuds at Rogelio's back, and the big man went over into the water with a splash.

He heard the sounds of footsteps running toward him from the far end of the dock—men who'd been hidden there among the pilings and the hawser coils, he realized—and then the engines of the cabin cruiser were coughing to life, Bahamian crewmen fore and aft shouting alarm and scrambling to cast their lines free. Other men were coming from the direction of land, knifing between him and the Cuban, who was running toward the car.

Someone on the boat was shouting at him, *Come now, come on now,* a voice cut off by a roar of automatic gunfire and ending in a scream.

He ducked behind one of the dock pilings for cover, groping inside the valise for his pistol. The steel of the pistol was cold and slippery, and heavier in his hand than it had ever seemed, and for a moment he thought that he might be caught in some terrible dream.

But the gunfire and the cries and the roaring motors and the biting odor of cordite that stung his nostrils came from no dream. In the next moment he had the pistol out and his hand was braced against the piling, and he was squeezing off round after round toward the vague shapes that advanced from the end of the cluttered pier.

He heard a groan and saw someone fall, heard the shouts of others now diving for cover. He heard popping sounds from the boat and realized that someone there had joined the firefight as well. Just pray they didn't mistake him for the enemy, he thought.

He glanced in the direction of the car and saw the Cuban clawing at the door. The Cuban was not armed. He never was.

"Get her out of here," the old man cried. He sent shots toward the figures that advanced along the shoreline. "Get out now."

He heard the Fiat's engine catch hold finally and the sound of its tires tearing at the pavement. A man rose from the shadows to order the car to a halt, a rifle poised as if to fire. The car's bumper broke him at the knees, hurling him skyward, the rifle exploding aimlessly as he flew.

The boat was swinging away from the dock now, its engines maxed, the water at the pilings churning to a froth. He heard footsteps nearing in the darkness and turned to fire, but there came nothing but dull clicks from his pistol. He rose up and swung, clubbing steel into the face of the man who was lunging toward him.

He felt hands clutch him briefly, then slide away. He was running toward the boat now, could still make it with a mighty leap. He saw a crewman poised at the rail with his hands outstretched like the hobo in some train scene from an old movie, ready to pull his desperate pal on board.

Come on, old man, you can do it. One last burst of speed . . .

And he might have made it, might have managed that terrific leap, except for the blinding flash that came, turning the darkness into a sudden negative of itself. Instead of leaping toward the boat, then, he was hurtling backwards, flung by a wave of heat and light that had once been the particles of a boat and its crew, now transformed into a roaring fireball, and just as suddenly it was nothing at all.

"¿Adonde?" the man with the automatic rifle asked, staring down through the still-swirling smoke at the motionless form at his feet. *Where do we take him?*

What was left of the cabin cruiser still smoldered nearby, a few spars jutting at an angle from the shallow marina waters. Though anyone nearby would have heard the shots or witnessed the explosion, there was little sign of it. Only the music from the *paladar* was silenced, and the lights of Havana still burned in the distance.

The armed soldier's superior, a man in a suit who carried no visible weapon, shrugged. "That depends," he said, then moved to nudge the form on the dock with the thick sole of his shoe.

There was a groan and a painful gurgling sound in response. Good, the man wearing the suit thought. It would not have gone well for them if their quarry had not survived.

The man in the suit used his heavy shoe again, then again, and finally turned to his underling with a smile. "We will take him to the Castillo Atares," he said, with a wave toward the distant city and the hilltop where their legendary headquarters was perched. "Where else do you think?"

2.

Key West, Florida, Present day

An especially bright day in the Florida Keys, the sky so blue, the nearby waters so turquoise-glassy, it seemed a crime to be doing anything that resembled work. Then again, it was his work that allowed him to be here in the first place, John Deal thought.

Were his estranged wife, Janice, around, she'd have termed it a conundrum, or something else vaguely Zen-like. But she wasn't around much these days, so Deal would settle for calling it a trade-off. Better to bust your butt in paradise than anywhere else, wasn't it? Nothing too hard to figure out about that.

"Here's a bunch of messages they said to bring down." It was Russell Straight, holding out a wad of pink memo slips in his big hand. He was practically shouting, trying to compete with the sound of a pile driver that was working the job site a dozen yards away.

"Thanks," Deal said. He palmed the memos and stuck them in the hip pocket of his khakis, his gaze on the piling that sank way too easily with every blow of the big machine smashing it into the earth. "We're headed for China with that," he called back to Russell, pointing.

Russell winced as the huge weight shot down the guidelines and slammed into the end of the girder. "That's what you get, trying to go deep on an island."

Deal nodded, but that didn't mean he agreed with the sentiment. The job site was situated on the eastern end of Key West, all right—one mile wide, four long, average elevation six feet above the surrounding Gulf and Atlantic waters—but they'd managed to set all the other support pilings for the main condo structure without a problem. It was just the last that was giving him fits.

A dozen feet below the surface, the piling had hit a pocket of sand that seemed bottomless, an ancient dune flooded over eons ago, but never dispersed before the next layer of an ever-evolving planet covered it over. They were thirty feet down now, according to the hastily painted gauge on the side of the steadily plunging beam. But there was nothing to be done but keep on going until they encountered limestone rock again. Pound and pray, he thought, something his old man might have said.

Russell waited for an upstroke of the pile driver before he spoke again. "The bookkeeper says she has to talk to you," he added.

"Then call her I shall," Deal said. He wondered vaguely where that odd phrasing had come from. It sounded to him like the ramblings of an other-era pirate. Too long down here, without the comforting press of civilization? Some form of island fever?

"Today," Russell added. There was a *ka-chung* as the hammer released and the pile driver slammed down its punctuation.

Deal glanced again at the piling. Still plunging through sand, he thought. Any minute now, there'd be voices from Peking rising up out of the hole. He glanced up into the brilliant summer sky, then back down at his watch.

"You had lunch yet?" he asked Russell.

"Never once had too much lunch," Russell said, patting his flat belly.

Deal nodded. Russell weighed two-forty and was no more than an inch or two taller than Deal's own six feet, but if there was any fat on that copper-skinned frame, you couldn't see it.

"Come on, then," Deal said. He lifted an arm to wave to the operator sitting in the air-conditioned cab of the pile driver. The man inside gave him what looked like a thumbs-up as the giant hammer slammed down again. Thumbs-up for what, Deal wondered? He turned away toward his truck then, motioning for Russell to follow.

"This is a lot better," Russell said, once they'd settled themselves at a table in the cool Pier House lounge.

Deal nodded. He felt something prodding him in the hip and reached to find the wad of memos Russell had given him earlier.

He tossed them on the table beneath his foreman's baleful gaze. "Don't you pretend I didn't give you those, now," Russell said.

Deal held up a hand in surrender, his gaze traveling over Russell's shoulder out the windows of the second-story lounge. A three-masted schooner was at anchor a hundred feet or so off the marina docks, its sails furled, its decks quiet. Deal had fleeting thoughts of Tahiti, flaming sunsets, grass skirts and flowers tumbling like snow. A dark silhouette on the central mast transformed itself as he watched, growing huge momentarily, then subsiding again.

"You ever see an osprey?" Deal asked Russell. Most of the company's work went on in Miami, but Deal had come down to Key West a year or so ago to see about this job, and now he was finding it hard to get the sand out of his shoes. He'd opened an office of DealCo in Key West, in fact, and had come to spend more and more of his time here. It had fallen to Russell to do much of the running back and forth.

"I don't get into fish," Russell said.

"It's a bird," Deal said. "Eagle of the sea. There's one right out there, perched on the mast of that ship."

Russell glanced out the window. "Looks like a crow to me," he said.

"It's bigger than a crow," Deal said. "Not to mention of a different color."

"Whatever," Russell said.

"I don't know that I've ever seen an osprey on a boat mast before," Deal said, thinking that there couldn't possibly be anyone on board. He looked at Russell. "Have you ever read *The Rime of the Ancient Mariner*? It takes up the matter of birds and boats."

"Every time I went to the prison library, they said that one was out," Russell said.

Deal nodded. "I've got a copy. I'll lend it to you."

"My stack is pretty thick right now," Russell said. He glanced toward the bar. "What's it take to get a drink around here?"

Deal raised his hand. In moments, a tall curly-haired guy with a square jaw, piercing eyes and wearing a floral-print shirt appeared from the service passage, wiping his hands on a towel. "What'll you have, Mr. Deal?"

"The usual for me," Deal said. "I'm not sure about my associate. He seems thirsty."

"We can fix that," the guy said, giving Russell his professional smile.

"Tom Selleck, meet Russell Straight," Deal said.

The bartender extended his hand. "Good to meet you. Tom is right, actually, but the Selleck part, that's just Mr. Deal's joke."

"He looks just like him, though, wouldn't you say?"

Russell looked at Selleck quizzically. "Now you mention it," he told Deal. "How about a beer, Tom?"

"You have a preference?"

"Give him a Red Stripe," Deal said. The bartender nodded and went off.

"Who's Tom Selleck?" Russell asked, watching the bartender duck into a cooler for the beer.

Deal thought about it. "Did they have television in prison, Russell?"

"Wasn't anybody like *him* on it," Russell said, glancing toward the bar. He turned back to Deal. "You know what they do to guys who say *actually* in the joint?"

"I can guess," Deal said. "Tom Selleck is an actor. He had a series a few years back. He played a private detective who lived in Hawaii."

"So you say," Russell answered. "Instead of fat and ugly like your pal Driscoll, he looks like our bartender?"

The affable Tom was back by then, with Deal's tea and a

squatty bottle of Red Stripe and a glass for Russell. "More or less," Deal said, downing half of his tea. He'd been out on the site since seven, and it had been hot even then.

Russell had a drink of his Red Stripe, then held the bottle away for inspection. His hand was so big he had to rearrange the bottle to finish reading the painted-on label. "This is from Jamaica," he said.

"So it is," Deal said.

"What are *you* drinking?" Suspicion was heavy in Russell's voice.

Deal held up his glass. "Iced tea," he said. "With Sweet'N Low." He patted his stomach.

"That's *all* you put in it?"

Deal leaned his glass toward Russell in answer.

"Sometimes you sound like you got a load on," Russell said.

"Sometimes I do," Deal said.

Russell shook his head. "Driscoll is like that," he said, after a moment.

"Like what?"

"Always wants to be the last man talking, you know?"

"I hadn't thought about it," Deal said. "But I am going to watch that about myself, from now on."

Russell had another swig of his beer. "Maybe you been spending too much time down here in the tropics. The heat cooks your brain."

"You'd be spending more of your time in Key West if Denise were still here."

Russell allowed himself a smile. "She likes Miami just fine," he said.

Deal smiled himself, thinking how the two had met in this very bar, how Russell had steadfastly denied any significant interest in the woman for so long. Whatever works, Deal thought, ignoring a little pang of wistfulness that rose and then popped like a bubble inside him.

He turned away to check the schooner again, but the osprey had disappeared. That was one of the things about Key West: Little amazements, how they come and go.

"Speaking of that fat-ass Driscoll," Russell said at his shoulder.

"What about him?" Deal said.

"He told me something interesting the other day."

Deal turned. "He's giving up his efforts to have your parole revoked?"

Russell ignored it. "He told me you used to be a cop."

"Did he, now?"

Russell ventured a laugh. "I told him he was crazy."

Deal finished his tea. He liked the tea they served here. It had a fruity, tropical undertaste that seemed to go with the setting. He'd assumed it was a house recipe. When he'd asked, Tom had informed him it was Lipton's.

"What did Driscoll say then?"

Russell looked at him more closely. "He said ask you."

"How much is riding on this, Russell?"

Russell leaned back in his chair. "I didn't say we bet."

"You didn't have to. How bad are you going to feel when you have to pay up, Russell?"

Russell narrowed his eyes. "You shitting me?"

"Driscoll told you the truth," Deal said.

"Bullshit," Russell said. "You're just going along with him."

Deal reached into his pocket, found his money clip, extracted a twenty and slid it across the table. Russell glanced down at the bill, then shoved it back. "Man," he said, shaking his head.

"Keep it," Deal said. "Call it gas money."

"Man," Russell repeated. He finished his Red Stripe, then turned to the darkened service entry, the twenty held high in his hand. "Hey, Magnum," he called. "Bring us another round."

Deal nodded as the bartender emerged and headed for the cooler. "You want to hear the whole thing, it might take two," he said to Russell. And then he began.

3.

Miami 1989

It was dusk on the way, the heat lifting up from the South Florida streets as if the lid of a giant pot had been lifted somewhere high above. Just a breeze rolling in off the steely waters of Biscayne Bay and down the concrete corridors flanking Brickell Avenue, Deal thought, but why couldn't a person imagine one of the Titans mucking about up there, past where the magic beanstalks end and some other world begins—right now, a curious, bad-news god checking what was cooking in the always boiling pot called Miami.

Crazy, sure, but your mind tends to wander, doing what he was doing. And so what if it was crazy? One person hears thunder and calls it a weather-related phenomenon. Why couldn't it just as well be the gods at tenpins?

"So, who do you like in the Super Bowl?" his partner asked.

Deal turned his gaze from out the open window of the Vic, glanced through the twilight gloom at Vernon Driscoll, who sat with both hands on the wheel, as if they were moving, as if they were headed somewhere. "It's August," Deal said. "I haven't given it a lot of thought."

Driscoll shrugged. "Time flies," he said. "Now's when you get the odds you like. Brownies and the Cowboys, that's what I'm thinking. Cowboys to cover."

"You must be bored," Deal said. So, he had giants lifting pot lids from steamy skies, Driscoll had the Super Bowl on the very opposite side of the calendar. Each to his own.

He turned his gaze back out the window. They had parked the unmarked car in the first slot on a side street off Brickell, just south of the Miami River, a stretch of the broad boulevard that had once been flanked by stately two-story homes occupied by the city's movers and shakers, now a man-made canyon with bank towers for walls looming high overhead.

As a matter of fact, Deal's old man had built the colossus catty-corner from where they sat, twenty-four stories of shiny black glass that reminded him of the obelisk in *2001: A Space Odyssey.* Awe inspiring. Mysterious. Nothing much inside.

The first two floors of the building housed the National Bank of the Caymans. The other twenty-two floors were largely unoccupied. The owners, whoever they were, must not have been concerned. Rent had held steady at $42 per square for four years, ever since the day his old man had signed off on the certificates of occupancy and gone on to the next distinguished set of clients.

"I don't get bored," Driscoll was saying. "I savor the nature of my work, even the most miserable, minutiae-ridden aspects of it, such as this."

"You have a screw loose," Deal said. There was an elevated plaza in front of the bank, with a big fountain surrounded by some black marble benches. During the day, secretaries came out to sit in the shade of the towers and eat their lunches and watch the water spritz over the bronze sculpture of Triton, who lay practically naked in the middle of the fountain. Now the plaza was empty, except for Triton, who lay back on one elbow looking just about as excited as Deal's partner.

"I do have a screw loose," Driscoll said. "Why else would I be a cop?"

"I'm a cop," Deal said, shifting his weight from one buttock to the other. He felt the nudge of a spring in the Vic's seat beneath him. How many had sat here before him, how many hours spent sitting and waiting for something to happen?

"You are a poseur," Driscoll said, his tone affable.

"The last guy told me that is still sucking soup through a straw," Deal said. He glanced down at his palms, brushing them as if there were dust there.

"There's not another person on the force who knows the meaning of the word," Driscoll said. "Besides, I didn't say you couldn't handle yourself."

Deal took his eyes off the façade of the bank building for a moment. "Why'd you let them stick me with you, anyway?"

"That's not the way it works, buddy boy. I just do what I'm told."

Deal stared at him. "My old man spread a little juice around, some of it came your way?"

Driscoll made a grunting sound deep in his throat. "He'd have to pay a hell of a lot." He examined one of his own thick hands, front and back, like maybe there was writing on one side, he'd forgotten which. "You like action, why didn't you become a fireman?"

"I thought about it," Deal said, "but my old man plays cards with the fire chief."

"He plays cards with the police chief, too," Driscoll said.

"But he doesn't like *him*," Deal said.

"You do have a screw loose," Driscoll said. "Anybody else wouldn't mind a little suck with the brass."

"Funny," Deal said. "That's exactly what my old man said when I told him I was going up for detective."

Driscoll sighed, an indication that went far beyond the shrug. "You could be building bank towers for offshore clients, knocking down some real jack, instead of sitting here trying to put them away."

Deal nodded. "Apparently this pisses some people in the department off?"

Driscoll raised an eyebrow. "It makes them think you've got a screw loose. Either that or your old man set you down here."

Deal felt heat rising up the back of his neck. Following graduation from Gainesville, he'd spent a few desultory years running from job site to job site as one of his old man's construction supervisors, marking time as an overpaid flunky, waiting to take over the reins of DealCo Construction when his old man got ready to chuck it in and move down to the Keys, sometime around the middle of the twenty-first century.

There'd been a hell of a blowup when he'd left the job, another one when he'd joined the force. His old man thought he'd lost his mind, snorted that Deal would be back, groveling for his job inside of a month.

But he'd stuck it out, spent three years on patrol, another

year and a half as assistant to the assistant chief, before he'd taken the shot at plainclothes. Schnecter, the detective they'd paired him up with after he'd aced the exam, had made the kind of insinuations Driscoll had brought up. The results had not been pretty. Deal was riding with Driscoll now, on probation, one slip away from directing daytime traffic out there on Biscayne.

"Is that what *you* think?" he said to Driscoll.

"I think you have a screw loose," Driscoll said, pointing across the seat. "You're going to pull that armrest off if you're not careful."

Deal glanced down, saw that he was clutching the Vic's door handle in a death's grip, his knuckles glowing in the gloom. He pulled his hand away, wiped his palms together, brushing away more imaginary dust.

"Your old man's okay," Driscoll went on.

"He ask you to tell me that?" Deal said.

Driscoll ignored it. "He builds things for slimeballs, that doesn't make him a bad person."

"Barton Deal, toast of the town," Deal said, his gaze steady on Triton, silhouetted against the tasteful nimbus of the façade lighting now.

"He's been Barton Deal for quite a few years, and he's still walking around on the outside," Driscoll said. "That ought to tell you something."

"Sure," Deal said. "He knows how to spread the grease."

Driscoll shook his head. Maybe he disagreed, or maybe he was simply dismayed by Deal's attitude.

"You broke in standing guard outside his card games," Deal went on.

"That was another day and time," Driscoll said. "Anyway, a guy likes to play hold 'em, that makes him a criminal? You can go buy yourself a ticket on a casino ship, right now, right over there on the river." Driscoll pointed toward the glowing lights of a ship tethered beneath the prow of a downtown hotel in the distance.

Deal glanced over. The Miami River wasn't much of a river at all these days, more of an estuarial canal that had been dredged to allow for steamship loading and unloading. There had once been a slough there draining the Everglades, back when they'd called the town Fort Dallas, after a far-flung Army post. Prehistory, by Miami standards. All of ninety-five years ago. Now it was drugs and illegal aliens stuffed in cargo containers coming up from the Caribbean, stolen automobiles and trucks and bicycles by the thousands heading back. To put a dent in that trade, they'd need the fort brought back again.

"It was a crime when it was happening," Deal said to Driscoll. "It still is, as a matter of fact."

"Well," Driscoll said, checking his watch, "it's the right night, isn't it? Maybe we ought to run on down to Casa Deal and bust him and his pals," Driscoll said. He was referring to the palatial bayside home not far from where they sat, the home where Deal had grown up, where his old man still lived and held court for the movers and shakers and favored clients of the moment, his mother in faithful if ever-more-blurry attendance.

Driscoll was warmed up now, waving a hand in the direction of the National Bank of the Caymans. "Why waste our time staking out a Dade County commissioner who's helping launder more cash than runs through Caesar's in a month of Sundays? So what if it's all to the benefit of the drug cartels and the petty dictatorships and the old Nazis still having their house parties in the jungle? We could put your old man and the fire chief in the hoosegow, make a real dent in crime down here."

Deal might have answered, but in the few weeks he'd been

riding with Driscoll he'd already learned that there wasn't much point in arguing with the man. He could point out that it was growing dark outside, a twenty-minute discussion would ensue, with no certainty about the outcome. Besides, he could grant anyone the oddity of the situation. How to explain what he'd done with his life? He wasn't sure he could explain it to himself.

"Maybe it's Freudian," he said to Driscoll. "I spent my whole life watching my old man skirt the law, I figure it's my job to make up for it somehow."

Driscoll stared back at him, a moment's disbelief flitting across his usually deadpan countenance. "You share these feelings with Schnecter, did you?"

"Schnecter thinks Freud is a boxer's first name," Deal said. He paused, taking in Driscoll's unprepossessing appearance: Sansabelt slacks straining at the gut, short-sleeved dress shirt half untucked, a slob horse player's mournful eyes and downturned lips. Never had looks been more deceiving, he thought.

Driscoll's reputation within the department was legendary, and never mind that as a young detective he'd spent time on "security" detail for various city officials. In one regard, Driscoll was right: In those days, the practice of keeping stick-up artists out of the mayor's crap game and reporters away from the cathouses he and his cohorts visited might as well have been printed in the job description.

When the chips were down, though, Driscoll was the guy you wanted at your back. He'd made his name during one of the political conventions of the late sixties, out on the Beach, tackling a crazed protester who claimed to be carrying a bomb and headed for the stage while Hubert Humphrey spoke. That action had gotten him decorated and led to assignment on a series of high-profile cases, a remarkable number of which he'd seen through successfully, including the first fall for Dagoberto Saenz, involving a complex kickback scheme connected to lucrative airport-maintenance contracts.

Two years ago, at an age when most detectives of like grade and service were safely ensconced behind desks downtown, some even retired, Driscoll had taken a bullet in the chest meant for a fellow officer who hadn't seen his assailant coming.

Most seasoned detectives would have resented Deal's presence—if nothing else, it was simply dangerous being partnered up with a rookie. But there hadn't been a hint of that from Driscoll. His Buddha-like nature seemed to accept it all. If this was a last shot, he'd drawn the best for a mentor, Deal thought, glancing at the stoic profile beside him.

"Where'd you go to college, anyway, Driscoll?"

"Is this a job interview?" Driscoll's gaze remained steady out the windshield.

"I'm just curious."

"I was home-schooled," Driscoll said. "Einstein used to come by every morning. Bugsy Siegel on the weekends."

Deal nodded. "I thought so."

Driscoll shrugged, glanced over. "I'm from West Virginia. I started Bluefield State. My folks moved down here, it took me awhile to finish up. I got a degree from FIU now, criminal justice."

"You have an interesting makeup for a Miami cop," Deal said.

"So do you," Driscoll said. "Guy joins the department dreaming one day he can bust his old man."

"That's not what I said."

Driscoll shrugged. "Same thing."

"Who's the last person won an argument with you, Driscoll?"

Driscoll thought for a moment. "Bugsy Siegel. Einstein was a pushover."

Deal nodded. How two civil servants passed their time together. Still, it was a monumental improvement over solitary traffic patrol, and Driscoll a major step up from Schnecter. "Speaking of criminal justice," he said, nodding out the open window. "Guess who's coming to dinner."

Driscoll turned to follow Deal's gaze, his hand already going for the portable radio that lay on the seat between them. A man in a good suit and carrying a briefcase was cutting across the deserted boulevard in front of them, purposeful strides carrying him in the direction of the bank:

Dagoberto Saenz. Twice indicted and thrice reelected county commissioner from the district north of Miami International, the cradle of crooked politicians in Dade County, a distinction that was saying something around these parts.

"He's crossing against the light," Deal observed. "We've got a case already."

Driscoll nodded, a rare smile tugging at the corner of his lips. "Oswald," he said, keying the radio. "You see who's on the way?"

"Roger that," came the response. Osvaldo, the techie on duty, was holed up in a tiny office on the fourth floor of the building beside them, monitoring an array of listening devices tuned to pickups secreted throughout the bank's inner sanctum. The stakeout had been operational for over a month now, but so far Saenz had proven uncanny in his ability to say nothing even the slightest bit incriminating during his visits to the executive offices.

What Deal had overheard resembled nothing so much as a slightly duller version of his own conversations with Driscoll, with the main difference being that Saenz and his cohorts tended to discuss the world of business instead of the world of sports. Who was in line for the landfill contract in South Dade? Was the free port project likely to get off the ground? Could Castro ever be convinced to trade in dollars?

"We're up and running?" Driscoll spoke into the radio, prompting another affirmative from Osvaldo.

"Loud and clear," the techie answered. "Somebody left the boardroom to go down and get the door, somebody else is mixing drinks." There was a pause before Osvaldo continued. "Sounds like *mojitos* to me."

Driscoll nodded and gave Deal what passed for a hopeful look as Dagoberto Saenz topped the steps of the plaza. A slab of dark glass swung outward as Saenz approached the building, and in moments the commissioner was inside.

"I'm going to try to patch you through," Osvaldo's voice came. "Turn off your scanner."

"It's off," Driscoll said. Deal had switched the Vic's radio off shortly after they'd parked.

"It doesn't sound like it."

"Trust me," Driscoll said. "We're silent."

"Shit," Osvaldo said. "I'm getting a lot of noise from someplace."

"Not from us," Driscoll insisted. He glanced at Deal, who checked the radio switch and shrugged.

"Hold on a second," Osvaldo's voice came again. "There. See what you get now."

There was a crackling noise from the speaker of the handheld unit, then the echoing sounds of a door closing as if at the bottom of a well.

"Commissioner," Deal heard someone say.

Driscoll gave him a smile. "Bingo," he said, in a soft voice.

"Alberto," came Saenz's response. "How good to see you. *Con mucho gusto.*"

"Yeah, yeah, yeah," Driscoll muttered. "Spill the beans, you assholes." There was a sudden burst of salsa music then, as if someone had abruptly switched the channels.

Driscoll rekeyed the radio, but the salsa music blared on. "What the hell? What's going on up there, Oswald?"

Driscoll banged the radio against his meaty hand, then gave Deal a questioning look. Deal took the unit and pressed the key himself. Frank Sinatra's voice now, "Strangers in the Night."

"Call Oswald on the cell," Driscoll said.

Deal snatched the phone from the glove compartment and punched in the number. The connection rang once before Osvaldo's voice broke in. "Don't waste your breath," the techie said in his nasally voice. "You guys are listening to the Chairman of the Board, correct?"

"That's right, Oswald. What's the trouble?"

"That's all I'm getting, too," Osvaldo said. He'd cut the feed from his listening equipment and his words now echoed over the radio Driscoll was holding. The sounds of Sinatra traced faintly in the background.

"Tell him to try the gun mike," Driscoll said. It was a device rigged to a boom that resembled a rifle stock. You pointed it at a window a hundred yards away and the thing could read the vibrations of someone talking in a room on the other side.

"Tell him I already did," Osvaldo said. "They must have pulled the curtains in the boardroom."

"Sonofabitch," Driscoll said, swinging his gaze toward the bank's façade. "Fucking bastards."

"They're on to us, then," Deal spoke into the phone. "They're jamming the equipment."

"We can't be sure," Osvaldo said. "Let me get to work up here." The phone connection broke. The sounds of Sinatra carried on over the handheld radio.

"They've probably known the place was bugged the whole damn time," Driscoll said, pounding the wheel with the heel of his palm. "No wonder Saenz has been so tight-lipped all along." He keyed off the radio and tossed it on the seat in disgust. "Now they're having fun. Frank Sinatra my ass."

Deal glanced at the building, a shaft of darkness deeper than the night sky. "Why do that, though?" he said. "Why go to the trouble?"

Driscoll shook his head. "Because they're assholes."

Deal gave him a look. "Or because they've finally got something to say to each other and they don't want to take any chances somebody overhears."

Driscoll shrugged. "Either way, we're screwed."

They sat in silence then, both of them staring across the broad avenue. Deal imagined Dagoberto Saenz inside the building with a glass raised to his partners in crime, some clever phrase passing his lips. He'd heard the man often enough on the evening news, never at a loss for words, nearly as good with the *bon mot* as Deal's old man. Get indicted often enough, he thought, maybe you learn to master the sound bite.

He was about to turn to share this observation with Driscoll when there was movement at the façade of the bank building again. The double doors swung open wide, and Saenz reappeared, moving quickly back across the plaza, his briefcase at his side.

"You see that?" Deal said, watching Saenz descend the steps.

"Yeah," Driscoll said. "It's a turd wearing a three-piece suit. Somebody call the *Herald*."

"Look how he's holding his briefcase," Deal said, pointing. "He was swinging it every which way when he went inside."

Driscoll gave him a look, then turned to stare at Saenz who stood at the curb now, waiting for the light to change. The case was in his right hand, his shoulder clearly drooping toward the ground.

"Looks like he's carrying lead all right," Driscoll said mildly.

"They loaded him down good, is what happened," Deal said, pointing. "He's carrying so much loot, he's afraid to cross the goddamned street."

"You could be right," Driscoll said.

"We could pop him," Deal said.

"We could, indeed," Driscoll said.

"But we won't."

"Right again."

Deal sighed, leaning back in his seat. "Because maybe all he's got in that case is twenty pounds of contracts, or half a dozen copies of the Cayman Island Yellow Pages. We'd blow a month-long undercover operation and end up with major egg on our faces."

"Give the boy a gold star," Driscoll said.

"We could run him over," Deal said, as Saenz finally stepped from the curb and into the crosswalk, "claim it was an accident."

"But he's waiting for the light this time," Driscoll said.

"That's a technicality," Deal said.

"Technicalities," Driscoll repeated. "That's what makes lawyers rich."

Deal laughed, though his heart wasn't in it. "How much you figure he's carrying?"

"A fucking lot," Driscoll said.

"Sonofabitch," Deal said.

"You're learning," Driscoll said. By then, Saenz was out of sight.

"Don't you feel the least bit like a stereotype?" Deal asked. They were still sitting in the Vic, outside a Krispy Kreme shop out on Seventh Avenue now, an Anglo holdout in what had largely become a Latin neighborhood over the last fourty years. Driscoll seemed to know every such outpost in the county. Ride around with him long enough, Deal thought, you might think Castro had never happened, Little Havana was just a myth.

Driscoll popped the rest of his doughnut into his mouth and brushed powdered sugar off his shirtfront. "I'm no stereotype," he said, swallowing. "You'll note I paid for my doughnut."

Deal nodded. "Thanks for the coffee," he said, raising the Styrofoam cup.

Driscoll waved it away. "I gave up coffee myself," he said.

"Was this some health issue?"

"Issue of stakeouts," Driscoll said, shaking his head. "I just got tired of peeing in a cup."

"That's an attractive thought," Deal said, glancing at his coffee.

"That's reality," Driscoll said, before his gaze turned suddenly intent. He was pointing at the radio, Deal realized. "Turn that thing up, will you?"

Deal glanced at him, then reached for the dial. ". . . Shots fired," the dispatcher's voice was saying. "Repeat, three-three-two at twelve-fourteen Bayview Drive. All units that can clear proceed to one-two-one-four Bayview Drive . . ."

Deal stared dumbly at the radio for a moment, feeling the same kind of numbness as when you hear your name called over a loudspeaker or you pick up the phone to find someone there even though you haven't dialed and there hasn't been a ring.

He turned to say something—he wasn't sure what—but Driscoll already had the Vic in gear, his foot mashing the gas pedal. "Hold on to that," he said, nodding at the coffee in Deal's hand.

"Right," Deal said, his mind still whirling. He tossed the coffee out the window as the Vic's tires squalled in a backward power slide. They were out onto Seventh Avenue now, still sliding backward as Driscoll yanked the shift into drive. The heavy car shuddered, then its tires shrieked again as the big V-8 kicked in, Deal back in action, slapping the magnetic blue flasher onto the Vic's roof without any prompting from Driscoll.

Half a block west in seconds, then a screaming left, and then another, and then they were powersliding out in front of the advancing traffic on Southwest Eighth Street, what passed for the Via Veneto or the Champs-Élysées where Little Havana was concerned, headed back in the direction from which they'd come, on their way to that impossible address, on their way to Casa Deal.

Driscoll held the pace at redline all thirty blocks back to Biscayne and another quarter mile southward down the boulevard, but eased off once they'd swung off onto the curving lane that flanked the bay. The distant end of the oak-shrouded street was alive with flashing cruisers, what seemed like half the force gathered in the few minutes it had taken them to arrive.

Deal was out of the Vic before Driscoll had fully stopped, the door slamming shut behind him and the older detective's "Easy now."

He was past the first phalanx of uniformed officers in seconds, his shield held high, and past the pair at the gated entrance ready to stop him, shield or not, when an older cop he recognized vaguely pulled his partner aside at Deal's brusque command.

"This is my old man's house. Get the hell out of the way."

The hallway in front of him led to a vast, high-domed and drafty room that was rarely used, except for the most formal occasions. His mother liked to tell visitors that Paul Whiteman's orchestra had once played there in the twenties, for the former owners, of course. His old man liked to add that Al Capone had been among the guests the night it happened. The things that made his parents happy, Deal thought, striding hard down the marble corridor.

His mother sat now on a Louis XVI love seat in a distant corner of the room, her forehead propped on her hand, a female officer at her side. A pair of detectives conferred nearby, one with a pad in his hand.

One of the men turned at Deal's approach, then relaxed at something his partner said. Deal realized that something had happened to his hearing. He was vaguely aware of words being spoken, but the sounds seemed odd and dissonant, washed over and distorted by a roar that was growing steadily inside his head. It had been growing since he'd heard the address crackling over the Vic's radio, he realized, growing louder with everything he'd seen and sensed since then.

His mother's gaze was teary and unfocused when she raised her head at his approach. Blasted out of her gourd, he saw, but nothing unusual about that. Behind the blur of alcohol, her game good-hostess gaze was gone, replaced by one of utter desolation. She put her hands out for him, but standing would have required something far beyond what she had left. The lady cop beside her seemed almost as distraught, Deal noted. The roar inside his head kicked up another notch.

"Where is he?" Deal said. He could barely hear his own voice. His mother's hands were still stretched toward him. Trembling, he noticed. Her son come home at last. "What's happened?" he said. The back of his hand brushed her weathered cheek.

She rocked backward, running her tongue over her lips. She reached one hand toward him, used the other to point. He saw her lips move, but whatever she said didn't really matter. He was already on his way to the study.

One of the detectives put out a hand to stop him, but Deal shook it off. There might have been footsteps following in his wake, but it was impossible to tell. It didn't matter. One man or two. It would have taken more than that.

A dozen paces down the hallway to the left, a dark corridor with rarely used guest quarters on either side, toward the open, glowing doorway ahead. He saw Ernie Martinez, an assistant M.E., standing inside the room mopping his brow with a handkerchief. The flash of a photographer's strobe ricocheted down the hall.

Martinez saw Deal coming and pointed. A uniformed cop met him at the doorway, but the guy was a step slow and thirty pounds too light. When the backpedaling cop hit Martinez, they both went down.

The two detectives from the Paul Whiteman room had caught up by then, each latching on to one of his arms. They couldn't have held him, though, not if he hadn't allowed it.

He didn't fight them, though, just held his ground, long

enough to see what he'd been expecting to see for a good long time now. What was left of his old man was sprawled in the big leather swivel chair behind the desk he'd bought in Cuba, though you'd have to recognize the blood-spattered, custom-made guayabera and the linen trousers he favored to realize who had been sitting there. The shotgun that had etched the particles that had once been his face and the top of his head up the side of the plastered wall and into the ceiling above lay across the desk where the recoil had sent it. Was the roar inside Deal's head even the tiniest fraction of what his old man had heard before the lights went out?

"Get him out," he heard someone say. "Get him the fuck out of here."

Not two men, not a dozen, he thought. The trouble's just beginning . . . but then he saw Driscoll's face in front of his, saw the big man's arms come his way.

"Let him go," he heard as Driscoll pulled him close. "Come on, Johnny-boy, you come with me."

"Funny thing about that desk," Deal said to Driscoll, who sat in a chair across the long mahogany table in the formal dining room.

An hour or so had passed. He'd helped get his mother into their longtime housekeeper's car, the two women headed now for the Grand Bay Hotel where there was the hope of some rest and, at the very least, a twenty-four-hour bar, courtesy of room service. During and after, there'd been a parade of department brass in and out of the house, but Deal had kept away from it. Maybe his father's corpse was still slumped in his favorite chair in that blood-splattered room; maybe it wasn't.

"What about the desk?" Driscoll said. He'd poured them each a drink from a decanter on a sideboard. He'd poured a couple of drinks in fact. Maybe his mother had the right idea after all, Deal thought, swirling what was left in his glass.

"The guy who owned it was a Cuban named Chibas, Eddy Chibas."

"That's funny?"

"He was a politician, the last honest politician in Cuba according to my old man. This was back in the forties. He was a real pain in the ass for Batista, but it wasn't going anywhere for him."

"You're right, it's a real scream," Driscoll said.

"I'm getting there," Deal said. "Anyway, this Chibas is so down and out about how things are going, he arranges a radio interview in his office there in Havana, where he lays out his case against the Batista government point by point, and when he's finished, right in front of the interviewer, mind you, he reaches into the drawer of his desk—that desk—and he pulls out a pistol and blows his brains out, right on the air."

Driscoll finished his drink, reached back for the decanter and poured another. "For a minute there, I thought you'd never get to the punchline," he said.

"What my old man found so funny," Deal continued. "Chibas couldn't even kill himself right. He went on so long with his speech, the station had cut away to a commercial. He shoots himself, my old man liked to say, while 'the Cuban people are hearing about "a spic and a span."' " Deal found himself shrugging in a way that Driscoll favored. "Everybody read about what happened, of course, but it wasn't exactly the drama that Eddy had in mind."

"I guess not," Driscoll said. He glanced up at Deal. "Your old man had a strange sense of humor."

"He bought the desk for a song," Deal said. "I think that's what he liked as much as anything. Brought it back on his own boat."

"I never heard that story," Driscoll said.

"Well, he had a million of them," Deal said.

Driscoll nodded. He had another sip of his drink, seeming to ponder something. "You have any idea why he did it?"

Deal looked at him. "You being a detective?"

Driscoll stared back. "I was just asking. You don't have to talk about it."

"I'm surprised it didn't happen sooner, that's all."

"You sure he was as upset with the way his life was going as you seem to be?"

Deal thought about it. "I'd say the facts speak for themselves."

"Maybe there were some health problems. . . . "

"My mother would have known, I'd have heard about it."

"You sure?"

"Reasonably."

"How about his finances?"

Deal raised an eyebrow. "You see any signs of poverty around here?" Deal tossed the rest of his drink back. "Look, Driscoll, when it comes right down to it, there isn't any logical reason to kill yourself, and the only guy who really knows won't be talking."

Driscoll dropped his eyes at that. He seemed about to respond when his gaze caught something over Deal's shoulder. "Hold on," he said, pushing himself up quickly from the heavy table.

Deal turned in his chair, his eyes widening at the unmistakable form in the doorway. A tall, angular-featured plainclothesman with a white-sidewall haircut from the sixties cut him a disdainful stare, the same expression Deal had knocked sideways a few weeks before. "Schnecter . . ." he said in disbelief, starting out of his chair.

Driscoll's heavy hand was on his shoulder in an instant, shoving him back in his seat. "I'll take care of it," he said.

Deal tried to shrug him off, but Driscoll's grip was unyielding. "I said sit down."

Schnecter looked away, stepping backward into the gloom of the hallway. Deal felt himself give. Driscoll shot him a last meaningful stare, then moved out into the shadows after the detective.

Deal heard murmurs passing back and forth, then Driscoll's "The hell you say." There was something else from Schnecter, then silence. After a moment, Driscoll came back into the room, his face solemn.

"What?" Deal said. As if anything could top what had happened so far. "My mother . . ." he began.

Driscoll cut him off with a shake of his head. "It's not about your mother," the big man said. He paused for a minute, cutting his gaze back toward the departed Schnecter. "They found some stuff in that hilarious desk you were telling me about, John . . ."

Deal stared, trying to read a sudden stiffness in Driscoll's posture. "What kind of stuff?"

Driscoll glanced toward the ceiling, clearly uncomfortable. "I can't get into it with you." When his gaze came back to Deal, there seemed a hint of pain in his eyes. "The captain needs to see you, John. This isn't good."

"What are you talking about . . .?"

Driscoll held up his meaty hand as if he were directing traffic. There were footsteps in the hallway again, several men this time.

"John Deal?" asked the first plainclothesman through the door. No one Deal knew, but he could guess what division the guy worked.

Deal nodded, and the detective displayed his shield. "Stoneleigh. Internal Affairs. I need you to come with me."

Deal glanced over his shoulder at the two burly uniformed cops who stood blocking the doorway. He turned to Driscoll, who held up his hands in a gesture of helplessness. "I'm sure it's all bullshit, John, but you gotta go with the man."

"I'll need your piece," Stoneleigh said.

Deal turned to stare in astonishment. "What the hell? What is this about?"

"Right now, it's about your piece," Stoneleigh said. "The rest of it you can take up with the captain."

Deal gave one last glance at Driscoll, but the veteran detective had his face turned away. Deal pulled open the flaps of his jacket then and felt Stoneleigh's practiced hand lighten his holster.

"It's a terrible thing, John," William Garrity said, as he ushered Deal toward a chair in his office. Garrity, a gravel-voiced Irishman who'd been around the department even longer than Driscoll, looked like he'd been called up straight from central casting. A pair of piercing blue eyes, steely hair swept back from a commanding brow, a way of moving that dominated the space—and usually the people—around him. He'd been chief of detectives for what seemed forever, turning his back on more than one offer to move on up the line. "Barton Deal was one hell of a man," Garrity added.

Deal nodded but didn't say anything. There was a certain resemblance between Garrity and his father, it occurred to him. Another larger-than-life dinosaur. It wasn't awe or disdain that kept him quiet, however. Just the feeling he was part of a play that was headed toward a scripted finish, no matter what lines he used.

Garrity gave him a clap on the shoulder, then turned to Stoneleigh, who'd stopped just inside the doorway, his two grim-faced yard dogs right behind. "We'll be fine, Detective. Just close the door on your way out."

Stoneleigh showed no surprise. He nodded and was gone in an instant. "Sit down," Garrity said, pointing to a tufted leather chair flanked by a side table with a reading lamp. In other circumstances, it might have sounded like an invitation.

It was a cozy enough place, Deal noted as he sat. Wood paneling, bookcases, plaques and trophies and manly bric-a-brac scattered about. You might take it for a reading room in a gentleman's club. The sixth-floor corner windows provided an impressive view of the Freedom Tower illuminated in the distance, a soaring neo-Renaissance relic on the bay front that had once housed the offices of the *Miami News,* then had later become a processing center for Cuban refugees. An émigré builder had refurbished the building and was angling for tenants with a sense of history. Garrity must have liked the view. He'd held the office long enough.

Garrity waited for Deal to settle himself, then perched himself on the corner of his desk. He pursed his lips thoughtfully, as if unsure how to begin.

"I knew your father well, John. He had a certain reputation, but I think that had more to do with some of the people he associated with than anything he did himself . . ."

"Big dogs draw lots of fleas," Deal said.

It stopped Garrity momentarily. "That's one way of putting it . . ." He cleared his throat and glanced at a manila folder that lay on the desk beside him. "Do you have any idea why you're here, John?"

"Not the slightest," Deal said.

Garrity nodded, fixing him with the same gaze he must have used on several thousand suspects in a forty-year-plus career. "From the moment you joined the department, there was talk—your father being who he was and all—then once you made detective, it only heated up . . ."

"Captain . . . "

"Let me finish," Garrity said. "You're here right now because your old man was a friend of mine. I never paid any attention to that kind of tongue wagging. In my estimation, Barton Deal was stand-up all the way. When I heard about what happened between you and Schnecter, that didn't bother me either. But John . . ." He broke off, then turned to pick up the folder beside him. "What the hell am I supposed to do about *this*?"

"What is it?" Deal said.

Instead of answering, Garrity tossed the thick folder to him, his gaze one of challenge. "It's hard for me to look at what's in that folder, John. Hard for me to believe you'd compromise the department that way, even harder for me to accept your old man would put you in such a position."

Deal stared at Garrity, thoughts forming and reforming in his mind quicker than he could possess any one of them. "I don't know what on earth you're talking about, Captain, but I can tell you . . ."

Garrity shook his head. "These documents were found in your father's files. It's all there, John. Reports in your handwriting, notes from your old man, financial transactions in payment for your services . . ."

Deal turned to the folder, flipped it open, saw a copy of one of the transcripts he'd signed off on: Dagoberto Saenz in conversation with officials of the National Bank of the Caymans. Beneath it was a note in his father's unmistakable hand dated a month before. "Johnny-boy," it began. The man hadn't written Deal so much as a Christmas card in the last five years. Deal glanced back at Garrity in disbelief. "This is all bullshit. I don't know who's responsible. . . ."

"Listen to me," Garrity broke in, his face darkening. He cut a glance at the doorway of his office and pushed himself away from his desk, looming directly over Deal now. "I don't want to hear it. I don't want to know about it. In fact, I do not give a good goddamn. I brought you in here for one reason and one reason only."

He snatched the folder from Deal's hand and shook it in his face. "I can make this go away," he said. "I will make it go away, in fact. But you are going to go away with it."

Deal stared, uncomprehending.

"You can stay and fight this, John, but you'll go down, trust me."

"You're asking me to resign?"

"The chief was no friend of your father's. He won't stop at driving you off the force. What's in this folder will send you to prison."

"What's in that folder is bullshit."

Garrity seemed not to have heard. "You're not the only one who stands to lose."

Deal hesitated, an iciness sweeping over him. "You'd go after Driscoll, too?"

"I wouldn't go after anyone. But you're not listening to me. No one wants a scandal. You don't want your mother dragged into court. Listen to reason, John."

Deal rose, swatting with the back of his hand the folder Garrity held. "Did Schnecter cook this up? Whose idea was this?"

Garrity took a step backward. "You can save all that, John. This room is clean. No one's listening. For the sake of your father, I'm imploring you . . ."

The broad windows at Garrity's back seemed to beckon. For a moment, Deal considered it: Drop his shoulder, drive ahead, find out if Garrity could fly. He'd been small at linebacker, by Gainesville standards, but he could stick.

"Don't let them do it to you, John," Garrity was saying. "Your old man would tell you the same thing. He knew when to pick his fights."

Deal stopped, blinking. The rage that had possessed him only moments before seemed magically to vanish.

Seconds ago, Garrity had seemed the very image of a devil in a dance. Now Deal found himself staring at a frightened, aging man. He saw the image of his father sprawled backward in his chair, saw his mother's desolated stare. At a certain stage of the game, everyone's dreams go flying, he thought.

What crazy dream had moved him to this pass, what kind of round-peg thinking in a square-peg world? The son of Barton Deal become a cop? How could such a notion end otherwise?

He reached into his pocket and saw Garrity start. A little pleasure in that, maybe. He withdrew the case and tossed the shield on the shiny desktop, and then he turned for the door.

"I'm sorry, John," he heard Garrity say.

"You don't know what sorry is," he said. And then the door was closed, and he was gone.

4.

Key West, Present day

"So that's how you and Driscoll hooked up?" Russell said. They were out on the street now, Deal's story finally finished, their sizable tab at the Pier House paid. He'd been locked so deeply into the memories of his Miami past that Deal felt a little light-headed now, navigating the bright streets of Key West.

They were headed down Duval toward the Key West offices of DealCo, passing a T-shirt shop with a rack dragged out on the sidewalk. Deal stepped down from the curb to let a tourist foursome pass between them: two dark-haired women in shorts and tank tops, probably sisters, two gut-heavy, close-cropped husbands in T-shirts and cut-off jeans. Canadians, Deal guessed from the season and the rare pink glow of their skin.

After they passed, Deal rejoined Russell on the sidewalk. "It was something else that brought us back together," Deal said. "Something that happened later, to my wife."

Russell gave him a look. "Anything I know about?"

"Some other time, maybe," Deal said. "It's too nice a day." And it was, he thought, glancing up into the slice of Wedgwood sky above the storefronts along Duval. Some heavy cumulus in the distance, out over the Gulf Stream, but if there was rain there, it was hours away.

Hot, of course, but it was August, and they were near the southernmost point of land in all the United States, closer to Havana than Miami. It was the kind of tropical day when you could break an honest sweat just thinking about work, but that was all right with Deal. He'd still go out with a crew some days, peel off his shirt, start framing alongside his men. A better workout than Bally's, and the jokes were better, the company far less genteel.

"You ever find who set you up?" Russell asked.

Deal paused at the bottom of the wooden outdoor staircase that ran up the side of a red-brick building to the offices he'd rented. There was a title-search and surveying company on the ground floor, its shades drawn shut, a CLOSED sign hanging in the window.

"Once that folder was gone," Deal said, shaking his head, "there wasn't much to go on. And with me being on the outside . . ." He trailed off, trying to stop his thoughts from squirreling back down those twisted memory trails.

"Maybe it was a setup, maybe it was just a convenient way to get me out. No doubt my old man was plugged into the department. He was plugged in everywhere. Anybody could have been feeding him information, even Garrity, for all I know." He gave a Driscoll-like shrug, implying a world of possibilities.

"What I found out soon enough was that Driscoll was right about my old man's finances," he said, his hand gripping the peeling banister. "DealCo was up to its eyebrows in debt. I had my work cut out just trying to keep the company afloat and my mother's doctor bills paid."

He glanced up at the doorway at the top of the stairs: DEALCO DEVELOPMENT it said in old-fashioned gilt letters across the beveled-glass insert. KEY WEST OFFICES was added just below. He gave Russell something of a smile. "It seems like that's what I've been doing ever since, just fighting to keep my head above water."

Russell followed his gaze up toward the doorway. "Even now?"

"Things are better," Deal allowed. "Maybe that's why I've been enjoying Key West so much."

Russell nodded, watching a young woman in a floral-print dress coming across Duval Street toward them. Orange dress with swirling white flowers, tanned and slender legs, flat white sandals that showed off her just-done, orange-tipped toes. She gave them a smile as she passed, on her way to unlock the door of the shuttered title-search and survey company.

"What's not to like?" Russell said, as the woman disappeared inside, leaving the smell of citrus cologne in her wake. "Good weather, rum drinks and beer, all this fine scenery."

"It is Lotus Land," Deal agreed, his thoughts drifting again. He, too, had met someone in Key West, just about the same time that Russell had met Denise. But what city was it that Annie Dodds enjoyed right now?

“You remember those phone messages?” Russell’s voice cut into his thoughts.

Deal came out of his reverie, gave Russell a helpless look.

“I didn’t think so,” Russell said. He reached into his pocket then and withdrew the pink wad, thrusting them Deal’s way. “And don’t forget to call the bookkeeper,” he said, pointing up the stairs. “You’re the boss of this outfit, okay?”

5.

DEAL'S CALL to his bookkeeper in Miami brought both bad news and good. The good news was that the trustees of a bankrupt development company for whom Deal had constructed a strip mall in South Dade had finally issued a check for his final payment, a year to the day after he'd finished the job. The bad news was that the automated payroll system they'd just had installed had run amok: Somehow $14,000 in checks had become $1,400,000. Luckily the mistake had been spotted before he'd turned his men into millionaires, but the replacement checks would have to be cut by hand and Deal's signature would be required on each.

"No way can I get up there tomorrow, Bernice," he told the bookkeeper.

"Who tells them they don't get paid?" Bernice replied, her voice nonchalant.

"Sign for me," Deal said.

"That would be forgery," Bernice said.

"You've done it before."

"For petty cash."

"What's the difference?"

Deal heard some tapping noises and the whir of an adding machine. "About thirteen thousand, eight hundred, and forty-two dollars," she said.

Deal sighed. "I trust you, Bernice. Sign the checks, will you?"

"I could clean you out, you know. You'd come home to nothing."

"It wouldn't be the first time," he told her. "If you do it, go somewhere nice. Find yourself a man." Bernice had celebrated her sixty-second birthday last month. She'd been married once, but it had ended sometime before the Beatles had played the Sullivan show.

"Did you ever watch *Psycho*?" Bernice asked.

"Sure," Deal said.

"Then you know what happens to thieving women," she said.

"Only in the movies, Bernice."

"You need to get back to Miami," she said. "I don't like the way you sound."

"I sound fine," he told her.

"Mrs. Suarez called from the concentration camp, by the way. She said to tell you everything was fine. She wanted you to know that she and Isabel will be released sometime next week."

Deal smiled. Mrs. Suarez was his tenant in the Miami fourplex he still called home. About Bernice's age, she'd played surrogate grandmother for his daughter all her young life. The two of them had been dragged along to a New Age spiritual center cum fat camp by his ex-wife, who was "concerned" about their daughter's weight.

"This is a crucial time in a young woman's life," Janice had told him.

"Isabel is ten," he'd said.

"She's gaining," Janice insisted. "She's ten pounds over normal."

"And an inch taller."

"She'll like it there."

"At fat camp?"

"That's not what it's called."

"What difference does it make what they call it?"

"They learn how to eat properly, that's all."

"Isabel already knows how to eat."

She ignored him. "She'll enjoy it," she continued. "They swim, they hike, they ride horses . . ."

"Clydesdales?"

"What are you talking about?"

"Great big horses for the big fat kids."

"Are you going to fight me on this? We've agreed on two weeks' vacation each with Isabel. You're free to take her wherever you like . . ."

"Who's going to be with Isabel while you're in the sweat lodges?"

"Mrs. Suarez has agreed to come along. She'd like to lose a little herself."

"I'll bet," Deal said.

"You don't have a clue about women, John. You like to think you do, but you don't."

"I'll grant you that much," he'd told her wearily, and the matter had been settled.

"Are you still there?" Bernice was asking. "I told you Mrs. Suarez called. . . ."

"I got that," Deal said. "I was just thinking about something."

"I think it's time you got back up here," the bookkeeper repeated.

"Next week," Deal told her. "Before Isabel gets back. I promise."

"There was a man in here looking for you," Bernice persisted. Deal thought he detected something in the bookkeeper's tone.

"A client?"

"He suggested as much, but he was a tight-lipped sort. He didn't want to talk to anyone but you."

"You tell him I was in Key West?"

"I didn't tell him anything," the bookkeeper said. "I didn't care for him. I explained that you were out of town and that if he wanted to leave his card I'd have you get in touch."

Deal sighed. "So give me his name and number."

"He didn't leave it. He said he'd be back."

Deal rolled his eyes. "Well, I'm sure he will. Give him the Key West number if he turns up again."

"That I'll do," she said.

"And you'll sign those payroll checks?"

It was the bookkeeper's turn to sigh. "If you really want me to."

"I trust you with my life, Bernice," he told her.

"Then you're a damn fool," she said. She'd hung up before he could say good-bye.

Following his conversation with Bernice, Deal turned his attention to some of the paperwork for the project he was involved in at the eastern end of the island. He might be having trouble getting his last piling properly set, but compared to the political hoops he had to jump through to move a project along in Miami-Dade County, this undertaking had been a breeze.

It hadn't hurt, either, that Deal had been willing to pick up the pieces of an unraveling project that the Key West city fathers feared might wind up in the wrong hands. Following the untimely death of Franklin Stone, the original developer of the property, several of the larger Florida developers, including one multinational firm, had made overtures to step in. But because the development encroached upon a wetlands nature preserve, the commissioners bowed to growing public pressure and agreed to keep Deal, Stone's original choice as builder and the "homegrown" candidate, on board. Nor had it hurt, of course, that Terrence Terrell, Dectra Software magnate, for whom Deal had meticulously restored a pair of historically significant bayside properties in Miami, had weighed in on his behalf. In any case, the job was his now, and Key West was beginning to feel more and more like home.

Part of the pleasure surely had to do with the fact that Deal was operating out of the shadow of his father's legacy. It was the first major project that he'd assumed outside Miami and, as he'd suggested earlier to Russell Straight, might well constitute a turning point in his dozen-year struggle to resurrect the business he'd taken on when there had seemed nowhere else to go.

If it were not for the fact of his daughter's ties to Miami, he thought, his life might easily segue to "The Rock," as some locals referred to Key West. But meantime, Isabel still had vacation time from school coming. She could spend her two weeks with him down here in the beachside apartment he rented, and after that, he would simply continue to manage the commute.

The thought of Isabel's visit prompted him to set aside the permitting sheets he'd been checking and start a list on a lined tablet. "Stuff for 2nd Bedroom," he jotted down. "Kids' sheets, bedspread . . . cartoon characters?" He paused. Maybe Isabel had outgrown such childish things. He scratched out "cartoon characters" and wrote in "something girly . . . ask clerk."

"Girly?" He stared at what he'd written, then scratched it out again. What was happening to his brain? Maybe Mrs. Suarez would have some suggestions, if she didn't come back from the Southwest a New Age convert, that is.

He heard a tapping at the door to his office, then, and glanced up, surprised to find the young woman from the survey and title-search company standing there. "Sorry," she said. "I didn't mean to scare you."

"That's okay," Deal said. He put his pencil down. "I must have spaced out. I didn't hear you come in."

"I used the inside stairwell," she said, shrugging. "The door wasn't locked."

Deal nodded. "I guess I forgot about that. I haven't been in here much."

The girl turned and glanced over her shoulder into the outer office where an empty desk sat. "You don't have a girl," she said, turning back to him.

"I'm working on it," Deal said. "The truth is, we're not really that busy yet."

She nodded. "You're the one putting up the Villas Cayo Hueso, out by the airport, right? The place Franklin Stone was going to build before he got killed?"

"That's right," Deal said.

She shook her head. "That's a big job," she said. "I'd say you're going to need some office help."

He smiled. "Are you applying?"

She shook her head. "Oh no, that's not what I meant. I was just saying"—she gave him a smile of her own—"I couldn't leave downstairs, anyway. That's my boyfriend's place."

"Ah," Deal said, lifting his chin in understanding.

"Somebody's got to keep things going until he gets back."

"Gets back?" He couldn't help but steal a glance at those long, tanned legs. The nails at the ends of her toes glistened like ripened berries.

"From Raiford," she said, with a toss of her hair. "He got caught out in the Straits with a load of square grouper." She paused, noting Deal's expression. "That's Conch for marijuana," she added.

"I'm familiar with the term," he said.

She gave him a speculative look. "Ray Bob Watkins," she said. "Maybe you've heard of him."

"Afraid not." Deal shook his head. Watkins Title Services was the name stenciled on the windows downstairs, he recalled. Somehow he'd never imagined anyone named Ray Bob in charge.

"It was a major setup," the young woman in his doorway was saying. "A friend begged him for a favor and then ratted to Customs. Now Ray Bob's doing three to five and his buddy is walking around scot-free."

"Ray Bob must be pissed," Deal offered.

She lifted one of her shapely brows. "I wouldn't want to be that guy when he gets out," she said.

Deal nodded. He willed his gaze up from those long and slender legs, only to find it settling on the inviting plane of her chest. Matching dimples at her breastbones, he noted. A gold chain bearing what looked like a miniature diamond-studded conch shell trailing into a dark furrow of cleavage. He had a sudden picture of Ray Bob snarling in his cell, rattling the bars with both his hands and feet.

"I didn't mean to lay all that on you," she said.

"Hey . . ." Deal said, turning his palms up to show it was okay.

"The truth is, I did have something of a proposition for you."

Deal considered a rejoinder or two, but he'd never been a rejoinder kind of guy, not when it came to women. He found himself simply nodding, as dumb as Og, the caveman hunter.

"I was just thinking," she continued, "since things are slow downstairs and all, and you're bound to need some help . . ." She gave a shrug that squeezed her shoulders together and deepened the furrow between her breasts, sending the conch shell into solid darkness. "What we could do is let people come up here through the downstairs entrance. I could even answer your calls and stuff. I wouldn't charge much, and it'd give me something to do, you know?"

Deal considered it briefly, long enough for the image of Ray Bob prying apart the bars of his cage to coalesce in his mind. "That's not such a bad idea . . ." He broke off then, staring into the earnest gaze before him. "What's your name, anyway?"

She laughed, a tiny, embarrassed sound. "Angie," she said. "Angie Marsh. I guess I should have mentioned that."

"You just did," Deal said. He rose from his chair then and came around to the front of his desk.

"I'm John Deal," he said, extending his hand. She reached and shook briefly, a dry strong clasp that suggested better than Ray Bob deserved.

"Pleased," she said.

"Me, too," he said. He could smell the faint hint of her perfume now and wondered if it had been wise to leave the protection of his desk. "I appreciate your coming up, Angie. I'll have to think about it, though. I mean, this is just a place to hang my hat right now, really."

She nodded, but there was a hint of disappointment in her eyes. "Sure," she said. "It was just a thought. If you change your mind, you know where to find me." She finished with a bright smile and turned toward the outer office. "I'll still keep an eye on things," she added. "No charge."

Deal gave her a smile back. "I appreciate it," he assured her. He tried to keep his eyes off her retreating backside, but it was a brief, unsuccessful effort. Any one of the dozen thoughts racing through his mind would have sent Ray Bob vaulting the twelve-foot, razor-wire fences of Raiford.

He walked to the door of the inner stairwell and watched her descend the carpeted steps, her silhouette a graceful, ever-shifting assemblage of curves and angles against the brightly lit landing below. She turned at the bottom and gave him a wave. Deal waved back, waiting for her to disappear before he closed and locked the stairwell door. Something of what Ray Bob must have felt when his cell door clanged shut ran through Deal as the stairwell bolt shot home. The only difference, he reminded himself, was that he was the one operating the lock.

He spent the rest of the afternoon trying to keep his mind on the heat and energy calculations the engineers had drafted for the first of the structures at Villas Cayo Hueso, and away from the various fantasies the visit from Angie had planted. Though the structures that would make up the development were framed of block and steel-reinforced concrete, capable—in theory, at least—

of withstanding Category V hurricane winds in excess of 150 mph, Deal had tempered Franklin Stone's original Mediterranean-inspired plans somewhat, replacing the outer finishes of stucco and red barrel tiles with a weather-resistant clapboard siding and bright tin roofing more in keeping with the indigenous architecture of the island.

It was a bit more expensive, but no less durable, and so what if it meant that the cost of materials and the increased air-conditioning load would cut into the profit margin by all of two percent? This was his project, now, not Franklin Stone's, and it was likely to be standing a long time after he was dead and buried, too. He wouldn't be able to take the two percent to the grave, either.

He closed the calculations file and leaned back in his desk chair, pleased at the feelings of self-righteousness that had stolen over him. He would never have chosen this career, no doubt about it, would never have willingly started down the pathway that was darkened by the colossal shadow of Barton Deal. But fate had guided him here, regardless, and maybe, just maybe, he was beginning to find real satisfaction in what he did.

He wasn't sure how his old man had felt about his work. By the time Deal had been old enough to wonder about such things, Barton Deal had already ascended far beyond the plane of sharing his innermost feelings with his only son. It simply wasn't the sort of conversation that larger-than-life figures carried on. His old man had a million aphorisms, of course: *Build 'em to last, boy. Never soap your nails. Measure twice, cut once. Pound and pray.*

Maybe he had loved his work at one point. But as for what was going through his father's mind—the last years of his life, at least—Deal had little clue. *Just because your old man built things for slimeballs doesn't make him a bad person,* Vernon Driscoll had told him once. Wouldn't it be nice to think so.

He shook off the thoughts and checked his watch to see that it was almost six. He'd have to hurry out to the site if he wanted to catch the crew supervisors before they went home. But he'd asked Russell to give him a call if there were any significant developments, and chances were they'd already be gone. If the boss was off the job, who'd be fool enough to stick around late?

He tossed the calculations file onto a stack that threatened to topple and stood up to stretch. Maybe he ought to reconsider Angie Marsh's offer, he thought, glancing at the various piles that mounded his desk. Either that or convince Bernice to come down from Miami for a week to get things in order.

He walked into the outer office, stealing a glance at the locked stairwell door. He felt a little twinge of shame, locking a pretty girl out of his office. She was just a person come to see a man about a job, he told himself. He'd sleep on the notion, see how her "proposition" sounded in the morning, he thought, then went out the door, shaking his head at the lurid thoughts that had leaped instantaneously into his mind.

6.

HE WAS a couple of steps down the outdoor staircase, still preoccupied with his unruly thoughts, when he saw the figures poised at the landing below. Deal stopped, his hand on the rough-grained railing, trying to reconcile the image of the two men staring up at him with any version of Key West life he was familiar with.

The man in the lead was silver-haired and tall, wearing a dark silk three-piece suit and a maroon tie. He stared up at Deal from behind a pair of stylish, tiny-lensed designer sunglasses, his chin tilted high as if to improve his aim. Behind him was a shaved-headed man who made Russell Straight look small, a portion of his bulk hidden beneath a loose-draped guayabera shirt.

"Mr. Deal?" the man in the suit asked, his voice as smooth as a radio announcer's.

"That's me," Deal said, still poised at the top of the stairs. He glanced out at the street where a Town Car with smoked windows was angled carelessly at the curb.

"How glad I am that we've caught you," the man said in a tone that affected great relief.

"I'm afraid you didn't," Deal said. "I've got a job to check on. I'm already late."

The man in the suit didn't budge. "Would that be the Villas project, Mr. Deal? The property Franklin Stone had acquired out near the Salt Ponds?"

Deal hesitated, glancing at his watch again. "If there's something I could help you with, maybe we could talk out there. I'd like to catch a couple of my men . . ."

"Perhaps we can save you a bit of trouble, then," the man said, a smile spreading under his blanked-out eyes. "We've just come from Villas Cayo Hueso, you see. And as Tomás here will verify, there wasn't a soul to be found, save for your watchman."

"Eddie?" Deal said. He wasn't so much surprised that everyone else was gone as he was that Eddie Hayduke had actually shown up on time.

"He did not provide us with his name," the silver-haired man said. "But he did give us this address."

Deal glanced again at the Town Car. "Are you down here from Miami?"

The question brought what seemed like a glare from Tomás, but the man in the suit gave a nod that was somewhere between acquiescence and denial. "We have in fact passed through Miami," he said.

Something occurred to Deal then. "You stopped by my offices up there, yesterday. Spoke to my bookkeeper."

It seemed to please the man. "Indeed we did, Mr. Deal. I've

been quite anxious to talk to you. I have a most interesting proposition, you see. And you are the very man I need."

"I didn't get your name," Deal said.

"No, you did not," the man agreed, smiling once again. He raised his hand and snapped his fingers softly. Tomás reached into a pocket of his guayabera and produced—rather deftly for a man his size, Deal thought—what appeared to be a business card. The man in the suit received the card over his shoulder without a backward glance, then extended it between his first two fingers toward Deal. A theatrical gesture, Deal thought, but he appreciated good theater as much as the next person.

"My name is Fuentes," the silver-haired man said, in his confident baritone. "Antonio Fuentes. And I have come a great distance to speak with you."

Deal descended the staircase far enough to take the card from the outstretched fingers. He glanced at the bodyguard, then more closely at Fuentes. His old man had been a great fan of the black-and-white gangster movies of the forties and fifties. Here was Cesar Romero in the flesh, he thought, unflappableness incarnate.

He examined the card Fuentes had handed him—no phone number, no address, no company affiliation, simply the name in a bold, flowing script. Deal gave Fuentes a questioning look, and the man made a placating gesture with his hands.

"Please, Mr. Deal," he said, indicating the office door behind him. "If I could simply have a few moments of your time. It is my earnest intention to make you a wealthy man."

Deal had to stifle a smile at the outrageousness of it, but then again, how often did people show up at his offices offering to make him rich? His old man had probably had characters like

Fuentes standing in line on a daily basis, but he was more accustomed to strip-mall developers beating him up for fifty cents off the square foot. He had another look at the cut of Fuentes's suit, then turned and headed for his door. "All right, Mr. Fuentes, you can come on up."

"How much do you know about Cuba, Mr. Deal?" Fuentes was sitting in one of the battered wicker cabriolets that had apparently served the former occupant of the offices as side chairs, his fingers tented over the plume of his dark red tie. He still wore his sunglasses, an affectation that Deal found annoying.

Deal glanced at Tomás, who remained standing, hovering at his boss's shoulder. He was about to answer Fuentes when something dawned on him. "Do you wear your glasses for a reason, Mr. Fuentes?"

Fuentes offered his saturnine smile. "Are you asking if I am blind?" He raised a finger to the side of his glasses, continuing before Deal could answer. "It is an unusual condition which makes my eyes extremely sensitive to light. In the sunlight, it is very difficult for me. Even here in this room, it seems quite bright."

Deal glanced about the office. He'd switched off his desk lamp on his way out earlier, leaving only the late-afternoon light reflecting through the single window on his left. Another half hour, they'd be sitting in the dark. "I'm sorry," Deal said.

Fuentes waved it away. "It's disconcerting, speaking to a man when you cannot see his eyes. I quite understand."

"You were asking me about Cuba," Deal said, trying to get them back on track. "What about it?"

"I was simply curious," Fuentes said. "How much you know, the level of your interest."

"I've lived in South Florida all my life," Deal said. "It'd be pretty difficult not to know a little bit about the place."

"Have you ever traveled there?"

Deal shook his head. "It's not all that easy. Are you trying to sell tickets, Mr. Fuentes?"

Fuentes laughed softly, but Tomás's face stayed stony. Deal found himself wondering if the bodyguard spoke English. He looked rather Teutonic, but he'd been fooled that way before. "I am not a travel agent, I assure you," Fuentes said. "I was simply curious."

"My old man used to go down to Havana before the revolution," Deal said. "He had a boat he liked to take there a couple of times a year."

"And you never went along?"

"I was in diapers," Deal said. "Besides, he was going down there to raise hell."

Fuentes nodded. "Havana was a good place for that, back then."

"So I hear," Deal said. "I'm sure there's a point to all this."

"Would you call yourself an impatient man, Mr. Deal?"

"I'm anxious to get rich, that's all."

Fuentes seemed pleased with that. "Havana was once a magnificent city," he said. "Is *still* a magnificent city," he corrected himself, "though it is crumbling as we speak."

Deal nodded. He'd heard the sentiment often enough from architects and others. "Are you Cuban?" he asked Fuentes.

Fuentes offered his smile before he answered. "I prefer to call myself a citizen of the world, Mr. Deal. But I do have a great interest in the country, and in its potential. That is what I have come to talk with you about."

Deal stared. "Are you sure you haven't got me confused with someone else?"

"Quite sure, Mr. Deal," Fuentes said, he shifted in his chair, leaning forward as if giving in to Deal's impatience. "You see, great changes are impending in this country to the south. Ninety miles from where we sit. Closer by half than to Miami."

"And it might as well be a thousand miles," Deal said.

"For now," Fuentes said, dismissively. "But these political impediments that seem so monumental at present will soon disintegrate into nothingness. Think back a few years. One day the Berlin Wall was standing, the next day Coca-Cola was flowing outside the Kremlin."

"The situation is hardly the same," Deal said. "There are plenty of Cubans in Florida who aren't exactly ready to buddy up with Castro."

It brought another dismissive wave from Fuentes. "Soon Castro will be gone," he said, "and with him will go the fuel that fires the political theatrics you refer to. There is a tide of dollars coming that will sweep all that away forever."

"That's a rather cynical position, Mr. Fuentes."

"I would rather call it optimism, Mr. Deal."

"I seem to remember a lot of people thinking they'd get rich once the Berlin Wall came down," Deal said. "But they forgot nobody had any money to buy all the Cokes and Levi's we were going to sell over there."

"Which brings us to the reason I've come to talk with you, Mr. Deal. I am not here to talk to you about trade. I'm here to talk about infrastructure."

Deal shook his head. "Then maybe you ought to get to it."

"You're a builder," Fuentes said. "And an intelligent man. I should have thought you'd have pieced it together by now."

"My grades were never that good," Deal said. "Why don't you help me out?"

"It's why I asked if you had ever visited Havana," Fuentes told him. "If you had, you would realize the scope of the work to which I refer. As one gauge, consider that the United Nations presently sponsors a multinational effort to restore certain of the most important structures in Old Havana. The entire budget of this enterprise is less than twenty million dollars annually. You have a practiced eye, Mr. Deal. If you were to survey Habana Vieja and the Malecón for yourself, you would see that twenty *billion* would scarcely scratch the surface."

Some of Fuentes's reserve had left him now, and his voice had risen to something resembling urgency. "Fifty years of neglect, Mr. Deal. Try to imagine Venice or Florence transported to the tropics and left for fifty years without a single coat of paint, a tightened screw, a roof tile replaced. The scope of the work to be done in restoration alone is enormous. And that does not take into account the amount of new construction that is inevitable: hotels, convention centers, marinas, state-of-the-art port and transportation facilities . . ."

"Who's going to pay for all this?" Deal asked.

"This is not Bulgaria we're talking about. People *want* to travel to Cuba, just as your own father did. Americans will flock there again by the hundreds of thousands, once the obstacles have been cleared and the amenities they seek are in place, and never mind any misguided rabble-rousers who don't wish to join the parade. The politicians who manipulate them now for profit will be the very ones reaping the rewards of a revitalized Cuba."

"Sounds like you've got it all figured out, Mr. Fuentes. I still don't see where I come in."

Fuentes paused and sat back in his chair, regarding Deal over his retented fingers as if he were a parent calculating how to handle a troublesome child. "I'll be honest with you," he said after a moment. "The truth is that you are convenient."

"I'm sorry?"

Fuentes leaned forward again. "You come highly recommended to us," he said.

"Us?" Deal said. He didn't imagine that Fuentes was talking about him and Tomás. He held up the card bearing Fuentes's name. "Just who the hell *is* us, anyway?"

Fuentes held up a hand meant to calm him. "I represent a group of businessmen, an international consortium with significant ties to interests in the United States as well, who have positioned themselves to be of aid as Cuba struggles to rebuild itself. Not everyone there—and I include some in the present government—is inimical to the prospect of increased foreign development, not even the involvement of individuals from your own country."

"Dollars have a way of making friends," Deal said.

"Exactamente," Fuentes said. If he had heard any irony in Deal's tone, he gave no sign of it.

"I'm a builder, Mr. Fuentes, not a politician. And the last time I checked, American companies weren't permitted to do business in Havana or anywhere else in Cuba. When and if that changes, I'd be happy to talk to you and your partners, whoever they are, about the various possibilities, but right now, I think that we're both wasting our time."

"I assure you that we are not," Fuentes said. He reached inside his suit coat and withdrew an envelope, then laid it on Deal's desk. Deal eyed it suspiciously. Blank, no addressee, no return address, the same cream-colored linen stock as the card Fuentes had handed him.

"What's that?" Deal said.

"Consider it a retainer," Fuentes said.

"For what?" Deal asked.

"For your services as a consultant."

"What if I'm not interested?"

"Why don't you open it before deciding?"

Deal gave Fuentes a look, then picked up the envelope, untucked the flap. Folded inside a sheet of thick stationery bearing Fuentes's name he found a cashier's check, made out to John Deal, drawn on a bank in the Cayman Islands. Deal checked the figures, then glanced back at Fuentes.

"You must have made a typo," he said. "My bookkeeper just did the same thing."

Fuentes smiled. "The amount is correct, I assure you."

Deal looked at the check again, just to make sure. "Why would you want to offer me a million dollars, Mr. Fuentes?" Deal's gaze traveled to Tomás as he spoke. The expression on the bodyguard's face suggested he shared the same sentiment. So much for questioning his grasp of English, Deal thought.

Fuentes made the dismissive gesture with his hands again. "It's simply a first installment. I told you it was my intention to make you a wealthy man."

"You'll have to do better than that," Deal said, tossing the envelope back on the desk. "I'd be interested to know who sent you here and exactly what services you think I can provide that are worth that kind of money."

"I'll be frank with you," Fuentes said, and for the first time his tone seemed sincere. "I'm here to take advantage of your pedigree. As you point out, you are not a political animal. Of the half-dozen builders of your rank in South Florida, you're the only person who wouldn't have thrown me out of his office the moment I broached the subject and the location of our undertaking. For another, your reputation is impeccable. In fact, it precedes you with our friends inside the ministries to the south. You may not have been aware of it, but your father had many influential friends in Cuba. And not all of them departed during the general Diaspora."

"So I'm an honest South Florida building contractor, and as far as Cuban politics goes, a don't-care-ified one-eyed cat. That's worth a million dollars?"

"We think it is," Fuentes replied. "You are able, honest, well respected, and you carry not an iota of political baggage. For what we hope to accomplish in the coming years, that makes you an extremely valuable person indeed."

"In other words, you're looking for a front man."

"Nothing could be further from the truth," Fuentes said. He pointed at the envelope lying between them. "I hope that the amount does not insult you."

Deal tried not to laugh. "I just take this million-dollar check down to the Bank of the Keys and cash it, that's it? No contract, no guarantees, no nothing?"

"Your acceptance of the retainer implies your partnership and willingness to represent our interests, of course," Fuentes said. "Among other things, we'd want you to visit Havana, talk with some knowledgeable people, see with your own eyes the scope of what I have been describing to you." He shrugged. "We want to be prepared to hit the ground running, as you say, the moment the political climate permits."

Deal stared at him, calculating. "If I were to do that, go over there and engage in any serious discussions about building anything in Cuba, and the word got back about what I was up to, I could forget about doing any more business in Miami-Dade County—they might even try to pull me off the port project."

Fuentes shrugged. "I understand there's a certain amount of risk." He paused and pointed to the envelope on Deal's desk. "But it is my contention that the rewards far outweigh the downside. Besides," he continued, gesturing at the site map of the Villas project that Deal had pinned to the wall behind his desk, "it's my understanding that you've come to enjoy your time in Key West. Your work with us should carry no political ramifications in this area. And there's no reason why you can't continue the project you've already begun while our planning goes forward elsewhere."

"I still don't know who you are or who you work for or with," Deal said. "Do you really think I'd take this kind of money from someone I didn't know?"

"It happens all the time, Mr. Deal."

"Not in my life," Deal said.

"Simply more proof that you're our man," Fuentes said, rising from his chair. "I would have been surprised and even disappointed had you snatched this offer." He leaned forward and spoke more softly, as if conveying some privileged message. "It is a delicate matter, of course, but I will see that you receive all necessary information regarding the nature and the makeup of our partnership. You'll look it over and make a decision. I've no problem with that, though I hope that I can count on your discretion."

"What makes you think you can trust me?"

Fuentes offered his smile again. "My confidence in your character is what has led me here, Mr. Deal."

Deal stood up then, too. He picked up the envelope and held

it out toward Fuentes, who was already headed for the door. "You'd better take your check, " he said.

But Fuentes continued on without breaking stride. "Keep the check," he said, holding up a hand. "Tear it up, burn it, cash it, do whatever you decide," he said, Tomás close on his heels now.

He paused at the doorway and gave Deal a meaningful glance. "You're a singular man, Mr. Deal. I look forward to doing business with you."

7.

"WELL," came the voice at Deal's ear, "isn't this a surprise?"

He turned from his seat at the Pier House bar to find Angie Marsh standing a few inches away, what looked like a frozen margarita clutched in her hand. The color on her neatly manicured nails matched that on her toes, he realized, and he wondered why he hadn't noticed as much before.

The fact that he was working on his second Meyer's and Coke while he waited for Russell Straight to show might have had something to do with it. When he slowed down, he tended to notice more things, simple as that.

For instance, he was very much aware that she had changed from her loose-fitting orange print dress into a pair of black slacks and a clinging white tank top that revealed even more of that lovely bone structure he had admired earlier, as well as an inch or so of bronzed skin just above her belt line. It had become abundantly clear to Deal that he would have to keep the inside stairwell door not only locked but possibly nailed shut as well.

Hire this woman as his secretary? Sure. And why not add Salome and Madonna to the staff while he was at it?

"Were you waiting for someone?" she asked.

"I am," Deal told her. "But he's late."

She regarded him for a moment. "What a coincidence," she said. "The person I was waiting for hasn't shown either."

"Have a seat?" Deal offered, indicating the stool beside him.

She slid in easily, brushing against his arm as she moved. She settled herself, smiled and took a sip of her drink, then made a show of checking her watch. "Ray Bob's about a year late, as a matter of fact. And I don't look for him for at least two more, even with time earned for good behavior."

Deal found himself smiling, then, just as quickly, glancing around the bar. There was a piano player working the lounge at the far side of the room where a few older couples looking spiffy in jackets and go-to-dinner dresses nodded along to "Fly Me to the Moon."

"If you're looking for any of Ray Bob's friends, don't bother," she told him. "The Pier House is a little reserved for that crowd." She made a face as she finished.

"Just how much did you and Ray Bob have in common?" Deal asked. He finished what was left of his drink and nodded his assent to a questioning look from the barmaid at the service counter.

Angie gave him a tolerant glance. "Hey, who knows what gets people together in the first place? Somehow it happens, then one day you wake up and look at who's lying next to you. By then, it's a little bit late to be asking the question."

She broke off for a sip of her drink. "But I'll tell you one thing, when the guy you're with takes a trip up the river, it tends to give you a whole new perspective on a lot of things."

Deal nodded. Her comment got him thinking briefly about Janice, or more precisely, about the two Janices he had known. The young, carefree, fun-loving woman he had married, and the wounded, inward-turning woman she had become.

And as always, there came the pang of guilt, the voice that insisted that it had all been his fault. Men who'd tried to kill him nearly killing her instead, not once but twice.

How do you begin to make up for something like that? he wondered. Just how?

He picked up the fresh drink the barmaid had brought and turned to Angie. "Do you visit him?"

"I've been up a couple of times," she said, glancing absently around the bar top as if she'd misplaced something. She turned back after a moment, offering a rueful smile. "You ever smoke? I quit like a year ago, but it's like sometimes I forget I don't anymore."

"My mother smoked a lot before she died," he said. "It sent me off the habit."

"Lucky for you, I guess," she said. "Anyways, it's not exactly a pretty picture, up there. Ray Bob could be tough to get along with even when he was walking around free . . ." She trailed off, then turned back to meet Deal's gaze.

"I write, end of every week, let him know what's going on with the business, which isn't all that much, tell him how his brokerage account is doing, things like that. It's more like a business report." She took some of her drink and gave her hair a toss.

"I'd like to think he'd do the same for me, even though he probably wouldn't," she added, a thoughtful look on her features.

"Whatever we had is gone, that's for sure. But I haven't had the heart to come right out and say so, him sitting behind bars and all."

"Given what you say about Ray Bob, that might be the safest time to tell him," Deal said.

She smiled. "You're probably right," she said. She sucked the ice of her drink dry and signaled to the barmaid for a refill. The piano player had finished with "Fly Me to the Moon," and was now belting out a by-the-numbers rendition of "Cabaret." Two of the well turned-out couples had begun to fox-trot on the small dance floor.

"How about you?" Angie asked, turning to him. "What happens in your life when you're not being a construction mogul? Is there a Mrs. Deal somewhere? Some little Deal juniors running around?"

"There is a Mrs. Deal, in fact," he told her.

"I should have guessed," she said.

"And I have a daughter, Isabel, who's ten."

"Wonderful," Angie said. "Where are they, at the beach or something?"

"Isabel's mother and I are separated," Deal said. "The two of them are out at a spa in New Mexico as we speak."

"That sounds nice," Angie said, examining a nail. "Just how separated are you?"

"It's been awhile now," Deal said. "Several years, in fact."

Angie considered what he'd told her. "Did she want it that way, or was it you?"

When Deal hesitated, she held up a hand. "Never mind, I already know."

He glanced at her. "Am I that obvious?"

"Don't ever play poker," she told him, rolling her eyes.

The piano player segued from "Cabaret" into "New York, New York," and more couples were up to dance. "Is that guy the worst or what?" Angie said.

Deal glanced at the piano player. "He's better than the last one they had."

"The guy with the bad hairpiece?"

"That's the one," Deal said, his gaze drifting into the distance. He wasn't going to mention the singer who'd been paired up with the guy. He hoped Angie Marsh didn't bring her up either.

"Can I ask you something?" Angie said.

He turned. "Are you feeling shy all of a sudden?"

"I just wondered if you had eaten yet."

"I haven't," he found himself admitting.

"And this guy you're waiting for, is he coming or what?"

Deal glanced at his watch, shaking his head. He'd given up on Russell Straight an hour ago, to be honest, even before Angie had turned up at the bar. A balmy summer evening, a guy who looked like Russell alone in Key West . . . well, Deal would get a play-by-play in the morning—if he allowed it, that is.

"So why don't I take you for dinner?" Angie was saying.

Deal thought about it briefly, imagining Ray Bob listening in on this proposition, yanking the bars of his cell apart like taffy. "That's nice of you to offer . . ." he began, but she cut in.

"Come on," she said. "You already turned down business. We can go for pleasure. I know this Mexican place out on Stock Island, if you'll drive."

Deal was about to decline when something—the effects of his drink, the guileless smile on the face of the lovely woman in front of him, or maybe the remnants of the sensible self that still lurked inside him—intervened. "Mexican?" he found himself repeating.

"You don't like Mexican?" she asked doubtfully.

"It's my favorite," he said.

"Then what are we waiting for?" she said.

In truth, Deal had no answer.

"This is an unusual car you've got," Angie said. She sat on the broad bench seat opposite him, her legs tucked beneath her, glancing around the cabin of the Hog as they drove slowly southward down Duval Street. He'd sent down the windows to let the stale heat out, then switched on the A/C to mix with the balmy summer air streaming through.

It was dark now, and the foot traffic had picked up, tourists aimlessly milling from one geegaw shop to the next or looking for a likely bar. Plenty of them had already settled at the Bull & Whistle, where the sounds of a bluesy guitar player filtered out the open windows onto the street. Several steps up from "New York, New York," Deal thought, considering the urge to pull straight to the curb, scratching the pretense of dinner altogether.

"The Hog is what everybody calls it," Deal told her. "It started out in life as a Cadillac."

Her eyes widened. "No kidding. What did you do to it?"

Deal laughed. "It wasn't me. A guy I was doing a job for went belly up in the middle of things. He gave me this for part of what he owed."

"And you took it?" She turned in the seat, peering through the cab window to what had once been the backseat of an automobile. Now the roof had been cut away, the backseat and trunk converted to a pickup bed by Cal Saltz, a man who had liked to dabble in the breeding of thoroughbreds and had wanted a more genteel way of hauling a bale of alfalfa out to one of his steeds on a weekend afternoon.

"I needed a truck at the time, and this seemed the next best thing," Deal said. "I keep saying I'm going to get rid of it, but there are a couple of mechanics up in Miami who love the thing. They keep fixing it up, adding one thing after another, and I haven't had the heart to make them stop."

She nodded, running her hand over the retooled leather seat between them. "Well, *some*body's been taking good care of it," she said. "And it's weird enough to be a real Conch-mobile. You could probably name your price for it down here."

"I'll keep that in mind," he said. They'd left the crowded downtown streets now, and Deal nudged the accelerator as they swung onto South Oceanside, a less traveled waterfront drive that would take them out to U.S. 1 and the short hop to Stock Island, the tiny island just to the north and east of Key West.

The sea breeze was stronger here, whipping through the cab of the Hog, carrying with it the tang of brine and beached seaweed, a smell that Deal had associated all his life with promise and adventure. And look where he was, after all, cruising the beach of an island paradise in a heavy car, a beautiful woman at his side, a couple of drinks in his belly and the night spread out before him.

He heard a sudden rustling of paper at his side and caught the flash of something vaguely white as it whipped past his face and vanished out the Hog's window in the slipstream. Something else was still whirling about in the vortex, thrashing like a crippled bird.

Angie's hand shot out and snatched the clattering paper before it flew out the window too. "What the heck?" she said, as Deal found the buttons for the windows and sent them gliding up. "Sorry," he told her.

"You ought to be sorry," she said, her mouth open. She held up the paper she'd snatched from midair, brandishing it at him. "Do you know what this *is*?"

Deal glanced over, saw her staring at him accusatorially, holding what seemed to be a check in her hand. The cashier's check Antonio Fuentes had offered him earlier, no less. He'd carried the envelope out of his office—he couldn't just *leave* it there—then had left it on the seat of the Hog when he'd gone into the Pier House and forgotten about it. If Angie had been a second slower, he thought . . .

"Thanks," he said, holding out his hand.

"Thanks?" she repeated. "I'm not sure 'thanks' quite covers it. How about, dinner's on me, can I buy you a new car, something like that?"

Deal smiled, still holding out his hand. "Dinner was on me to begin with," he told her.

"You just ride around with million-dollar checks flying around your car? I think you need a better filing system. Look, we could close up Watkins Title and I could go to work for you full-time . . ."

"It's a long story, Angie," he said.

"I'll bet it is," she said.

"Can I have the check?"

"Sure," she said. She pulled the check back to her breast. "Just indulge me for a minute, will you? I never held a million dollars before."

He shook his head. "It really isn't what you think," he said.

"Well, I'm glad you told me, because I would have sworn I was holding a cashier's check with a one and six zeroes printed on it."

"Angie . . ."

"Oh, here," she said, sounding exasperated, reaching to tuck the check in his shirt pocket as they slowed for the traffic signal at the junction of U.S. 1. He felt her hair brush his check, felt her breath on his neck as she leaned close. "Money's way overrated, anyhow, or so I've heard."

The "Mexican place" Angie suggested had turned out to be terrific, run by a pair of brothers from Jalisco who had originally come to Florida to toil in the agricultural fields south of Miami. The place was small, a dozen tables or so, half of them on an outside deck covered with an awning, the last empty one of which they had snagged upon arriving.

"You like the margarita?" Angie asked him, as their waitress, the daughter of one of the brothers, they'd discovered, deposited their second round and left.

"I'm going to guess it's better than the one you had at the Pier House," he said, raising his glass to meet hers.

"I had two at the Pier House," she said. "And, yes, this is better. It's the real thing. No lemonade. Just lime juice, tequila, some triple sec and ice."

"Spoken with authority," Deal said.

"I spent a little time in Mexico," she said.

"This was before Ray Bob?"

"It's been such a nice night," she said. "Are you trying to ruin it?"

"Just asking," he said. "How about, 'What took you to Mexico?' "

She thought about it a moment. "An airplane," she said finally.

"Okay," Deal said. "It can remain a mystery."

"I was a teacher," she said. "I took a job teaching at an orphanage in Chihuahua."

Deal stared, trying to reconcile Angie the teacher of orphaned Mexican children, with Angie the companion of Ray Bob Watkins, flamboyant Key West drug runner and convicted felon. "Another surprise," he said. "Where'd you go to school?"

"Scottsdale Community College," she said.

"As in Arizona?"

"As in," she agreed. "My dad was in the service. We moved around a lot."

He nodded, still trying to build the bits and pieces he'd gleaned into a cohesive whole.

"I've only got an AA," she was saying, "but I found out that's all I needed for the job. The orphans didn't seem to mind."

And why would they? Deal thought. Then something else occurred to him. "You speak Spanish, then?"

"Fluently," she said.

He shook his head, recalling his fractured conversations with their server. Angie had listened patiently, making her own requests in English. "How come you don't . . ." He broke off, waving his hands about their surroundings, trying to find the way to say it.

". . . order my *flautas* in Spanish?" she finished for him.

When he nodded, she went on. "I'm not in Mexico anymore, and I'm not Spanish. I only speak the language when I have to."

"That's an interesting take," he said.

“I’m an interesting person,” she told him.

He laughed. “I’ll drink to that,” he said. “So what’s the Chihuahua–to–Key West connection?”

Her expression dimmed. “There are cockroaches everywhere,” she said.

“Is this where Ray Bob comes in?”

“I thought we had an agreement,” she said with a sigh.

“I’m sorry,” he said.

“You don’t have to talk about your million-dollar checks.” She shrugged. “I don’t have to talk about cockroaches.”

“I told you, I don’t even know if that check is real.”

“It looked real to me.”

“You know what they say about appearances.”

“No,” she said. She put her glass down, then lay her hand on top of his. “Why don’t you tell me about appearances, John?”

He took a breath. What the hell? What the living hell? “A guy showed up in my office this afternoon, late, after you’d gone home.”

“How do you know when I went home?”

He stared at her, every bit of his innate, fight-having-a-good-time reserve suddenly vanished. “I heard you close the front door of Watkins Title. I went over to my window and watched you walk down Fleming Street, right out of my life.”

She paused a moment. “That’s sweet,” she said, finally, her eyes on his. “But I wasn’t gone for long.”

“You weren’t,” he agreed. This is Key West, he was reminding himself. Such things as this could happen here. One could let them happen.

“You were telling me about this man in your office,” she said.

“You sure you want to hear?”

"Of course," she said. "If he's the one who gave you the check."

"He called himself Antonio Fuentes. He wanted me to build some things for him in Cuba."

"Is that allowed?"

"Not presently, but someday. He's betting on the come."

"He must have a lot to bet," she said, pointing at his shirt pocket where the check still nestled.

Deal shrugged. "Maybe."

"Are you going to take his money?"

He gave her a smile. "You think I should?"

"Does it matter what I think?"

"I was just curious."

"Too bad," she said, dropping her gaze. "I was hoping that it mattered."

"It's more complicated than it seems," he said. "I mean, you don't just take a million dollars from someone you don't even know."

"You don't?"

"Of course not. Who knows what this guy really has in mind."

She thought for a moment. "Still, it seems like he's the one taking all the chances. You're the one who's got the check."

He stopped. "Sure, but who knows what he's after?"

"What you're saying is, someone comes along and offers you something that seems almost too good to be true, you don't want to take it."

"In this case, sure."

"In every case?" She had his hand in hers now and was staring at him intently.

His drink was nearly gone, he noticed. Somehow hers seemed to have vanished as well.

Their waitress, someone who would have struck him as a lovely woman under ordinary circumstances, was whisking by their table toward the kitchen. "The check?" Deal managed quickly as the woman strode by. She nodded, without breaking stride. Deal could have sworn he saw her hiding a smile as she disappeared.

Angie directed him back onto the island, down North Roosevelt this time, past Sears Town and its attendant strip-mall fallout, on across First Street and then White, until they were once again beneath the leafy canopy that shaded the streets of Old Town, the area that Deal had come to think of as the true Key West. Away from the hectic bustle of Duval, Old Town was an eclectic mix of grand Victorians built by the seafarers and wreckers who had founded the place, cheek by jowl with modest saltbox cottages that would have looked at home amidst the dunes of the northeastern shore.

To Deal, who'd grown up in brightly lit and pastel-stuccoed Miami, these secluded streets and their clapboard houses exuded a fairy-tale charm, lending even this drive an out-of-time, otherworldly feel.

"Down there," Angie said, pointing out a lane obscured by shrubbery. One of the more impressive Victorians, converted now to an upscale bed-and-breakfast, took up the corner just ahead.

Deal slowed and swung the Hog into a turn. Branches brushed the sides of the doors as they went. "We could park on the street," she told him, "but then we'd have to walk."

"Perish the thought," Deal said, peering down the tunnel of greenery ahead.

"Right in here," she said, pointing to a suddenly appearing turnout off the narrow lane.

Deal obeyed, the lights of the Hog washing over the front of a neatly painted cottage just off the lane, nearly hidden beneath a looming banyan tree and fronted by a tangle of crotons and waist-high asparagus ferns. There was a tin-roofed porch running across the front of the place, with a wicker chair posted on one side of the entry and a motor scooter perched on the other.

"This is home," she said, pointing. "We could have taken my scooter, I guess, but somehow it wouldn't have been the same."

"How did you ever find it?" Deal said. He cut the motor, then the lights, leaving the faint glimmer of moonlight filtering through the overhanging limbs.

Angie's arm lay on the back of the seat behind him, her fingertips lightly poised on his shoulder. He felt light-headed but knew it wasn't the drinks. Maybe it was a dream, he thought. And why try to rouse yourself from a dream like this?

"A friend rented it from the guys who own the B and B up front," Angie said, pointing through the gloom. "When she moved out, I took over the lease."

"It looks great," Deal said. "Like Hansel and Gretel."

"You should come see," she said, one finger at his collar.

He turned. She leaned forward. He felt her lips on his. Dream or not, he thought, right thing or wrong, such thoughts no longer computed, whisked away like Fuentes's envelope out the Hog's window.

He was vaguely aware of the crinkling of paper as he pulled her against him. "The check," he heard her say, her lips at his ear.

"Forget it," he said. He levered himself out from behind the wheel, sliding down with her onto the broad seat of the car. For once, he thought, a reason to love this ungainly car.

His hand found her breast, he felt hers at his shirtfront, felt a button pop. "But John . . ."

"Forget the check," he repeated. And so they did.

Deal awoke with his head jammed into the corner of the passenger seat, his chin pressed nearly to his chest. Angie lay with her cheek pressed against his chest, her breathing quiet and regular, until he tried to ease away from the armrest that seemed to want him in a headlock.

"Hey," she said sleepily, lifting her chin. "Look what happened."

"Just look," Deal said. He levered himself up a bit, working his neck muscles against their stiffness.

The moon had shifted, sending more light from its new angle. He glimpsed the graceful curve of a shoulder, the rise of her hip, a tangle of clothing on the floorboards. "Good thing we didn't park on the street after all," Deal said.

"Mmmm." Angie made a sound of agreement, nuzzling against him. After a moment, she raised her head to look at him. "Maybe it's time to go inside."

Deal managed to bring his watch around into the light. Almost five, he saw. In less than two hours, his crews would be at work. "Almost time to go to work," he told her.

"On Saturday?" she said. "Don't construction moguls take the weekends off?"

"Maybe some do," he told her. "The rich ones."

"You're rich," she said, rearranging herself against him. "I happen to know."

"Not anymore," he said. "We vaporized that check. I felt it go up in one flash of heat and smoke. There's a scar here, right on my chest."

"No such luck," she said. She pushed herself up on her forearm, allowing him a view of her breasts as she reached for something on the dashboard.

"I saved you," she said, turning back, the check between her fingers. "That's twice."

Deal shook his head. "How'd you manage that?"

She smiled. "You were preoccupied," she said.

"I'd really better get you inside," he said.

She felt him shifting beneath her. "Don't you want to rephrase that statement?" she said.

It took him a moment. "Come on," he said. "I'll never make it to work."

"Whatever you say," she said. She found her top amidst the tangle on the floorboards and deftly pulled it over her head and into place. It gave Deal a momentary pang, like watching a moment's rewind of a breathtaking piece of film.

She opened the passenger door of the Hog and stepped outside to don her slacks, an equally downbeat moment, Deal thought, as the last pale glimmer of untanned flesh disappeared. He struggled into his own clothes in the meantime, finding one of his deck shoes under the seat, another on the dashboard. Maybe that's where she had stowed the check, he thought, sliding out into the moonlight to join her.

"You sure you don't want to come in?" she asked, pausing at the stairs to the porch. She was carrying her shoes in one hand, along with a ball of white lacy fabric that he first took to be a handkerchief.

"That's the very problem," he told her. "I'd love to. But I've got to be out there first thing."

She shrugged. "Suit yourself," she said.

"Maybe I could get a rain check," he said.

"Maybe," she said. Her tone was noncommittal, but her expression suggested otherwise. "Work hard," she said. She took one backward step up and leaned to kiss him quickly. In the next moment, she turned and was gone.

8.

DEAL NAVIGATED the Hog through a network of back streets southward across the island to the condominium complex where he'd rented his apartment, rubbing his stiff neck all the way and debating whether or not he should try for one more hour of sleep. But the chances he'd be able to wake up again were about the same as being able to pry himself out of Angie Marsh's cottage on time, he thought. He'd make himself a pot of coffee and head on out to the Villas, be there when the crews and the machine operator showed up, make sure things were right.

On the right, he passed the glowing bulk of the Casa Marina, the hotel Henry Flagler had intended as the showpiece of his Florida chain back when the mogul was in his heyday, and one of the few outposts of commerce in this far-southern part of the island. The hotel, eighty years old but aging nicely, was another

Florida monument to unqualified ambition, one Deal's father had been particularly fond of, and the family had stayed there several times in Deal's youth, Barton Deal never passing by one of the sepia-toned photos in the lobby without delivering some snippet of history.

"There's the man who invented Florida," his old man was fond of saying, pointing at a portrait of a mustachioed Flagler. The man had built a series of hotels down the east coast of Florida—St. Augustine, Ormand Beach, Palm Beach, Miami—along with a railroad to bring the crowds to them—and then, in the ultimate display of hubris, had planned to make Key West his terminus, hopscotching the railroad a hundred and fifty-odd miles over mostly open water to the Southernmost Point.

He'd somehow managed to pull the feat off, and even the fact that the rail line had been quickly blown to smithereens by the ungodly Labor Day Hurricane of 1935 had not dimmed his old man's enthusiasm for the undertaking. "Flagler was a goddamned pyramid builder," Barton Deal would proclaim loudly, happier if there were other tourists passing within earshot. "Wore seven-league boots. The kind of man in short supply these day."

Seven-league boots, Deal thought, turning eastward now, toward his complex. Surely that's what his father aspired to wear. And perhaps he had, by some lights anyway. Mighty big shoes to fill.

He was at the foot of South Roosevelt now, turning into the complex, pushing the button on the ponderous gate opener, finding himself wondering what his old man would have to say about his evening's experience. The dangers of staying up too late, or getting up too early, he was thinking, listening to the clanking of the heavy operating chain as the gate drew back. His old man would scoff at the notion of any guilt, to be sure. And he'd be even more impatient with Deal's tendency to deny himself pleasure, so he wasn't really sure if they could discuss anything about his encounter with Angie. "Hell's bells, boy. You're going to look *that* gift horse in the mouth?"

Still, Deal thought. Still . . .

. . . for so many years, he had harbored the hope that somehow he and Janice would find their way back together, that he could climb the mountain of guilt he'd built, see past all the impediments she'd piled up . . . denial, hope against hope, those had been his mainstays, for above everything, there was his daughter, Isabel, to think about.

Enough, he told himself, as the gate finally swung open to allow him access. He would think about it all tomorrow, as the lady once said, or at least wait for the cold light of day. In the meantime, a shower, a strong cup of coffee, a few aspirins to lighten the throbbing in his stiff neck. He glanced at the corner of the seat where he'd been wedged, asleep, shaking his head now. Sure, it had been enjoyable, what had led up to that nap, but wouldn't it have been just as much fun in a proper bed?

He left the car in the designated space beneath the building, then walked past the thick pilings to the seaward side of the complex. The front entrance was closer, but he favored the back steps, where he could get a dose of the sea breeze heavy in his face, and the reassuring slap-slap of the waves as well.

This place had some advantages, then, he was thinking, but if he'd been more patient, he might have found himself a cottage like Angie Marsh's, a hideaway in never-never land, and it was a short hop from that thought to the memory of the lacy panties she'd been holding as she kissed him good-bye, and an even quicker hop to the memory of that same bit of lace peeling away . . .

"Nice night for a walk, Mr. Deal," came an unfamiliar voice from the shadows.

The sound caught him like a blow. Deal stopped short, his hands raised in reflex. "What the hell?" he said, his eyes combing the darkness.

There was a tile-topped table and a clutch of lawn chairs arranged about a common area just ahead. Deal saw a shadowy figure rising from one of the chairs, the glow of a cigarette rising up, turning bright, then arcing away toward the sand.

"Don't be alarmed," the man said.

"Okay," Deal said, gathering himself. He checked the shadows, wondering if the man had company. "My alarm is off. Way off. Who the hell are you?"

The man was walking toward him now, and Deal drew back. Was there a pistol in that outstretched hand? Did he have a chance at making it to cover behind one of the support pillars?

"Relax," came the voice. A flashlight snapped on, illuminating what looked like a wallet in the man's outstretched hand. A badge case, Deal realized. Black leather surrounding a gold-and-silver shield, a photo ID beneath a plastic liner on the opposite side.

"I'm with the Department of Justice," the voice behind the flashlight said. "Does the name Fuentes mean anything to you?"

9.

"You were waiting out on that patio all night?" Deal asked, examining the shield under the bright fluorescents of his condo's kitchen. Norbert Vines, the ID read. He was a bland-looking guy in his thirties, shortish dark hair, a face that looked like it had been designed to be forgotten.

Vines shrugged as he took his shield back. "More or less," he said.

" 'More or less'? What does that mean?"

"It means we've had our eye on you for a while, ever since Fuentes turned up at your offices in Miami." Vines pulled a package in a courier pouch from under his arm and dropped it on the granite-topped kitchen table, some pages of typescript sliding free.

"Fuentes had this sent over for you, by the way," Vines said. "It must have fallen open after it got here," he added.

Deal stared at the man. The ache at the back of his neck had inched upward, turning into the beginnings of a real skull-pounder. He massaged his neck, wondering if there'd been somebody skulking in the bushes outside Angie's place, earlier. The possibility made him want to drop his shoulder and charge, send Vines backpedaling out the door and over the rail beyond.

"Look, I'm sorry if I frightened you out there," Vines said. "It's not my idea of fun, staying up all night, you know."

"Then why bother?" Deal said.

"Because it's important that we talk to you," Vines said.

"Who's this 'we'?"

Vines cleared his throat. "I'm part of a special-investigations unit within the Department of Justice," he said. He tapped the pocket where he'd replaced his shield, as if Deal might have forgotten. "You've been helpful to us in the past. It's our hope you'll be willing to be of help again."

Deal shook his head. "You must have made a mistake, my friend. I'm a building contractor . . ."

"You worked with Talbot Sams," Vines interjected, his tone more forceful.

It stopped Deal, a wave from the past washing up over him like a blast from the surf outside. Just when you think a memory might be safely buried, he thought, it's suddenly there again, as alive as the moments themselves . . .

. . . Deal entering the remote field offices of the company to find a man with a badge like Vines's, offering to keep him out of jail in return for the head of a client. Deal had had little choice but to comply, but things had not gone as anyone planned . . .

"*Worked* with Talbot Sams?" he managed. "Are you crazy? You're talking about a man who tried to kill me."

Vines shrugged. "Sams had an agenda of his own, I'm not

disputing that. But the fact is that he was within the agency's employ. He was carrying out an investigation of a highly sensitive nature when he . . ."

". . . when he did his damnedest to kill me and a bunch of other people I know," Deal finished.

He'd cut Vines off because he knew what was coming. The man might not have been callous enough to blurt out the details, but there was no disputing that a rogue agent named Talbot Sams was two years or more dead, and Deal had had his hand on the knife that killed him.

The fact that he'd learned it was Sams who had likely driven his father to his suicide had some bearing on how Deal felt about the matter—not to mention that Sams had been intent on plunging that same knife into Deal during the course of their struggle—but it was another chapter in his life that he wasn't eager to revisit, not with this stranger standing in his kitchen.

He stopped, refocusing on Vines. "The way it started with Talbot Sams, he came by my office uninvited one day, then pressured me into feeding him some information. That wouldn't be what you had in mind, would it?"

Deal was trying to stop the images that paraded through his mind, but it was hardly the sort of thing he'd ever forget. Talbot Sams had had a storied career as one of the Justice Department's in-house spooks, an undercover agent with more latitude and less oversight than any CIA agent ever dreamed of. He'd made a fortune by picking and choosing which of his targets to run to ground and which to blackmail, using the same tactics to pressure informants into cooperating when it suited him. He'd forced Barton Deal to help him with more than one of his schemes and—like father, like son, Deal supposed—had tried to do the same to him. Except it hadn't quite turned out the way Sams had planned. Instead of pocketing a fortune, Sams had ended up dead.

Vines held up his hands in a placating fashion. "I'm not here to pressure you, Mr. Deal. I'm here to plead with you." He gestured at the packet lying on the table once again.

"Your buddy Fuentes is involved with a group of people who make the notion of sleazy seem attractive. Some of them we've been aching to put away for years. Most of the individuals are from South America, but their influence is wide-ranging. They have ties to drugs, death squads, worldwide terrorist organizations."

His eyes met Deal's. "You were in the profession once; you ought to appreciate what we're up against."

Deal stared, fighting the urge to laugh. *The profession.* As if he'd signed up for a fraternity that never let you go. "That's something I don't talk about," he said to Vines, evenly. "Ever."

"That's understood," Vines nodded, his voice softening for a moment. He glanced away quickly—as if he'd read the dismissal files, Deal thought—and who was to say he hadn't.

"But we need help," Vines said, turning back, "and you're in a position to provide that help. That's the truth of it. That's why I'm here. Fuentes has a travel invitation for you in that packet. All we're asking you to do is accept."

Deal sighed, his hand going to the back of his aching skull once more. "If you're after Fuentes and his cohorts, why not go pick him up? Why are you bothering me?"

"You know it's not that simple," Vines said.

"I don't know anything," Deal said.

"Fuentes is a middleman, that's all, the consummate broker. We're not interested in him, and his backers are well out of our reach."

Deal stared at Vines in astonishment. "Are you looking for me to go after one of these people?"

"It's nothing like that." Vines shook his head. "We're looking for information, that's all."

Deal stifled a bitter laugh. "That's all Talbot Sams wanted. A little information."

"I can't speak to what passed between you and Talbot Sams, Mr. Deal. I can only speak for myself, and for the interests I represent. We'd like you to take Antonio Fuentes up on his invitation to visit Cuba. It's as simple as that."

"I'm an American citizen," Deal said. "I'm not allowed to go to Cuba."

Vines seemed not to hear. "Fuentes may have no scruples, but he does have influence. There may be no other person, in fact, as practiced as he in brokering arrangements that channel illicit monies into legitimate enterprises worldwide."

"Imagine my surprise," Deal said. "I took him for an honest old guy who needed a carport built. Now you tell me he's a money launderer."

Vines made a waving motion with his hands, brushing it all away. "We have reason to believe that among the men Fuentes is in contact with in Cuba is a person of extreme political importance." He paused then, for emphasis. "We believe that this person is poised to assume the presidency once Castro is out of the way."

Deal stared at the man for a moment. "Maybe that's a reasonable assumption," he said, "given what Fuentes and his crowd seem to have in mind. So what? I still don't see where I come in."

"There's been no end of speculation as to who's next in line over there," Vines said, "but no matter who it is—even if it were Castro's brother himself, and we very much doubt that it will be—there will be undeniable and massive changes in how our government and Cuba's interact."

"Is this the kind of pep talk they gave Teddy Roosevelt before he charged up San Juan Hill?"

"It's not going to be gunfire that determines the course of the next round of political change in Cuba, Mr. Deal. This time it's going to be dollars. Whomever Fuentes is in contact with, that's where the real power is located. You can trust me on that."

"I wouldn't trust you to lock the door on your way out, Vines."

The man was unfazed. "You have a unique opportunity to help change the course of history; that's what I'm trying to convey to you. You can be a part of the solution to an immense political and social problem that has plagued this country for almost fifty years. Right now, people are out there in those straits, riding inner tubes and smugglers' boats, risking their lives to try to get to this country," Vines said. He swept his arm vehemently toward the tasteful, wood-shuttered windows of the condo.

"At the same time, you've got the Florida exile community, working the other side," he continued. "They're one of the most powerful lobbying group in Washington, clamoring for an agenda that makes the NRA look like a pack of liberals." He shook his head as if bewildered by his own words. "The heartache, the expense, the strife for everyone . . . you can be a part of the solution to all of it."

"What if he's the wrong guy?" Deal said.

Vines stared back, puzzled. "What are you talking about?"

"Say I come up with the name, you don't like who it is."

Vines threw up his hands. "Then we'll deal with it, if you'll pardon the expression. It's the *information* we're after. The ability to prepare to respond. That's the key . . ."

"Forget it, Vines," he said. "Go find yourself another contractor."

"You are the right man," Vines said, his tone resolute. "You have no political agenda. Your reputation is impeccable." He paused, an odd expression crossing his features. "When it comes right down to it, we want you over there for the same reasons Fuentes does."

"I must be doing something wrong," Deal said weary. "I am attracting entirely the wrong class of client."

"Ah, yes," Vines said, as if he had forgotten something. "There is that, too." He reached into the pocket of his coat and withdrew an envelope, then held it out toward Deal.

"What's that supposed to be?" Deal asked.

"We don't expect you to take time away from your business affairs without recompense," Vines said. He extended the envelope another inch, practically waving it under Deal's nose.

Deal's curiosity got the better of him. He took the envelope and peeled it open under Vines's watchful eye. Another cashier's check, he saw, another offshore bank. Not quite as many zeros as on Fuentes's check, but not bad for a few days in sunny Havana.

"Government work pays a lot better than I remember," he told Vines.

"Some of it may," Vines said. The tone of his voice made Deal wonder if he'd finally struck a chord.

"I wish I could help you out," Deal said. He handed the check back toward Vines who stared as if it were a snake in his outstretched hand.

"I don't know where you got that," Vines said, indicating the envelope, "but it certainly wasn't from me."

Deal didn't miss a beat. He crumpled the envelope and tossed it onto the kitchen counter. "We've wasted enough time, Vines. I want you out of here, now. I've got work to do."

He started forward, ready to brush by the man, but Vines didn't move. "You're a tough one to convince," he said, with something like a smile on his face. "They said you would be, but I had no idea it would be this difficult."

"Is that right?" Deal said, sizing the man up. "We've been through fraternity, liberty and cold, hard cash. What's next, rubber hoses?" Vines was barely six feet, maybe went one-seventy. "You have some help on the other side of that door?"

Vines shook his head, and Deal thought the man's expression shifted toward something resembling sadness. "It's about your father . . ." he began, then faltered when he saw the look in Deal's eyes.

"You'd drag my father into this?" Deal felt his hands clenching. The hell with it, he thought, let Vines bring in his hidden SWAT team for backup. He was going to put an end to things right now. It was getting light outside, maybe one of his neighbors would be up early, hear the ruckus, they'd call the cops and bail him out.

"Hear me out," Vines said, raising a warning hand. "Just give me one more minute. If you don't want to listen to any more after that, I'll leave."

Deal hesitated, caught by some flicker of sincerity in the man's gaze. "It better be goddamned good, Vines."

Vines nodded, edging away a millimeter or two, perhaps. "Your father died under something of a cloud, I can appreciate that . . ."

"I'd call it more than a cloud," Deal said. "More like a hurricane. Category Five. It's been blowing for a dozen years or so."

"Barton Deal's reputation was greatly diminished," Vines continued. "And you've suffered as well. A promising career upended, a life spent since trying to rebuild a once-powerful firm . . ."

"I appreciate the condolences," Deal said. "But your minute's just about gone."

"I can make it go away," Vines blurted.

Deal shook his head. "What are you talking about?"

"That cloud, that force-five hurricane you were just talking about," Vines repeated. "I am in a very real position to put a few things right for you."

"You'd have to be quite a guy, Vines," Deal said.

"Just listen," the man said, his confident tone at odds with his unprepossessing appearance. "I know all about you, dammit. You've been bearing this cross for a dozen years. I can help you get it off your shoulders."

Deal blinked, not sure if he should let Vines continue or drop him with the punch he'd been yearning to throw at someone since the night he'd found his father in his study all those years before, since the moment the captain had offered him that holier-than-thou opportunity to slink off from the department and into the night.

Just one dead-solid-perfect blow of retribution. That's all. Maybe Vines wasn't the perfect candidate, but he was suddenly looking pretty promising.

"For the love of God," Vines persisted. "What I'm offering you just doesn't happen in this business. Not in my experience, anyway."

Deal felt himself teetering on the edge of some vast abyss, but whatever was down there in that darkness, it was impossible to fathom. Rage? Madness? Simple oblivion?

He was exhausted, his head pounding, his emotions bouncing wildly inside his skull. "Get it out, Vines. Get it over with."

"When Talbot Sams came to you for help some time back, he told you that your father had been one of his informants for years. He told you furthermore that he'd approached your father at a time when he had compromised himself with a certain group of clients and made a proposition he could not refuse: Your father was to feed information along to Sams about certain unsavory characters DealCo did business with and by doing so could keep himself out of prison, am I correct?"

"Of course he got to make a few bucks in the process," Deal said, unable to contain himself any longer. "Sams became a kind of procurer by the time it was over. He'd send the scuzzwads my old man's way, let him build hotels for crooked pension funds, banks for Colombian drug lords, then bust the bad guys when the time was right." He broke off for a moment and threw up his hands in dismay.

"It was an arrangement that made Sams a legend, I gather, and unless I'm mistaken, he managed to skim off a few bucks for himself. I guess my old man was able to live with it for a while, but in the end that's what killed him. He blew his brains out, but it might as well have been Sams who pulled the trigger." Deal's chest was heaving by the last of it. He felt as if he'd picked up a safe and chucked it out the window at Vines's back.

Vines stared back, his voice soft now. "Everything you say makes perfect sense," he said. "But can you prove it?"

Deal scoffed. "Of course I can't. That doesn't mean . . ."

"I can." Vines cut him off.

Deal stopped, staring. Vines reached into his pocket and tossed a key onto the tabletop beside them.

"What is it?" Deal asked, his gaze moving from the key to meet Vines's intent gaze.

"A key to a safe-deposit box," Vines said. "Inside it is everything from Sams's own files pertaining to his arrangements with your father. Sams was a very thorough man, Mr. Deal." He paused and shrugged. "He came on board when Nixon was vice-president. Maybe they shared the same mentality, a compulsion to document even the crimes they committed.

"In any case, it's all there. Proof that he blackmailed your father, the illicit business arrangements authorized by Sams himself, a record of wire transfers, everything."

Deal stared down at the key, then back at Vines. "So I take a trip to Cuba with Fuentes, you give me back my father's reputation?"

Vines looked away for a moment. "Don't think that I'm comfortable with any of this, Mr. Deal. I don't call the shots. I just do what I'm told."

Deal nodded, his mind traveling back to that dreadful night, the sight of his father sprawled backward in his chair. "It all comes a little late for my old man, doesn't it?"

Vines turned back to him, his gaze as close to sincere as it was likely to get. "Sure it does," Vines said. "But it's not too late for you."

Deal shook his head. "What are you talking about?"

Vines gestured at the key. "Along with everything else, there are copies of the documents Sams planted in your old man's office, the stuff they found the night he died."

It took a moment, but the import of what Vines had just told him seemed to reset the ground beneath Deal's feet. "It was Sams who set me up, got me tossed?"

Vines looked away. "I'm sorry. It doesn't do much good to say that now . . ."

Deal laughed, but it was a strangled, off-key sound. "Not Schnecter and his pals, then . . ."

Vines had a plaintive look on his face. "It can't change what's happened, but it vindicates you and your old man, John. At least there's that . . ."

At least there's that, he thought. How much of every bit of effort of every day had he spent trying to find some way to make his life seem right? Every setback, every blow along the way not just bad luck, not just part of life, not to him.

He'd taken every punch with the inner certainty cosmic forces were at work, that it was his Job-like lot to reel and reel and keep himself standing upright for more. Now here was a man named Vines standing before him, suggesting that it didn't have to be that way; it didn't have to be that way anymore.

Deal took a deep breath, gesturing at the key that lay between them on the table. "How do I know all this material you're talking about really exists?"

Vines reached into his pocket and withdrew a computer disk. "Much of what I'm talking about, you'll find a copy of it on here. It's an encrypted file. You can open it, you can read it, and then it's gone." Vines gestured through the doorway into the living room where Deal had set up a desktop computer in anticipation of Isabel's arrival. "I wouldn't try copying it if I were you," he added.

Deal eyed the disk, then gestured at the key that lay on the table. "I just take that to the bank, everything's mine?"

"You'll need a second key, and some authorizations, but once you're back from this run to Havana, you'll have our complete cooperation." Vines gave him what passed for a smile. "You get to keep that, too," he said, pointing at the wadded envelope on the nearby counter.

Deal felt his lip curl. "Not to mention the satisfaction that I'm doing my patriotic duty?"

Vines nodded. "It's quite a package, when you put it all together."

"And why should I trust you to come through?"

Vines shrugged. "The information we're talking about is of no value to anyone but you, Mr. Deal. Talbot Sams is dead, his criminal activity a matter of record. If you're willing to be of assistance, we have no reason not to hold up our end of the bargain."

Deal found himself thinking of Fuentes, who suddenly seemed the soul of magnanimity in comparison to the man who stood before him. Fuentes, after all, was just an ordinary criminal who wanted to cut him in on the action, and rather handsomely at that. How on earth could you characterize people like Vines?

He thought next of Fuentes's check, tucked safely inside his wallet, those printed red numerals fairly pulsing in his mind's eye. There'd been no mention of any million-dollar check by Vines, which had to make him wonder.

One man seemed intent on filling Deal's pockets with cash, and another seemed equally intent that he let it happen, and give him back his father's soul in the bargain.

"All I have to do is go over there, keep tabs on who I meet?"

Vines glanced away momentarily. "That's just about the size of it."

Deal heard something in his tone. "What else, Vines?"

Vines turned back. "Just a couple of procedural details, that's all."

Deal caught a hint of pink sky out the kitchen window, and glanced at his watch with a sigh. "I'm going to make some coffee, and then I'm going to go to work," he said to Vines. "You've got ten minutes to tell me exactly what you want me to do over there."

"I can do it in five," Vines said. He was actually smiling as he handed over the disk. Then he reached into his jacket to pull an envelope from his pocket.

10.

"STAND UP," said the man in the suit, driving his foot into the old man's side. "Don't you see who it is?"

The old man had been sleeping, his buttocks resting on the concrete floor, his back propped against the wall of his cell. It was a preferable arrangement to using the thin mattress, which was infested with lice.

He had been dreaming of his preparations for a hurricane. He'd ordered truckloads of styrofoam packing peanuts brought to his house, and was engaged in filling all the spaces of every room, as if it were one huge multicompartmentalized box to prepare for shipping. He had reasoned that with all that packing jammed inside, nothing could break, even if the strongest winds hit. He was going to be the last item packed, just sit down in his favorite recliner with a cooler of beer at hand, have the fellows from the truck blow in the last of the styrofoam peanuts, pack him up tight, right in place, let the four winds blow.

That's when the kick awakened him, more or less. He peered up at the two men who had entered his cell and blinked in the bright light. He had no idea what time it was, for there was no window in his cell and the bulb that dangled from the high ceiling was always on, except for the times he had managed to knock it out with a toss of his shoe.

They'd beaten him the first couple of times he'd done it, then finally wised up and taken his shoes. They didn't make you a prison guard because you were smart, not even in Cuba.

He recognized the man in the bad suit as someone who had participated in the beatings. Certain things were hard to forget. But the other one, a bearded man in green Army fatigues, he was not so certain of.

"Stand up!" the man in the suit was shouting. "Salute your *comandante* . . ." He was positioning himself for another kick when the bearded man stopped him.

"It is not necessary," the bearded man said.

He knelt down, his eyes level with the old man's. "Do you know me?" he asked, his gaze keen on the old man's eyes.

"Now I do," the old man said with a nod.

"Of course," the bearded man said, a smile playing at his lips. He glanced up knowingly at the man in the suit.

"You're Jesus Christ," the old man said. "Come to save me at last."

The man with the beard hung his head. "I think you are playing games with me," he said. He directed the first of it to the floor, then brought his gaze back to meet the old man's. "My friend of so many years, how could you forget?"

"We were friends?" the old man asked.

"Good friends," the bearded man replied.

"Then why don't you get me out of here?"

The bearded man smiled tolerantly. "Joseíto here has questions for you. Important questions. There are people who wish me harm, old friend. You know these people, and you know of their plans. If you will only speak of these things to Joseíto then you will be on your way." He waved as if the notion were impossible not to grasp.

"People want to hurt you?"

"It is a lamentable truth," the bearded man said.

"You must be important, then."

The bearded man shook his head and glanced up at the man in the suit. "Leave him to me," the one in the suit said. "If there is anything left in that brain of his, he will speak it. If not..." He shrugged.

The bearded man turned back. "You hear what Joseíto says, old friend." He paused and waved a hand about their surroundings. "And this place where you are, it belongs to him. What am I to do?"

The old man blinked. "Let me go," he said.

"If you will only help Joseíto, it will be done."

The old man glanced up at the man in the suit, then back at the one with the beard. "Were we really friends?"

The bearded man's gaze seemed to draw inward. He drew a breath before he answered. "Yes," he said, finally. "We were friends."

"Did I ever do you any harm?"

The bearded man stared back. "I do not think so," he said.

"Then you should get me out of here," the old man said. "You'll rest easier if you do."

The bearded man sighed. He stood up and gave his companion a look that suggested perplexity.

"I will fix him," the man in the suit said.

"Another time," the bearded man said. He motioned for the man in the suit to precede him out the door. And they were gone.

11.

"A MAGNIFICENT SIGHT, wouldn't you gentlemen agree?" It was Antonio Fuentes come to join Deal and Russell Straight at the rail of the lavishly appointed Hatteras, waving his hand now in the direction of the looming headlands above Havana Bay, just off the yacht's port side.

"Awesome," Deal said, his eyes on the cliff-top fortress that commanded the entrance to the vast bay ahead. It was a word co-opted and drained by a generation of wave-rippers, stoners and skateboarders, but still it seemed appropriate for what he saw jutting into the sky above him, an enormous stone fortress that seemed to have grown up from the very rock beneath it.

"Be a good place to set up your guns," Russell offered. Sheets of spray unfurled from the yacht's prow, spangling the view into something approaching magic.

"The Spaniards thought so," Fuentes said. "They mounted a dozen enormous cannons inside those walls." He flashed his smile as he gestured. "The Twelve Apostles, they were called. A rather effective deterrent in those days."

Deal nodded, his eyes tracing the irregular lines of the massive battlements. It was Morro Castle up there, he knew that much, built in the late 1500s by the descendants of the original conquistadors, to safeguard the outpost called Cuba they'd wrested from the natives.

Look upon this work, ye mighty, and dismay, he mused, a version of a line from a poem he'd studied in college springing to him, some ruler's dare from the past to the foolhardy of the present.

Sure. The castle was just a showpiece now, but if he had been a pirate or plunderer with an eye on the sprawling city laid out below, the sight of that imposing fortress would certainly have given him pause. Then again, he thought, given their present purpose, perhaps he should feel pause right now.

"As if that weren't enough," Fuentes said, pointing toward the foot of the cliffs, "each night a great chain was raised from the bottom of the sea and stretched across the entrance of the harbor. It made the city virtually impregnable."

"They must have had plenty to worry about," Russell said.

"Cuba has always been coveted," Fuentes replied. He gave Deal a meaningful look.

"The most beautiful island that eyes have ever seen," Fuentes intoned, gesturing over the bow at the vista sprawled before them. "Do you know who wrote those words?"

"Christopher Columbus," Deal said, offhandedly.

Fuentes smiled again, and this time it seemed genuine. "You

surprise me, Mr. Deal. This from a man whose grades were not so good . . . ?"

"It was just a guess," Deal said. "I didn't think it was Ronald Reagan."

Fuentes smiled. "So you say." He nodded.

Deal glanced at Russell, then turned back to the view. Let Fuentes think he knew everything in his mind, he thought. It was probably better that way.

The waters of the Florida Straits, placid enough to begin with this day, had calmed even further as they approached the island, the swells subsiding steadily as the corrugated thumbprint of land grew steadily larger at the juncture of pristine sky and sea. He could only imagine Columbus, staring off at this lovely island after months at sea. It must have seemed a suitable payoff, even for such monumental efforts as those.

Their own had been a quick and uneventful crossing—he'd boarded Fuentes's yacht around eight and could guess without looking at his watch that it wasn't yet two. After a glance at what was on the disk Vines had given him, he'd spent a hectic day preparing his crews at the Villas for his absence and convincing Russell Straight to join him.

He'd confined his story to the vaguest details of Fuentes's proposition, leaving any mention of Vines out of it. For now, there was no need to revisit those matters with Russell, who'd been pleased enough to join him as it was. His girlfriend in Miami had grown accustomed to his periodic absences, and if Russell had no special interest in Cuba, he certainly wasn't unhappy about a few paid days off the job.

Deal had returned to his condo early in the evening to pack a few things, then tried to phone Janice to let her know he'd be away for a long weekend. He'd ended up having to leave a message on her cell phone, then left another detailed set of instructions for Bernice on the machine at his Miami office. He'd picked up a sandwich at Fausto's market, munched on it absently in the parking lot, then finally stopped struggling against the matter that had been bothering him the entire day.

He'd started the engine of the Hog, and after a few minutes' searching, managed to find his way back to Angie Marsh's tucked-away cottage, still uncertain what he was going to say to her.

As it turned out, his apprehension was wasted. Though the motor scooter was still perched where he'd seen it, and a melting glass of ice tea on the table beside the wicker chair suggested she'd certainly not been gone long, his knock at the door brought no response.

He'd tried Watkins Title and dropped by the Pier House as well, but had had no luck. In the end, he'd returned to the still-deserted cottage, where he'd tucked a note in the screen describing an unexpected business trip to the Caymans. Close enough, he thought, with a sidelong glance at their host. At least there was a Caymans bank involved.

He'd dropped into bed, exhausted, waking shortly before their appointed meeting time with Fuentes. He'd meant to drop by Angie's cottage on the way out of town that morning, but had hesitated, debating with himself: He had left his phone number on the note, after all, and time was getting short, and he was beginning to feel too much like a schoolboy anyway.

Sex in the front seat of a car, unanswered notes tucked in a sweetheart's door? Besides, what if he dropped by her place, only to find that she wasn't alone? No, he'd thought, he would be gone just a few days, and the separation would be good. He'd have a chance to sort things out, see how he felt when he returned. With that thought in mind, he'd driven resolutely past the looming Bed-and-Breakfast without a backward glance and made his way across town.

He'd arranged to leave the Hog in the parking lot of the Pier House, then had walked across the street to the Mallory Docks, where he found Russell already waiting. The two of them were ferried from the docks out to Fuentes's yacht on a tender boat piloted by a taciturn Conch who professed no knowledge of the *Bellísima* or the man who owned her.

"Lot of big, expensive boats come and go around here," the man had said with a shrug. "I don't ask a lot of questions, myself."

Fuentes had had no qualms about Deal's announcement that Russell would be joining them. Apparently, traveling with the taciturn Tomás suggested to him that anyone of importance needed a spare linebacker or two in attendance.

In any case, Fuentes had been there to welcome them on board and usher them inside a teak-paneled stateroom, where Russell devoured first one plate and then a second of the elaborate breakfast buffet laid out. Deal had merely picked at his food, and once again scanned the financials and other documentation Fuentes had sent over in the courier pouch.

There was no way of determining the precise identities of the principals behind Fuentes's undertaking, but the anonymous thumbnails before him suggested that at least one notorious South American political boss was involved. And whatever the identities of the half dozen individuals profiled, there seemed to be tremendous financial firepower in reserve—assuming, of course, that it was all true.

But why wouldn't there be some international consortium of the very powerful gearing up to snatch what they could of the island he was presently looking at, Deal wondered? Vines seemed to believe that such a scenario was under way. And there had been a series of groups intent on that mission for the past five hundred years, after all. First had come the Spaniards, then the Americans and finally the Mob. Even the Russians had tried their hand at Cuba for a few decades.

"You want some of that lunch they put out?" Deal came up from his thoughts to find Russell at his side, pointing inside the afterdeck stateroom where one of Fuentes's mates busied about the buffet table.

Deal followed Russell's gesture, absently fingering one of the tiny plastic disks in his pocket. One of Vines's "procedural details," he thought, ruefully. About the size and weight of a watch battery, the thing had one dark, irregular side, cooked up to resemble a chunk of dried chewing gum, while the other side was smooth, with a covering that peeled away, allowing it to be stuck onto any hard surface.

"Doesn't matter where you put it," Vines had assured him. "It'll pick up conversation anywhere in a room."

Vines had given him a dozen of the things to scatter in what he deemed "useful" locations during his stay in Cuba. When Deal had expressed doubt that anything so small could send a signal all the way back to the United States, Vines had shaken his head at Deal's naiveté.

"It doesn't have to," he said. "Why do you think we still maintain a U.S. Interests Section in Havana? There's a state-of-the-art listening station you wouldn't believe set up inside the place. These things will beam in loud and clear that far."

"Then why not let your spies go plant the bugs?"

"Cuba is a closed society, my friend. They can't get to where you're going. That's the whole point," Vines told him. "You can start with Fuentes's boat."

Which was something he hadn't gotten around to quite yet, Deal thought, breaking off his replay of the conversation. He wasn't an undercover agent—even when he'd been on the force, the notion of deception had never appealed to him. He was who he was, and these days he was a goddamned building contractor.

What had ever possessed him to go along with Vines on this? He took another look at the approaching shoreline, then gave Fuentes a sidelong glance.

"Maybe I'll get a little something," he said.

"Of course," Fuentes responded, with a grand flourish.

"How about you?" Deal asked. He realized his fingers had turned sweaty on the disk in his pocket. Some spy, he thought. But then again, Vines had been a little light on the training.

"Not just now," Fuentes responded with another dramatic wave. "I am enjoying the view."

He turned back to the rail then, and Deal quickly followed after Russell, who was already hovering over the table inside. As he surveyed the room, Fuentes's mate disappeared into the galley, from where issued the sound of pots being stowed, along with the clank of plates and crockery.

The heavy teak buffet table seemed a likely place to plant one of the bugs, Deal thought. It was surely permanent—the thing would have to be taken apart to move it from the room—and it had a spacious-enough overhang where he could hide the disk.

He watched Russell mounding what looked like tuna salad onto his plate, debated briefly about enlisting his help, then thought better of it. He reached back into his pocket and found the tiny tab with his thumb and forefinger, and, with the thing still hidden, peeled the protective covering away. He had the device out of his pocket and was about to step up to the table and press it to the underside of the lip when Fuentes's mate popped back out of the galley.

"Mr. Deal," the man said in his faintly accented English. "Allow me to help you . . ."

"Just getting some coffee," Deal said, hastily reaching for a china cup and saucer.

The mate reached quickly for the cup, but Deal grabbed it back with his other hand. The mate was resolute, however—this was a man who'd clearly been put on this earth to serve.

His hand darted swiftly to the edge of the delicate saucer and pulled it deftly away from Deal. He was about to lift the heavy silver coffee decanter to pour with his other hand when his eyes widened at something.

"Dios mío," the man muttered. He glanced up at Deal, his face ashen. "My apologies, Mr. Deal."

Deal's gaze was locked upon the man's finger, which scratched away at the china saucer, trying to dislodge the wad of gum stuck to its rim. Deal glanced back at the mate, his astonishment shading gradually toward dread. So much for spycraft, he thought. What in God's name was he to do? Russell, meanwhile, sent him a curious look, but didn't leave off working on his still-unfilled plate.

"Raúl," the mate called sharply toward the galley.

A young Hispanic man appeared in the doorway, concern on his face. *"¿Qué pasa?"*

"¡Mira!" The mate thrust the cup and saucer at his helper, a dark expression on his face.

"It is inexcusable," the mate added to Deal. "The boy is an idiot."

"No," Deal said, abruptly, his brain beginning to function at last. "It's my gum."

He thrust his hand up as if to snatch the plate away, sending both cup and saucer flying. The mate and his assistant stared in dismay as the delicate china struck the parquet floor and shattered.

"I'm sorry," Deal said. He started forward toward the mess, shards of china grinding beneath his sole.

"Let the boy get it," the mate said, tugging at Deal's sleeve. "You came for coffee."

Raúl had already ducked into the galley and was back in an instant with a broom and dustpan. In moments, he'd swept up the broken pieces and was gone. Deal heard the clatter as the dustpan was emptied.

Deal allowed himself to be steered back to the buffet table, where the mate poured his cup of coffee. "Nothing else?" the mate inquired, handing Deal the cup. "You are certain?"

"I'm fine," Deal said. The mate gave him a curt nod and hurried off into the galley, where he began to deliver a fusillade of angry Spanish at the unfortunate Raul. While Russell finished the building of a mammoth sandwich, Deal pulled a second of the disks from his pocket and quickly affixed it to the underside of the table.

"What the hell was that about?" Russell asked, finally glancing up, but Deal was already on his way out the door.

"You are just in time," Fuentes said, as Deal emerged on deck.

Deal nodded, wondering if Fuentes could hear the pounding of his heart. The man seemed oblivious, though. He was turned back toward land, his hand raised in the now familiar dramatic gesture.

They were less than a mile out from the coast now, and a string of impressive, Renaissance-style buildings had come into view, perched improbably above a huge seawall at the rocky, crescent-shaped shoreline and stretching away endlessly into the distance. It reminded Deal, who was still trying to get his breathing under control, of the striking view from seaward of the Art Deco hotels strung along Ocean Drive.

But, however impressive that sight was, it was only a few short blocks. This array seemed to go on forever, its graceful curving aspect only adding to the allure.

"The Malecón," Fuentes said, following Deal's gaze. "Miles of it. It looks rather grand from this vantage point, does it not?"

Deal glanced over. Fuentes's eyes remained hidden behind his dark glasses, but he had shed his suit in favor of a pair of buttery linen slacks and a long-sleeved guayabera of a slightly darker shade. He wore a cap with an elongated fisherman's bill and a flap that extended down the back of his neck. Maybe the man suffered from some form of albinism, Deal thought. Or maybe it was just a lifetime living under rocks.

"Grand?" Deal agreed, grateful for Fuentes's preoccupation. "I guess that's a good word for it. It looks almost surreal, Florence by the sea or something."

"Best to see it this way to begin with," Fuentes said, nodding his approval. "That is one reason we came by boat."

"I'm not sure I follow," Deal said.

"Once we are there," Fuentes said, gesturing toward the shore, "you will understand what I mean. Better your own eyes tell you than my words."

Deal took it in without comment. He glanced toward the

land again, noting that they had changed course slightly. They were heading west now, running parallel to shore.

"We're not going into the harbor?" he asked, a bit disappointed not to sail in beneath the prow of that massive fortress that hovered in the sky.

Fuentes shook his head. "It is the commercial port which lies that way," he said, using his chin to point back toward the castle. "We will dock at the Marina Hemingway. Arrangements are made more simply there."

He flashed Deal a hint of his all-knowing smile and paused before changing tacks. "I'm pleased that you were willing to take this journey, Mr. Deal. I'm confident that great things lie ahead for us all."

"A few years in a dungeon?" Deal said with a backward glance at the room where he'd planted his bug. Images from old movies spun through his mind, men in iron masks digging through rock with knives and spoons and fingernails.

It brought a hearty laugh from Fuentes. "We've hardly come here to plot the overthrow of the government," he said. "Our presence is welcomed here by many men of influence, I assure you. We will be discreet in our discussions, of course, but we have nothing to fear."

Deal nodded, but he was hardly convinced. He suspected that the real reason that they had come by boat was to avoid the annoying niceties of Customs. Despite the embargo and the travel restrictions, pleasure craft plied the waters between Cuba and the States with relative impunity. Even flying indirectly to Cuba, with an intervening stop in Canada, Jamaica or Mexico, left a paper trail that was easily traced by U.S. authorities.

While no one had ever been jailed for making the trip without a proper license, there'd been plenty of fines doled out, especially when friends of the Cuban exile community were occupying the White House. At the very least, they were traveling off the radar screen of the American government, Deal thought, or certainly Fuentes would assume that they were.

Barton Deal himself had favored a sail to Cuba for much the same reasons. His father had used the old port of Cojímar, just east of the city, an ancient fishing village where Hemingway had moored his own yacht, *Pilar,* and was said to have met regularly with Carlos Gonzáles, the true prototype for *The Old Man and the Sea,* but Deal knew that his father had docked at the more modern Marina Hemingway at least once. He'd returned grumbling about it, though: "Papa wouldn't have set foot in the place," he'd said. "Not a Hemingway thing about it."

"We're coming up on Miramar," Fuentes said, gesturing at a point of land that jutted into the sea not far ahead. "That's the River Almendares," he added, pointing at a cleft that separated one spit of land from the next. "We'll be putting in soon."

Deal nodded, pushing himself from the rail as the awesome sweep of the Malecón began to fade behind them. As they rounded the point, the seawall and its bulwark of rock and the modest surf disappeared, and the shoreline was transformed into a ragged blend of trees and waterfront housing, the sort of view he might have encountered virtually anywhere along the Florida coast south of Miami.

Up ahead he could see a long breakwater jutting out from shore, marking the entrance to the Marina Hemingway, he supposed. He could make out a line of red-tiled roofs poking above the treetops just inland, resembling nothing so much as a seaside complex in any one of a hundred South Florida communities.

Quite a contrast—he'd have to give Fuentes that much. One

moment he was staring at medieval Europe dropped down at seaside in the tropics; the next he was back in condo land.

The *Bellísima* made its way past the end of the breakwater and slowed, its big engines shuddering as it made the turn inside the protected waters. Just ahead, Deal saw a pelican drop into the water toward some unseen prey, as swift and as forceful as feathered lead. He glanced inside the screened afterdeck, where Russell Straight still grazed among the delicacies laid out on the buffet table.

"It looks a little like Boca Raton around here," he said to Fuentes, as they slowed to no-wake speed. They had entered a narrow channel now, flanked on either side by a series of three-story condominiums, their screened porches and cabanas arranged to offer a view of the murky canal and the occasional passing yacht. A few hundred yards ahead was the marina basin itself, where a welter of conning towers and sail masts poked up, bobbing alongside the docks.

"Indeed," Fuentes said, sounding as if he took it for a compliment. "But it's nothing to what was planned before the revolution." He swept his hand over the adjoining rooftops. "There are several hundred acres still untouched here. A silent fortune just waiting to be mined."

Deal nodded as if he agreed, but inwardly his spirits sagged. He was having a hard time matching up these surroundings with the images of an intolerant dictator haranguing the masses on the evils of capitalism.

"Most of this has to have been built since the revolution," he found himself saying to Fuentes.

"You are quite correct," Fuentes said.

"Fidel's been in the condominium business all along?"

Fuentes smiled. "What you see here is the result of foreign investment," he said, "monies which have reached the country in limited amounts, and in a few selected areas. After all, if you keep a lid too tightly on a boiling pot, Mr. Deal . . ." He trailed off with a shrug. "But this is only a mere suggestion of what is to come."

The engines of the *Bellísima* had ground nearly to a halt now, and Deal realized they were easing broadside toward a larger dock that sat apart from the crowded basin. Russell joined him as a deckhand and tossed a line to a counterpart standing on shore, just opposite the forward rail, and another pair performed the same aft.

"I guess we're here," Russell said, and Deal nodded, feeling an odd, unexpected sensation as he watched the dock glide up to meet them. On the way across the Straits, he hadn't thought much about the political aspects of what Vines had told him, but suddenly he couldn't help considering the prospect for a moment.

What if it were true, the intrigue that Vines had choreographed for him? What if the men he met here were indeed the ones who would change the land that lay before him forever? Hard to imagine anything other than the closed-off, cauldron-of-trouble Cuba that he had known all his life, and just as difficult to believe that anything he might do could influence such a monumental change. But on the other hand, the very concept was enough to nudge at his heart rate.

. . . *with a wild surmise,* came the phrase into his mind. How the poets had described the early explorers' view of the unknown Pacific regions they'd encountered. At the time an English teacher had required him to memorize the lines, Deal had had no idea what *"wild surmise"* was, but now he thought he had an inkling.

"Take a look at *that,* would you," said Russell, taking his arm and pointing.

The condos had curved away from the docks here, leaving room for a service road to make its approach. At the end of the lane, where the pavement widened beside a rusting storage shed, sat two cars parked at the end of the pavement: One was a hulking vintage Cadillac from the fifties, black with bulbous white-walled tires and a chrome sun visor that ran along the top of the windshield like a glinting eyebrow; the other was a Mercedes sedan, not new, perhaps, but still impressive enough to Deal's eye. In a country where an American automobile hadn't been imported in more than forty years, he suspected that these two vehicles constituted a significant portion of the flagship fleet.

"We must rate," said Russell at his side, and Deal could only nod his agreement.

One of the hands had already secured the ship's gangway to the dock and had assumed a position of rigid attention on shore. The ship's engines died away, replaced by the revving motors of the automobiles. The driver of the Cadillac emerged to stand by the nose of his idling machine, though the doors of the Mercedes remained closed, its occupants, if any, hidden behind a screen of dark tinted glass.

Fuentes had a hand on Deal's shoulder, urging him toward the gangway. "Welcome to Havana, Mr. Deal," he said, with his saturnine smile.

Deal glanced about, noting that one of the deckhands was at the rear of the gleaming Cadillac, loading their bags into the cavernous trunk.

"How about Customs?" Deal asked, as Russell passed between them, shaking his head in disbelief, his eyes wide, as if drawn toward the vintage car by an otherworldly force. "Immigration, all the little things like that?" He had the rest of the disks Vines had provided him clutched in his fist, ready to scatter them like seeds if the prospect of a search presented itself.

Fuentes gave him another hearty laugh. "Everything is taken care of, Mr. Deal. Rest assured. You have nothing to worry about."

Funny, Deal thought, his clutched fist relaxing as he stepped to join Fuentes on Cuban soil. Those were the last words he'd heard from Norbert Vines as well.

12.

"WHO'S IN the Mercedes?" Deal asked, pointing as the Cadillac followed the lead car past the gated marina entrance toward a junction with a highway. A slender, dark-skinned man in a set of faded green khakis stood at the intersection, waving them on, his hand raised to halt a tiny, smoke-belching car that was lurching toward them from the west.

Deal had already slipped one of Vines's devices into the crevice where the seat was joined. Vines had told him that the removal of the covering activated the devices. For all he knew, their conversation was going out on the Voice of America.

"Friends," Fuentes said, glancing ahead amiably.

He was sitting across the broad backseat, his fingers comfortably tented beneath his chin. Even with Russell's formidable presence between them, there was plenty of room. In the seat beside the driver sat Tomás, his gaze fixed on the road before them.

Deal nodded. "It's good to have friends," he said. He gave another glance at the tiny car that the guard had forced to a halt. A Fiat, he realized, twenty years old if a day. Blue smoke swirled in a cloud that enveloped even the guard, but the man seemed not to notice.

"It is indeed," Fuentes said.

"It seems some of yours are quite powerful," Deal said, wondering if the seat padding would muffle their conversations. But where else would you stick a wad of gum? He held up the packet Fuentes had sent along in Key West.

"Those are often the most valuable sort," Fuentes said. He stared out the window as if he were a tourist intent on the view.

The road had widened, Deal saw, its narrow two lanes turned to a broad boulevard divided by a well-tended median and flanked by fifties-style homes on broad lots, impressive enough by anyone's standards.

"This is Miramar," Fuentes said, gesturing out the window. "And there just behind you, the area of the Country Club," he added, pointing over Deal's shoulder.

Deal turned and glanced down a side street, caught a distant glimpse of an even more impressive set of homes. "Who lives in these places?" he heard Russell ask. "El Presidente and his posse?"

Fuentes gave Russell a tolerant gaze. "Actually, the president keeps a series of residences, for security reasons, most of them quite modest. The preponderance of the homes in this area is occupied by foreign emissaries, businessmen and the like. Some are embassies."

He fixed his gaze on Deal, then. "As I have been telling you, it's not all hovels and grass shacks down here." He flashed them both his all-knowing smile.

Deal nodded. "Let's say that I were to get involved with your enterprise," he began.

Fuentes gave Russell a glance that affected surprise, then turned back to Deal. "I would like to believe that you already are involved," he said.

"I'm talking about the real thing. Cashed your check, signed on, went to work," Deal said. "Just who is it I'd be dealing with?"

It brought another look of feigned surprise from Fuentes. "With myself, of course."

"And all these partners I was reading about?" Deal gestured with the packet once again.

"What about them?"

"Are these people I'd have any contact with?"

Fuentes gave him an inquiring look. "Not ordinarily, I should think. These are world travelers, men with a broad array of interests. Perhaps you might come in contact with someone at a social occasion, but in the everyday course of business, I'd call it most unlikely. Why do you ask?"

Deal shrugged, casting a sidelong glance at Russell, who kept his gaze straight ahead, his expression studiously neutral. "I think I ought to know who it is I'm working for, that's all. I'd feel a lot more comfortable that way."

"Well, Mr. Deal, let us say that a person in your position were to accept a commission from a multinational corporation, a Bertelsmann, perhaps, or a Vitech, seeking to build an offshore headquarters or a warehouse complex somewhere. Whom would you be working for in that case?"

"I'd know where the money was coming from, at least."

"And given the recent track record of these corporations, what assurances would that provide?" Fuentes gave him an ingenuous stare as the heavy car rumbled across a bridge—perhaps the one that had been pointed out to him earlier, Deal thought.

An enormous, oddly shaped bus passed them going the other way, belching diesel exhaust in its wake. "A camel," Fuentes said, pointing out his window.

Russell's head swiveled. "Say where?" he said, his tone disbelieving.

Fuentes smiled from behind his tiny glasses. "The autobus," he said, gesturing. "They call it a camel for its hump."

Russell peered out the window at the departing bus. "Because it's pretty damned ugly, that's what I'd say."

"Ugly, perhaps," Fuentes allowed, "but certainly efficient."

He could agree with that much, Deal thought. It looked as if the population of a small city might be jammed inside the bus, more the size of a train car than anything he'd seen in Miami.

The canopy of trees had fallen away altogether, he noticed, and the boulevard had become a broad highway running along the verge of the seawall, the whole sweep of the Malecón opening itself before them once again. In the distance, Deal could make out the profile of the massive castle rising above everything. It was quite a sight, he thought, as the familiar tang of sea breeze poured through the open windows, one that seemed to dominate the city from any perspective.

He forced himself from the view at last and turned back to Fuentes. "Let's just say that the chance to meet the people I'd be working for would give me peace of mind."

Fuentes seemed to think about this. "For now, why not think of yourself as working in my employ, Mr. Deal," he said at last. "I'm a reasonable man, with nothing to hide . . ."

It brought a laugh from Deal, a sound loud enough to prompt Tomás to turn his stony gaze upon them. "I'm sorry, Fuentes," Deal said, ignoring the bodyguard, "but you make the Sphinx seem forthcoming."

Fuentes reached across Russell's impassive form to pat him on the knee. "I appreciate your concerns, truly I do. I'm a cautious man myself. Believe it."

He broke off to fix Deal with a stare. "I would not have lived this long if I were not." He leaned back in his seat then, gesturing out the window at the seawall where a pair of lovers sat entwined.

"I'm sure I will be able to satisfy something of your curiosity in time," Fuentes continued. "But, for now, I simply ask that you be patient. Look around this magnificent city. Breathe in its essence. Speak to our associates. Once you have a better grasp of the scope of the enterprise before us, you will feel quite differently, I am certain of it." He turned back to Deal, his tone earnest. "You are a builder. You take pride in your work, this I know about you. Here you can indulge the passion for your craft as nowhere else on earth."

They were well down the Malecón by now, passing the façade of a multistoried building that might have stood for a doge's ruined palace, had they been in Venice. The building's ochre paint had worn nearly to the color of the underlying concrete skin, and the many tall windows on the lower floors were boarded over.

A dark-skinned man in an undershirt and drooping trousers stood in the once grand doorway, a cigarette dangling from his lips, scratching his underarm idly while an infant in a diaper climbed about the steps below. Whatever had stood on the lot next door had crumbled into a pile of brick and mortar at least twenty feet high.

"What happened there?" Russell said, a low whistle emitting from his lips.

"Raúl," Fuentes called sharply and the driver braked, piloting the Cadillac toward the curb before the ruined building. *"Un momento,"* he added, then gestured for Deal to get out.

Deal glanced at Russell, who shrugged, then levered his door open and stepped up onto the curb. The sun was hot, the air thick with the humidity familiar to him from Miami, but the breeze off the bay was stiffer than he might have expected, whipping his hair, snapping at the collar of his polo shirt. Russell joined him on the curb, working his big shoulders as he stared at what lay before them.

"Looks like the Bronx to me," Russell said, staring at the giant pile of rubble where a building once stood.

On the steps of the building next door, the man in the undershirt had scooped the infant to his hip, and the two of them stared down at the entourage that had pulled up as if something of great import was about to occur.

"But that's not your ordinary tenement," Deal said, gesturing at the tattered palace where the pair stood watching.

"Now you see what I was talking about earlier," Fuentes called as he came around the back of the Cadillac to join them. "From a distance, you apprehend the beauty that once was. Up close, you see what is."

He gestured along the Malecón before them, where a series of once-grand buildings marched off into the distance like embarrassed dowagers, their façades wiped nearly clean of paint by the ceaseless breeze, many with their windows blank and boarded, their impressive porticos sagging toward collapse. Here and there, scaffolding crept partway up a façade, but Deal saw no one at work.

"Reminds me of this hooker I knew in Atlanta," Russell Straight said, one hand massaging the opposite bicep. "Woman had to have been something once."

Deal's eye had been gauging the unsorted pile of rubble before them. He saw the hint of a staircase jutting above a tangle of fractured beams, and just beyond, the corner of a mattress sandwiched between concrete slabs. "I'm going to guess that nobody brought this building down on purpose, Mr. Fuentes."

"Very good, Mr. Deal," the man replied. He glanced up at a series of scudding clouds that briefly darkened the harbor sky. "There is a saying here: 'When it rains, it is good for the crops. But today buildings will fall in Havana.' "

"Was anyone inside this one when it came down?" Deal asked, his eyes still roaming the tangle.

"Perhaps," Fuentes said, shrugging. "There generally is."

"Shoo," Russell Straight loosed a breath at Deal's side. "Work from now till kingdom come, you couldn't straighten this place up."

Hard to argue with that sentiment, Deal thought, though he suspected Fuentes would put it another way. He was still thinking of what Russell had said when a few drops of rain splattered the dusty sidewalk in front of them, and Deal turned to the building next door. The man in the undershirt and the infant had disappeared, the deserted entryway gaping back at him now like a broken smile.

The rain picked up a bit, turning to a summer squall, and Fuentes gestured toward the car, where Raúl and Tomás stood, each with a hand on a door. "Quickly," Fuentes called. "We've seen enough, I think."

He'd seen plenty, Deal thought, with one last backward glance, though maybe not enough. And then he was running after Russell and Fuentes through the chilling rain.

13.

THE RIDE on down the Malecón offered more of the same: a kaleidoscope of beauty and ruin, punctuated here and there by sweeping plazas, most of them well traveled by dark-skinned pedestrians who seemed untroubled by the steady rain, and surrounded by an ever-present bevy of taxicabs, many of them Fords and Chevrolets from the fifties. Most sported mismatched fenders and door panels, taillights that seemed to have been stolen from tractors, windshields cracked and bound with tape. . . .

Emilio and Rodríguez, the two Miami cabinetmakers turned precision auto mechanics who lavished so much attention on the Hog, would love this living automotive museum, Deal mused. If there was endless work in architectural restoration ahead, the prospects for automotive couldn't be far behind.

"The U.S. Interests Section," said Fuentes, pointing out the window at an incongruous multistoried building of mirrored glass. "It was once the embassy, but . . ." He threw his hands up as if the change were a deep mystery. Deal stared out at the nondescript façade of the building, wondering if there was really a roomful of men behind those blank windows, hanging on their every word.

"They worried someone's going to break in or break out?" Russell said, pointing at the series of armed guards posted along the sidewalk in front of the building.

"A precaution, or perhaps a bit of drama," Fuentes shrugged. He pointed to a plaza that fronted the building, this one of considerably more modern design. A series of Bauhaus-inspired girders curved over the central area, and on the far side rose an enormous billboard depicting a young boy clutching the strands of a barbed-wire cage.

"The Plaza de la Dignidad," Fuentes explained. "During the crisis of Elián González, the park that stood here was replaced with a place where demonstrations could take place in view of the section."

He lifted an eyebrow at Russell, then fixed his gaze on Deal. "Perhaps there is no longer an embassy, but it is still an important place in Havana."

Deal nodded. Before Elián, whose mother had drowned while accompanying him on their desperate voyage to the United States, had been returned to his father in Cuba, everyday life in Miami had ground nearly to a halt. He'd had calls from friends in other parts of the country, most of them demanding some explanation for the incomprehensible furor they'd seen reported for weeks on the nightly news. "What the hell's all the fuss about?" they'd wanted to know.

"Just how much time do you have?" had been Deal's stock

reply. As a father, he'd been torn by the urge to see a young boy reunited with his only surviving parent. On the other hand, he understood all too well the passions of an exile group who had made their way to safety wanting to welcome and embrace that living symbol of their cause.

In the end, there'd been no satisfactory solution, and though the boy had been returned, heads had rolled, a presidential election decided by the outcome. In one regard, Vines was right, Deal told himself. So much still depended on this tiny island.

He came away from his thoughts to see that their car had turned off the broad avenue, headed south now into what seemed a business district. The rain had lessened to a drizzle and the streets were steaming as the sun began to break through the clouds.

The sidewalks were crowded, he noted, a few men in suits, more in guayaberas, some in T-shirts and gimmee caps. And everywhere, women toting webbed shopping bags and trailing doe-eyed children.

"This here is a country of brothers," Russell noted. And Deal found himself nodding agreement. Black skin, caramel, bronze and every shade in between out there, he noted, but few fair-complexioned Castilians such as Fuentes among them.

"Not so long ago there were many Russians," Fuentes said. "And before that"—he smiled—"many Americans. But now . . ." His voice trailed off as he repeated his gesture of mystification.

Deal nodded, listening idly while he scanned the crowds outside. He was watching what seemed like a pair of lovers parting at the street corner opposite, a man in a dark silk shirt, his jet-black hair swept back, bending to plant a kiss on the cheek of a slender young woman. She raised a hand to his cheek in response, then turned to duck into a waiting taxi.

The scene had raised an unexpected ache in Deal, a feeling almost inexplicable at first. In the next instant, as a flood of images swept over him, he understood. Angie leaning over on top of him, bending down to kiss him as they moved in time . . .

He blinked away the memories and glanced again at the street corner, but the man in the dark silk shirt was gone and the taxi disappeared as well. He shook his head at the feelings that had swept over him. Come all the way to Cuba, caught in the crossfire between government agents and international scam artists, and still he couldn't get her out of his mind. Big trouble there, Deal thought. Real trouble.

Fuentes was studying him, he realized, as their car slowed for another turn. "I know you must be exhausted," the man said, "but there is one last stop I'd like to make before we reach your hotel."

Deal glanced at Russell, who gave him a "Who, me?" look in return. "We're with you," Deal said.

It brought a smile from Fuentes, who leaned forward to tap their driver on the shoulder. The man nodded as if it had all been prearranged.

In seconds the Cadillac made another tight turn, carrying them down what looked like an alleyway, barely wide enough for the car to move. The passage was jammed with pedestrians who seemed unconcerned by the appearance of this massive car. As the prow of the Cadillac inched forward, they spread apart in waves, mounting the narrow sidewalks that flanked the roadway, then re-forming in the car's wake.

"You think that car of yours could make it?" Russell turned to Deal with a smile.

Deal shook his head. "I wouldn't want to try it."

"We are in the old city, now," Fuentes said, gesturing at the looming walls ahead. "There are buildings here that date from the 1500s. Once, a great wall surrounded everything," he said, "but that was taken down."

Deal noticed a rumbling beneath their tires then and realized they were traveling on cobblestones. On his left, an undifferentiated expanse of stucco fell away, replaced suddenly by a shaded courtyard with an elaborate fountain. On its far side he had a glimpse of an intricately carved church façade, the sight forming and vanishing as rapidly as an image in a dream. Medieval Europe in the tropics, he thought. How could such a thing be possible?

"Just here," Fuentes was calling to their driver then, and the Cadillac finally ground to a halt.

Fuentes leaned to speak to Raúl in rapid Spanish, then turned to usher Deal and Russell out into the street. Hardly had they alighted than the car was off again, leaving the three of them standing in the cool, dimly lit passageway. "I asked Raúl to deliver your bags," Fuentes said. He gestured after the departing car. "Your hotel is just down there a block or two, and as you can see there's no place to park in these quarters."

Deal nodded. It seemed twenty degrees cooler in the drafty passageway. Across the narrow street was what looked like an apothecary's shop out of Dickens, racks of oddly shaped bottles and ceramic containers crammed onto wooden shelves that reached toward vast ceilings, brass-trimmed urns glowing red and blue and green spaced about the marble counters. He felt light-headed for a moment, as if he'd been transported in time as well as space.

"Are you feeling all right?" Fuentes asked. "I can have the car brought back . . ."

Deal shook his head. Even Russell was staring at him in concern, he noted. "I'm fine. A walk sounds great, to tell the truth."

Fuentes nodded. "We won't stay long here," he said. "But I thought you'd want to see this right away."

He stepped between the two of them then and pressed a button set in a plate near a doorway in the wall. Deal heard a faint buzzing sound, and in moments there came a grinding noise as the heavy door swung open.

"Señor Fuentes." Deal heard an enthusiastic voice from the darkness inside. *"¡Con mucho gusto!"*

In moments a young man with a bushy head of hair had stepped out to embrace Fuentes energetically, his dark curls bobbing.

"Carlo," Fuentes said, stepping back to gesture at Deal and Russell. "These are my friends from Miami. Mr. Deal, Mr. Straight, this is Carlo Vedetti, architectural director for the United Nations project in Havana.

Vedetti's eyes lit up as if they were emissaries bearing gifts from China. "Mr. Fuentes exaggerates," he said, shaking hands. "I direct myself only, but please, come in, come in."

He led them inside, down a dim corridor that might have been a cave passage, then swept aside a curtain, ushering them into a brightly lit room that had been set up like an artist's gallery. Deal went inside, blinking, realizing that they'd entered a converted storefront through the rear entrance.

On the far side of the room, a spacious bank of windows opened onto another narrow street, much like the one they'd stepped in from, pedestrians hurrying to and fro without so much as a glance inside. The walls beside him were hung with photographs of churches and Renaissance buildings as well as a series of colorful architectural renderings.

"This is Habana Vieja," Fuentes said, gesturing at the welter of images about them. "The object of Señor Vedetti's crusade."

Vedetti nodded good-naturedly. "I am from Italy," he said, as if that explained everything. "What we are trying to do means much to me."

Deal nodded. "I told Mr. Fuentes it looked like Florence by the sea."

"Only larger," Vedetti said, his expression turning sober for a moment. "There is so much to be done. And our race is with time . . ." He trailed off, then fixed Deal with a look. "I have heard of your own work in architectural restoration, Mr. Deal."

Deal opened his mouth to protest. "I've done a little such work," he told Vedetti. "Nothing on this scale . . ."

"No, no, no," Vedetti protested. "Everyone knows of the legendary DealCo Development in Miami, and your own work on the MacLemore Estate on Biscayne Bay adjacent to Vizcaya"—he threw his arms open wide exuberantly—"everyone knows of that project. It is quite important work . . ."

Deal glanced at Fuentes, who nodded as if at a prize pupil. The old fox had probably had Vedetti prepped, but what the hell, the MacLemore restoration was one of the most satisfying pieces of work he'd done since he'd taken over DealCo. Specifically, Vedetti was referring to the fifteen-acre, thirty-five-room neo-Renaissance estate built in the 1920s just south of downtown Miami by a pioneering department-store owner.

The MacLemore family had eventually died off and the enormous place had sat vacant for several years before software mogul Terrence Terrell had purchased it in the 1990s, then set Deal to work. It was an Addison Mizener–designed coral-rock-and-marble masterpiece that rivaled Vizcaya, the nearby former Vanderbilt home and now museum, but because the MacLemore estate had always been in private hands, relatively few knew of it.

Deal had been at work at the estate for several years now, and could probably spend the rest of his life on the job, assuming Terrell's interest and cash flow held out. Keeping old buildings shored up was tough enough in any climate, but in the tropics, the battle was fierce. Still, in a city like Miami, where "historic" might well refer to anything prior to *Miami Vice,* he took particular pride in helping to restore a building that another buyer might have razed in a heartbeat to make room for a forty-story condominium tower.

He moved close to some of the drawings mounted on the walls, Vedetti following closely behind. "It is a monumental undertaking that lies before us," Vedetti said, gesturing, "but at least we have begun to identify the scope of the problem." He managed a wan smile for Deal.

"Were Señor Vedetti being candid," Fuentes chimed in, "he would tell you that he has performed miracles with the little money he has to work with, virtually all of it channeled to him from outside Cuba."

Vedetti gave Deal an apologetic look. "Cuba is a poor country, Mr. Deal. When it is a choice between food and medicine . . . well, how can I complain . . ." he raised his hands in a gesture of helplessness.

"Nonetheless, things might have turned out differently over these past forty years had not Fidel Castro been a man of the provinces," Fuentes said, tilting a photograph of a ruined church façade toward them. "In truth, the city has never truly captured the imagination of El Presidente. Say what you will about his practices and policies, he had no intentions of setting up court in

Havana. He was never comfortable here. Certainly, he has not been interested."

Deal took it all in as he browsed the magnificent series of images—palazzos, churches, public buildings—moving finally to a part of the wall where a pushpin-studded aerial photograph of the city had been mounted, with a series of boundary lines overlaid, marking off different districts. After a moment, he was able to identify the first landmarks he'd spotted off the rail of the *Bellísima:* the harbor and the headlands where Morro Castle loomed; then he traced the inward curve of the bay all the way westward to the point where the River Almendares flowed, and, just beyond, the breakwater and canals that marked the Marina Hemingway complex where they had come ashore.

"The Old City is here, some three hundred and fifty acres in size," Vedetti said, coming to join him. He pointed to a vaguely thumb-shaped section that sat across the mouth of the harbor from the castle and ran inland along the western shore. "There are roughly three thousand buildings within its borders, about one-third of them of extreme historic importance, some three hundred fifty of those built prior to 1800."

He paused, then gestured again at the map. "Most of our work is within Habana Vieja, though we have also begun to identify structures of interest in other areas, such as Centro Habana and Vedado as well." He pointed at the districts next to the old city, moving westward in order.

"A white pin indicates a project completed, or nearing completion," Vedetti explained. "The green pins designate those where work is in the planning stages or about to begin. Yellow are buildings that have been designated as worthy of restoration."

Deal nodded. It crossed his mind to ask Vedetti what the significance of the gum wad now affixed to the back side of the huge image was, but the giddy thought passed. Contenting himself with the thought that he was becoming proficient as a spy, and that in any case, he'd soon be rid of Vines's devices, he forced himself back to the moment.

There were hundreds of pins on the map, only a handful of them white, green, or yellow. "What about the red ones?" he asked.

Vedetti gave his wan smile. "You are familiar with the concept of *triage,* I presume?"

"That's where the dude's still breathing, but he won't be too much longer, not without a hell of a lot of work," Russell Straight cut in.

Vedetti's smile sagged a notch, but he nodded agreement.

"Then it looks like this whole city is on life support," Russell offered.

"That's one way of putting it," Vedetti said, with something of a sigh. He turned back to Deal. "We are very near the endgame, from an architectural standpoint, at least. We do everything we can, of course, but meanwhile I keep praying for some miracle."

"And it will come," Fuentes said, clapping his hand on Vedetti's shoulder. "You are a miracle worker yourself, and others will follow in your footsteps." He paused to send Deal his all-knowing gaze, before turning back to the architect. "But we have stolen enough of your valuable time, Señor Vedetti."

"It is my pleasure," Vedetti said, and to Deal it sounded like he meant it. "Men of your stature have the capacity to be of great assistance to our cause," he added.

Deal shot another glance at Fuentes. A notorious international money launderer and a Miami building contractor by default. If Vedetti truly had his hopes pinned on the likes of them, he feared that Russell Straight's assessment of the situation was accurate after all.

"What you're involved in is wonderful," Deal managed, extending his hand to Vedetti. "I'll be glad to help any way I can."

Vedetti clasped his hand as if it were a lifeline. "Your very presence is already of great help, Mr. Deal." He paused and lowered his voice, even though they were the only ones in the gallery. "Señor Fuentes has shared something of his intentions," Vedetti said solemnly. "And your place among the members of his team means much."

Deal turned to Fuentes, about to protest, but found the man engrossed in the study of an architectural rendering. What the hell, Deal thought. No need to air such details in front of Vedetti. Given what he was up against, the poor guy needed all the encouragement he could get. Let him think it was the next thing to Donald Trump and I. M. Pei dropping by for a visit, then. Deal could have it out with Fuentes later.

"It's been a pleasure, not to mention an education," Deal said, gesturing at the images that surrounded them.

Russell Straight nodded his agreement. "Good luck," he added.

Vedetti gave them a gracious bow. "I wish you both a most pleasant and rewarding stay in Havana," he said.

"We can find our way out, Carlo," Fuentes said, his hand on the curtain that shrouded the rear passageway.

Deal gave a last glance at the pin-studded map, then turned to follow the others out. He caught Vedetti's sincere gaze again as he was about to duck behind the curtain, and paused to wave. A good man, he thought. Someone he would enjoy talking with more.

"Maybe you'll come to Miami one day," he said.

"We will meet again." Vedetti smiled back. "Of that much I am sure."

Deal heard the door grinding open at the end of the passage, then. He returned Vedetti's smile, then the curtain dropped, and he was gone.

14.

"Joseíto has been to talk with you, I see."

The voice reached the old man as if from the distant rim of a deep well. Light up there, he saw. The promise of a life.

He was lying with his cheek pressed to the gritty floor, he realized. He didn't think he had simply fallen asleep that way. His head throbbed, more so than usual, and his tongue probed a spot where he felt certain there had been a tooth not long ago.

"Joseíto assures me you know nothing," the voice came again.

For a moment it appeared to the old man that there were several bearded, fatigue-clad men sitting on the edge of his cot and speaking to him. After a moment the images resolved into one. He tried to push himself up from the floor, but his arm would not cooperate. Broken, he assumed. Perhaps gone altogether, came another thought, though a downward glance assured him it was not the case.

In a bit, he felt a prickling return to the balky limb and realized it had only gone to sleep from the awkward position he had tumbled into. He also saw that his trousers were bunched at his knees, his underwear ripped and tossed aside.

Joseíto had been there, yes. He remembered now. A tractor battery trundled in, balanced on the lip of a handcart, a set of jumper cables clamped to the terminals. Joseíto had donned a pair of linesman's rubber gloves and held the cables in display. A clump of steel wool in the jaws of each cable, and what a shower of sparks when he brushed the wiry clumps together.

"Cojones," Joseíto had crooned, as others had torn at the old man's clothes. He had leaned down, then. "You think you have big balls."

Feeling had returned to the old man's arm, and along with sensation came the pain. Still, he managed to fasten his trousers about his waist and push himself back to his place against the wall. He blinked and glanced about the cell. Just one bearded man sitting there, yes, an unlit cigar between his fingers, watching.

"Where is Joseíto?" the old man asked.

"Would you like me to call him down?"

"Do as you please," the old man said.

"Joseíto was troubled that I would not permit him to join us," the bearded man said. "He feared that you intended me harm."

The old man stared at him. "He should have told you about the lice in that mattress you're sitting on."

The bearded man paused, then glanced down at his side.

"Fire up that stogie, why don't you. Maybe it'll chase the bastards away."

The bearded man had regained his composure. "I've dealt with lice before," he said, bringing his gaze back to level.

The old man nodded. "Me, too."

They stared at each other for a moment. "Joseíto suggests that you are of no further use to us," the bearded man said finally. "He feels that you are occupying space better employed in more worthwhile pursuits."

The old man considered this in silence, then nodded. "So you've decided to let me go."

It brought a tolerant smile from the man sitting on his bed. "You haven't lost your sense of humor, old man. I always appreciated that in you."

"The higher up you go, the harder it is to laugh," the old man said.

The man on his cot studied him for a bit. "I suggested to Joseíto that you had truly been injured in that blast," he said. "I reasoned that perhaps there were doctors who might help."

"An explosion?" the old man said.

The bearded man continued as if he hadn't heard. "Joseíto considers himself more able than any surgeon, of course. If a rock had thoughts, Joseíto could coax them forth."

"And turn a blind man lame," the old man said. There was the faint tinge of scorched flesh still hanging in the room. But strangely, pain was not so much an issue. When everything throbbed, no single ache could rise above the clamor.

The bearded man stood, brushing at the seat of his pants. "We have excellent medical facilities," the bearded man said. "Equal to the best anywhere."

The old man nodded. He felt his head begin to sag. "Where are we, anyway?" he asked.

But when he looked up, the bearded man was gone.

15.

NEARING SIX NOW, Deal saw, as he followed Fuentes and Russell away from the gallery entrance and down the still-crowded narrow lane. Fuentes had his arm about Russell's broad shoulders and seemed to be pointing out features of interest as they moved along. Fuentes's lips moved rapidly and Russell's head was nodding in time, the two of them dodging the on-coming foot traffic like a sack-race team.

Deal heard the sound of a hiccupping motor a few feet be-hind him and turned to see a young woman on a motor scooter weaving through the foot traffic as easily as an eel through bot-tom grass. He stepped onto the narrow sidewalk as the scooter zipped past, the driver exposing no small amount of her health-ily tanned thighs. He turned, about to hurry after the others, and nearly collided with a wizened little man bearing several days' growth of beard and missing his top dental plate.

"Cigars!" the little man barked at Deal in a rasping voice. "Monte Cristos, Cohibas, Romeo y Julieta . . ."

It took Deal a moment to realize what was going on. "I don't think so," he said.

The old man shook his head and moved closer. "Rum!" he added, and nodded in the direction of the departing motor scooter. *"Chiquitas,* too."

One-stop shopping, Deal thought, a smile crossing his face.

"Come," the old man said, pressing a grimy card into his hand. "I show you something . . ."

"Vamos, abuelo," Deal heard at his ear. It was Fuentes appearing from the crowd, Russell at his side.

Deal turned back, but the old man had already melted away into the crowd.

"He was begging?" Russell asked.

"He wanted to sell me some cigars," Deal said. "Or rum. Or a girl. My choice."

Russell nodded. "Maybe we ought to get him back here."

Deal had a look at the card the man had given him. On one side was a drawing of a woman in a Betty Grable–like pose he assumed was intended to be provocative, along with some printed Spanish he couldn't decipher. On the other side something had been scrawled in pencil. "I am your friend," it said, in quite legible English. Deal glanced off in the direction the hustler had taken, a question forming in his mind.

Probably just your typical hustler's gamesmanship, he thought, but then again . . .

"You'll get a lot of that," Fuentes said, joining them. "But there's no danger."

Deal slipped the card into his pocket, still uncertain. Spies slipping him secret messages, glimpses of Angie on crowded street corners. He *did* need rest.

Russell, meanwhile, gave Fuentes a look that suggested danger was the farthest thing from his mind, but Fuentes seemed not to notice. "Your hotel," he said, pointing across the crowded lane. "It's just there."

Deal followed Fuentes's gesture toward an unpretentious entryway just a few yards catty-corner from where they stood. A series of shuttered, wrought-iron balconies studded the building's cut-stone face, many of them bearing flower boxes that spilled bright color through the railings.

"There are the grander hotels farther out along the Malecón," Fuentes said, "but I prefer it here in the Old City." He stared at Deal from behind his tiny glasses like a seabird with obsidian eyes.

The man was seeking approval, Deal realized, and he lent it with a nod. "It looks fine," he said, and meant it.

"It was built as the palace of a duke in the early 1800s," Fuentes said, ushering them across the street. "Now it has been restored as a hotel."

"One of Carlo Vedetti's projects?" Deal asked. A pair of doormen in casual dress flanked the entryway, watching them without appearing to watch. An unarmed policeman ambled by, his baton crooked at his elbow, his gaze lighting upon them, then moving on.

Fuentes shook his head. "One of the few private projects I mentioned," he said, showing them through the door. "Come, I think you'll find it more than satisfactory."

He ushered them into a cool marble lobby that by Deal's standards could certainly have served as the entryway for a duke's palace. He motioned for the two of them to wait, then stepped into an adjoining room to confer briefly with an attendant who stood behind an elegantly carved reception counter.

"This is more like it," Russell observed. "Take a look at that."

Deal followed his gesture into a spacious atrium that lay beyond. Dominating the center of the area was an ornate fountain, surrounded by several little conversation islands where upholstered sofas and chairs had been clustered. Soft light filtered down from a stained-glass skylight some thirty feet above, and the occasional cry of a macaw echoed from somewhere in the surrounding foliage.

"How do you square this with what we saw this afternoon?" Russell said, uncharacteristic awe in his voice.

"I'm not sure," Deal said, marveling at the cool elegance before him.

"More evidence of what I've been telling you all along," Fuentes's voice came to them. He was back from the reception desk now, two middle-aged bellmen tagging in his wake. "Your rooms are ready, your bags already taken up," he announced, before taking a glance at his watch.

"I'd intended that we have dinner together," Fuentes continued. "But I'm afraid something's come up. I'd like us to have breakfast together, if that's all right. Some of the people we'll be doing business with would like to meet with us in the afternoon, and I'd like to go over a few particulars beforehand . . ."

"You told Vedetti I was already on board this project?" Deal cut in.

Fuentes paused, waving the suggestion away. "Carlo is an enthusiast," Fuentes said. "I assure you . . ."

"How about these people we're meeting tomorrow?" Deal pressed on. "Do they think I'm on board, too?"

Fuentes sighed softly, glancing at the bellmen who waited at a respectful distance. If they had the slightest interest in what was being discussed, there was no way of telling. "I will introduce you to these men from Havana as John Deal," he said, "son of the legendary Barton Deal and a rising star of capitalism in his own right."

"Fuentes . . ." Deal tried, but the man was sailing unflappably on.

"I will tell them that if everything that *they* propose finds merit in your eyes, then perhaps they will have the privilege of entrusting their most ambitious undertakings to your hands."

Deal fought the urge to roll his eyes. "Let's just be sure that you and I are on the same page, here. I agreed to come to Havana and have a look around, talk to few people, *then* I'll let you know what I think. Are we together on that?"

"Of course," Fuentes said, affecting surprise. "I understand your wishes perfectly. But," he said, lowering his voice and drawing closer, "no purpose is to be served by suggesting that you and I are anything but united in our goals. Do you follow me, Mr. Deal?"

Deal glanced at Russell, who stared on impassively. "If you want me to let these people—whoever they are—think that you and I are partners, I'll play along, up to a point. But make no mistake—I'll make up my own mind about where you and I go after that."

Fuentes smiled and reached to clap him on the shoulder. "I have no fear as to what your decision will be," he said, indicating their surroundings with a sweep of his arm. "How many men are given the opportunity to rebuild an entire country, after all, particularly one as magnificent as this?"

Deal nodded, wondering briefly if his old man had ever listened to such proposals. "I'm ready for a shower now," he told Fuentes. "We can talk some more at breakfast."

"Of course," Fuentes said. "I've made dinner reservations here at the hotel, and Raúl"—he broke off to point back toward the reception area where, Deal realized, their driver was perched in an overstuffed chair leafing though a newspaper—"will return with the car at your disposal for the evening. You'll find him a most knowledgeable guide," he said, with a meaningful glance at Russell.

"You mean he knows where all the good cigars are?" Russell asked, his expression blank.

"All that and more," Fuentes said, equally deadpan.

Something occurred to Deal then. "Then you're not staying in this hotel?" he asked.

"Alas, not." Fuentes shook his head. "But I will see you in the morning, though not too early. I will call you first." He paused then and gave them each a birdlike nod. "Have a most enjoyable evening," he added.

He turned then, giving an inaudible snap of his fingers that Raúl had already anticipated. The driver had folded his paper under his arm and was already moving smartly toward the door to usher his employer out.

"The dude's got an act, you have to give him that much," Russell observed, as the two disappeared into the stream of foot traffic outside.

Deal nodded absently. He'd been thinking much the same thing, in fact. Whatever Fuentes was, and whatever eventuated from it all, this act *was* a great one. It was the sort of thing Barton Deal would have loved.

16.

HIS "ROOM" turned out to be a suite, Deal discovered: bedroom, sitting room and cavernous bath featuring a bidet and a Roman tub, all the rooms meticulously detailed, with marble floors and high ceilings, the furniture tasteful and period-styled. What a waste, he thought, images of Angie flitting quickly through his mind once again.

And who had footed the tab for such a restoration? he wondered, as he threw open the tall shutters and found himself on a tiny, second-floor balcony overlooking the street where they'd all been standing less than an hour ago.

While Fuentes had told him that a day laborer might earn $25 a month in Havana and skilled craftsmen not much more, materials alone would have eaten up a major chunk of an $18 million budget, he was thinking. In Miami, it would take all of that and more just to bring a similar-sized Art Deco hotel on South Beach up to snuff.

He watched the steadily flowing foot traffic for a bit, noting that most of the children he saw were carrying what looked like sherbet cones and that a significant portion of the adults were hard at work on the cones as well. He glanced at his watch—maybe it was sherbet hour here in Havana, he thought, then caught sight of a street vendor with an ice-cream cart farther down the narrow passage.

A flower vendor had stationed a similar cart on the street just opposite his perch, and Deal caught a faint, jasminelike scent rising from the clusters of unfamiliar white blossoms that filled the containers. As the vendor finished with a customer, his gaze traveled upward and Deal found himself lifting a hand.

"How much?" he called, struggling to recover his meager fund of Spanish. "Cuantos?" he added, pointing down.

The man smiled. "One dollar," he said.

"Sold," Deal called. He fished a dollar out of his pocket and wadded it into a ball, then dropped it to the vendor.

The man caught it deftly, jamming the bill into his pocket without bothering to smooth it, then turned to pluck what seemed like several bunches of flowers from one of the plastic buckets in his cart. In a smooth motion, he wrapped the flowers in a section of newspaper, twisted the bottom end tight and held the bundle up as if were a newborn, motioning for Deal to catch.

Deal leaned and caught the spinning bundle as it rose, washing him with its fragrance. *"Gracias,"* he called to the vendor, who waved back as if he'd transacted business this way a thousand times. Passersby grinned up their approval as Deal stood with the giant bouquet in his arms. Fuentes had welcomed him to Cuba earlier, he recalled, but this seemed to be his moment of arrival.

He walked back into the room and found a smallish plastic wastebasket in the bathroom, then arranged the flowers in it and filled it with water from the tub spout. He took his makeshift arrangement into the sitting room and slid aside the phone and television on a marble end table to make room for the spray.

Now it truly seemed the quarters of a duke, he thought, standing back to admire his own handiwork. He'd never done such a thing in his life, it occurred to him—carry his own flowers into a hotel room—and he wondered what had possessed him to do it now. In the next moment, he found himself thinking of Janice: What would she say to such a gesture? he wondered. And along with the question came a pang. Wasn't it sad she had never had the opportunity?

He shook himself away from the thoughts and walked into the bedroom, found his suitcase on a stand and unpacked; the few shirts and slacks he'd brought went into an ancient armoire, the rest of his things into a drawer in a massive chest opposite the foot of his bed.

He showered, then shaved again—another unusual act for him—then padded back to the bedroom to dress in a fresh pair of khakis and a polo shirt. *New man,* he found himself thinking, as he examined his image in the armoire's mirror. And perhaps he was.

It had been a long time since he'd gone anywhere that had surprised him with its character, and that was what he was feeling now: that pleasant glow of discovery. He'd felt a hint of it when he'd gone to Key West to complete Franklin Stone's star-crossed project, and it was with him even more strongly now.

And why not? he thought. Why shouldn't he indulge this unexpected surge?

He'd spent a dozen years in Miami, trying to hold his marriage together, trying to find a way to live down his old man's mistakes, raising a daughter and trying to make a life. Wasn't it natural to gravitate toward some release?

Never mind Fuentes and his kill-you-with-kindness manipulation, never mind whether everything that Vines had promised was equally bogus, he told himself. He'd stumbled into an amazing place. He felt a kind of wonder. He'd come out of it with that much, at least.

He returned to the sitting room and sat on the couch, glancing at the blank eye of the television that sat incongruously on a wooden table in a corner. Curiosity alone might have prompted him to turn it on, but he was hesitant to mask the low murmur that rose from the street below his balcony. It was like a stream flowing past, he thought, the notion a comforting one. Despite everything—the hardships, the politics, the separation from loved ones—the stream of life flowed on.

He came awake with a start to the pounding at his door—nearly dark outside, he realized, trying to calculate how long he'd been out. He reached to switch on a lamp, then shoved himself up from the couch and padded groggily to open up.

"You in there?" he heard Russell Straight call.

"Hold on," Deal said, fumbling for the lock.

"I thought maybe you and Raúl took off without me," Russell said, as he strolled inside the room. He took a moment to survey the room, nodding with satisfaction.

"Yours is almost as big as mine," he said, "except I didn't get flowers."

Deal started to tell him the story, then decided against it. His own moment, he decided. He didn't need to share it.

"Last time I stayed in a room this big, there was a dozen other guys in it," Russell said, "most of them with tattoos."

Deal nodded. "Probably a lot of people in Havana living that way right now," he said.

"Yeah," Russell offered, "but even so, the place doesn't seem *beat,* you know what I mean?"

"I do indeed," Deal said. He had finally noticed what Russell was wearing. "Where'd you get that?"

Russell glanced down at the front of the guayabera, then smiled at Deal. "Across the street," he said, gesturing vaguely out the window. "I took myself a little stroll." He broke off to smooth the front of the cream-colored shirt with his hands. "What do you think?"

Deal nodded. "It's you, Russell." The truth was that Russell, with his strong bronzed features and chiseled build, would have looked good in sackcloth and ashes.

"Hundred percent cotton," Russell said. "The polyester was a little cheaper, but I like the real thing, you know?"

"I didn't realize you were such a shopper," Deal said.

"Hey," Russell said, lifting his hands, "when in Rome . . ."

Deal nodded, trying to imagine himself shedding his polo shirt for a guayabera. Maybe there was a limit to this new-man thing, though.

"You been sleeping?" Russell asked, staring at him more closely.

"I guess I dozed off," Deal said, checking his watch. He'd been dreaming of restoring that amazing tenement building they'd stopped by earlier that day, he realized, only in his dream the Malecón had become South Beach, and Fuentes and Vines were part of his labor crew.

"I'm ready to eat, myself," Russell said.

"I could do that."

"Except that joint downstairs strikes me as a little stuffy."

Deal shrugged. "Then let's go somewhere else."

Russell nodded. "The guy who sold me the shirt was telling me about these paladars. They're like restaurants in private homes, where the ones in hotels and stuff are supported by the government. This guy says you get the best food in a paladar."

Deal shook his head. "You amaze me, Russell. Guayaberas, paladars . . ."

Russell gave him a look. "You got to go with the flow, bro'."

"Let's do it, then," Deal said. He reached into his pocket to make sure he had his key, then stepped for the door.

Russell took a last look around the room. "Nice flowers," he said, then followed Deal out.

17.

"I've got a great idea," Deal told Russell as they reentered the hotel from dinner at the *paladar* that Fuentes's driver had taken them to, a madeover apartment on the third floor of a crumbling building in Central Havana. "We find the worst, beat-down warehouse district in Miami, and we put a restaurant on the third floor of the scroungiest building we can find. We'll call it El Paladar. We'll make a fortune."

Russell glanced over. "You have to admit the food was good, though."

Deal nodded. There'd been no steak, no shrimp, no shellfish of any kind on the menu—all such items reserved for the state-sponsored restaurants, they'd been told—but the items that had been available were as inventively prepared as in any chichi restaurant in Miami Beach, he thought. "I'm going to take this up with Fuentes in the morning," Deal persisted. "What a concept—terrific food in Albanian surroundings."

"You must have had one too many *mojitos*," Russell said.

"Or one two few," Deal said.

He heard the muffled sounds of a bass from the direction of the vast atrium and turned to find Russell rubbing his hands in anticipation. "Well, what do we have here?" Russell was saying.

The big man was pointing across the courtyard at a set of French doors behind which it seemed a party was in full swing, a blast of salsa issuing clearly, as a pretty young woman in a cocktail dress stepped outside.

"It is the *discoteca*," one of the bellmen flanking the entrance offered. "Live music," he added, with a meaningful nod at the *señorita,* who ducked into a nearby rest room. "Very good place."

Russell gave Deal an inquiring look. "How about a nightcap, then?" he asked.

Deal shook his head. "I've had enough for one day," he said. He glanced at his watch. He'd tried getting in touch with Isabel earlier and had meant to try again before he turned in, but it would have to wait for tomorrow, now. The last thing he wanted was to get up close and personal with a bass-pounding band. "You go ahead," he told Russell. "I'll catch up with you in the morning."

The young woman had emerged from the rest room, her gaze sweeping over them and holding on Russell for the tiniest fraction of a second. If she'd held it an instant longer, Deal thought, fire alarms would have gone off.

"You sure?" Russell said, his own gaze drawn to her retreating profile.

"I'll call you as soon as I hear from Fuentes," Deal said. "You go ahead and have fun."

Deal took the tiny elevator up alone, its cage lurching along in fits and starts as if driven by the pounding bass beneath him. The look that girl had given Russell had started him thinking of Angie again, and the wave of confusion that followed was trending toward a headache that threatened to spring into life with the same beat of the *discoteca*'s band.

The door of the elevator finally shuddered open and he stepped quickly out of the tiny compartment, vowing to find the stairs in the morning. He never took elevators one flight up. Why was he doing such a thing now?

He moved along the corridor toward his room, trying to banish the thoughts that had crept into his brain. He had enough things to worry about without getting involved with someone at this point. It had been a godsend, really, this trip, whatever else came of it. He and Angie, that had been one of those crazy, unexpected things. Better it should stay that way. But what was this pang that kept gnawing at his gut?

He stood at the door of his room, hesitating. Maybe he should go down and have one more *mojito* with Russell Straight. Maybe that was all he needed to get his mind off things. But that was crazy, too. He was tired, and if he knew anything about his job foreman, the man would already be deep in conversation with the girl who'd glanced at him, even if not a word of the other's language was being spoken.

He smiled then and moved to slide his key into the lock of his door, surprised to find it swinging inward freely at his touch. *What the hell,* he was thinking, one foot already inside the doorway before he thought better of it.

He was poised, hesitating between the impulse to flip the

wall switch just inside the door and the urgent warning that told him to turn and flee, when a hand clamped onto his shirtfront, yanking him violently forward, and another clamped over his mouth.

"Forgive me, Mr. Deal," he heard a familiar voice whisper at his ear. "But these walls have ears."

A flashlight beam snapped on, illuminating a face before him in a garish glow. Vedetti, he realized. Another man in the shadows at his side. A third was holding Deal firmly in a powerful grasp.

"We mean you no harm," Vedetti said in an urgent whisper, holding his finger to his lips.

The faint chirping of a cell phone sounded, and the man at Vedetti's side answered in Spanish. The man than handed the tiny phone to Vedetti.

The first cell phone he'd seen on the island, Deal thought dumbly, his mind a whirl of thoughts. "Listen," Vedetti said, thrusting the phone to Deal's ear.

"John," Deal heard the woman's voice on the other end. He knew it instantly and felt that he had somehow slid into a dream. "It's Angie. Please listen. Go with them, John. I'm here, in Havana. They're going to bring you to me. Go with them. I'll explain everything when I see you. Please go with them, John."

Vedetti pulled the phone away then and snapped the connection off. "Can I trust you?" he asked, his gaze boring into Deal's. Deal did his best to nod against the powerful grasp that held him.

Vedetti gestured with his chin, and Deal felt the grip loosen at his neck. In the next instant, brain gone white with fury, he was lunging toward Vedetti, his hands outstretched . . .

. . . and then everything was black.

18.

"YOU DANCE very well," the woman said to Russell, smiling at him from her place at the bar. The band was on break now, and while recorded music still blared from the speakers, it was almost possible to hear. Delia, she'd said her name was. A tawny woman with a lithe body that moved about the dance floor with enviable grace. She was dark-skinned, but fine-featured, her blood a blend of African and Indian, he guessed.

"Not half as well as you," Russell said. He mopped at his brow with a bar napkin, trying not to let his gaze go too far down the plunging neckline of her dress.

"It is what I do." She gave him a measured smile. "If you come to my studio, I will give you a lesson."

"I bet you could," Russell said.

"In the samba," Delia said.

"That's exactly what I meant," he said.

She patted his knee, then turned to finish her drink. The bartender leaned in, and Russell made a signal for another round. The woman intervened, however, holding up a finger to stop the barman.

"Perhaps you would like to go someplace quieter?" she said.

Russell regarded her more carefully. "What about your friends?" he asked, gesturing at a corner table where several couples were gathered, chatting animatedly in Spanish.

She turned to share his gaze. "It is fine," she said, unconcerned. She turned back to him, her gaze neutral. "There is a café nearby. A different kind of music."

"Quieter," Russell repeated. The thought crossed his mind that he was sitting with a working girl, but he could always deal with that issue later. Whatever she was, she was a stunner: jet-black hair that made even her coffee-colored skin seem pale in comparison, full breasts and a flat belly, legs that stopped the show when she danced. He'd seen old movies where smooth-talking white guys dropped into clubs and discovered babes they promised to turn into stars. Here he was looking at one.

She gave him a shrug. "Whatever you like," she said.

Over her shoulder he saw the members of the band beginning to reassemble on the tiny stage. "Sure," he said, "let's do quieter, then," and held out his hand.

"And what is it that you do in Miami?" she asked, her hand resting lightly on his arm as they walked down the narrow street, away from the hotel.

"I work for a builder," he said. "I go around, make sure guys stay busy on the job."

"There would be plenty of work for you in Cuba," she said.

"How's that?"

"In our system, everyone works," she said, "but sometimes not so hard."

Russell nodded. "Some things are the same all over." He heard a car motor start and glanced down a side street, where a dark sedan of a type he'd never seen was pulling out of the lot, pausing to let someone standing at the curb get in.

"What is it?" she asked.

He shook his head absently. "Just a guy who looked familiar," he told her, as the car sped away down the side street. It was dark, and he'd just had the briefest glimpse, but it was hard to mistake that wild head of hair.

"An American?" she asked.

He shook his head. "Somebody I ran into down here."

She gave him an appraising look. "You know what a man from your country told me once?"

"No," he said, glancing after the departing car once more. "What?"

"You all look so much alike."

He turned back. "Are you kidding me? Some cracker said that to you?"

She shrugged, then looked at him more closely, "What is cracker?"

"That's American for dickhead," he told her. He put his arm around her shoulders and moved them on down the street. "A blind dickhead," he added, feeling her snuggle in tight.

"We call this music *son*," she told him. They sat together on a wicker love seat at the rear of the tiny club, watching a group energetically at work on what he thought of as a bluesy version of the salsa they'd been dancing to earlier. "Do you like it?" she added, glancing up at him.

He nodded. Count Basie does Cuba, he was thinking, but kept it to himself. "It's quieter," he said, bringing a smile from her. "How old are those guys, anyway?"

She turned back to the stage. "Some are in their seventies," she said. "The singer is eighty. He has a granddaughter in Miami," she added, pointing to the gray-haired leader keeping languid time with an oddly elongated percussion gourd. "Maybe they will tour there one day."

He stared at her. "Tour?"

"They are famous, you know. All around the world."

"Except in Miami, I guess."

She raised her eyebrows. "It is difficult, going to America, even for them . . ." She gestured with her glass, then turned back to him, her gaze unflinching.

"You want something else?" he asked her.

She shook her head and put her glass down on the table in front of them. "I don't think so," she said. "How about you?"

"I'm ready," he said, his eyes on hers.

"Good," she said. And they got up to go.

When they returned to the hotel, the *discoteca* was still going strong. If anything it looked to Russell as if the crowd inside the room had grown, if that was possible.

She stopped him just outside the doors and nodded to the

young man who now stood sentry at the entrance. "Just one moment," she said, then ducked inside.

Russell and the bouncer stood regarding each other silently. He had an inch or two on the guy, and maybe twenty pounds, but the kid didn't seem intimidated. After a moment, Russell gave him a nod, and the kid nodded back. Some things were the same everywhere.

She came back out just as the group segued from one number directly to the next, smiling up at him. "There," she said, taking his arm. The kid was staring elsewhere now.

"You went to talk to you friends?" Russell asked her.

She gave him a frank look. "It was necessary to speak to someone," she said.

It took him a moment to understand. Finally he took her arm and moved them along toward the elevator. "You mind if I ask you?" he said, as he pressed the call button.

"Yes?" she said, her gaze unflinching.

"You're not working here, are you?"

Her expression darkened momentarily, then just as briefly the shadow passed. She squared her shoulders and stared back at him, evenly. "I am having a very enjoyable evening," she said, before pausing. "How about you?"

He smiled as the elevator door slid open. "Our chariot awaits," he said, offering her his arm, and then they stepped inside.

"You are still awake," Delia said, nuzzling close beneath the single sheet that covered them.

"Just now," he corrected her. He'd been dreaming of floating on his back on a soft, spongy cloud while a beautiful woman rose and fell above him, her face shrouded by the tumbling dark locks of her hair, one soft cry after another issuing from her throat like music that couldn't find a way to stop.

No dream, at all, he was thinking, just a drowsy replay. His arm went about her smooth shoulder and pulled her close, heat from her hips and breasts like coals.

Just about as likely as a dream, though, given what he'd come through. Who'd believe him if he went home and told about it—Russell Straight in a grand hotel in Havana, Cuba, with this woman too impossible for words—and no one left to tell besides.

His brother gone, and his mother too, heartbroken to have one son killed and another go to prison. His father dead, too, but that one with good riddance. Someone Russell might have had to finish himself if another man hadn't beaten him to it.

Then he pushed all that from his mind and focused instead on the feeling of that mass of curls resting on his shoulder. "You are *very* much awake," she said, her hand slipping down beneath the sheets.

"Never going to sleep again," he told her, rising up on one elbow. He flung the sheet aside, saw nothing but paradise ahead. In no time the clouds were rocking once again.

19.

DEAL AWOKE as he was being levered out of the backseat of a dark sedan, one pair of hands at his back, another pulling him forward. His own hands had been bound with tape of some sort, he realized, and a length of cloth had been wrapped about his mouth as a gag. More tape had been looped around his ankles, forming a loose hobble.

"Is awake," he heard someone say, then felt fingers tug at the knot at the back of his neck.

"I am sorry," he heard a voice from the darkness. "It was for your own protection . . . and ours, of course."

Vedetti, he thought groggily, blinking his eyes into focus. There was a pounding behind his right ear where he'd been clipped, but it didn't seem serious. Whoever had hit him knew what he was doing.

The gag was pulled away, and he worked his dry lips, trying to formulate a response. They were somewhere in the countryside, he saw by the dim moonlight, the car pulled up in a dusty clearing outside what looked like a farmhouse overhung by trees and surrounded by thick undergrowth. Locusts screeched in the empty darkness surrounding them, keeping time to the pounding in his skull. Shout all you want to out here, he thought, get a worse headache in return.

"What the hell's going on, Vedetti?"

He felt a hand on his shoulder, propelling him forward. He nearly toppled over and realized he'd been hobbled by a binding at his ankles. "Where is Angie?" he managed. "What have you done to her?"

"Inside, Mr. Deal," Vedetti's voice came. "Everything will be explained."

Deal felt the grip at his arm tighten, the same guy who'd clipped him back at the hotel, he judged. He took a series of mincing steps across the clearing but balked at the approach to the porch steps.

"Cut him loose," he heard Vedetti say. "Where do you think he's going?"

There was a grunt from behind him, then Deal felt something brush his pants legs near his ankles. More tape there, he thought, as the bindings were cut, then peeled away.

He broadened his stance to steady himself and glanced around the clearing, realizing that Vedetti was right. The vegetation surrounding them looked as dense as anything that choked all South Florida when you got half a mile from developed land. He wouldn't get a dozen yards in that tangle.

"Come now, Mr. Deal," he heard Vedetti from the porch above him. "There are persons most anxious to speak with you."

Deal glanced up, fighting a bitter laugh. "That's what I've been hearing ever since I came to Cuba," he said.

He felt a shove between his shoulder blades then, and felt a lightning surge of anger sweep over him. He allowed himself to stumble forward, then ducked and spun around, driving his elbow into the stomach of the man who had pushed him.

He heard a satisfying whoosh of air escape the man as he folded over, clutching his stomach. Deal raised his knee, and there came a muffled crunching sound as the man went over sideways with a gasp.

Deal heard footsteps rushing across the porch toward him and spun once more, clutching his still-bound hands together. He caught the man who was diving toward him with a solid, two-handed blow on the side of the jaw, sending him sprawling into the dust beside the first man he'd dropped.

That one was struggling to his knees and Deal had raised his hands to deliver another blow when he felt the cold press of steel against his cheek. "That is enough, Mr. Deal," he heard Vedetti's voice at his ear. The pistol barrel ground against his cheek for emphasis. "Are you listening to me?"

Deal nodded slowly, carefully lowering his hands. Vedetti backed away cautiously as his men picked themselves up out of the dirt.

"Cabrón," the stocky one who had shoved him muttered, taking a step toward Deal.

Vedetti called something in rapid-fire Spanish, and the stocky man hesitated. He gave Vedetti a look and then backed away.

"Can we please go inside, now?" Deal heard Vedetti say. "Quietly."

"Why not?" Deal said. And began to mount the stairs.

20.

HE WAS moving through the door of the farmhouse into a wavering pool of light cast by a kerosene lantern when he saw her, the sight striking him more powerfully than any punch he'd taken that night.

"Angie?" he managed. He could hear the disbelief in his own voice.

She stood in slacks and blouse behind a wooden table in a rustic kitchen, her hair pulled back severely, flanked by a pair of stern-faced men who looked strangely familiar. One was tall with long black hair swept slickly from his forehead, the other a wizened older man who seemed a ringer for the street hustler who'd slapped a picture of Betty Grable in his palm earlier that day.

"I am Angelica," she said, her gaze holding his steadily. Finally, she turned and spoke to someone over his shoulder. "Cut his hands loose," she said.

"But . . ." Vedetti protested at his shoulder.

"What are you waiting for?" she snapped. "Do you think he's going to hurt me?"

Deal stared, still stunned. A goddamned good question, he was thinking, as he felt Vedetti's knife slice neatly through the tape at his wrists.

The woman standing before him was clearly Angie, but his mind was having grave difficulty accepting that fact. An entire section of his brain had been given over to feelings of tenderness, erotic fantasy, uncharacteristic, long-buried notions that had threatened to change his life. Now all of it was being shaken loose, images of a woman moving urgently above him replaced with a brief glimpse of someone he barely knew offering a caress to a dark-haired man on a Havana street, then disappearing into a taxicab.

"You get around," Deal managed. "You sure as hell get around."

She stared back at him defiantly. "Don't indulge yourself," she said, evenly. "There's more at stake than you know."

Deal glanced around the dimly lit room, gradually accepting what seemed impossible. Half a dozen hard-faced men standing about, every one of them as attendant to this woman's authority as a pack of hounds. What in God's name had he stumbled into? Mata Hari's nest? The lair of the Black Widow?

Whatever it was, one truth had settled upon him as certain and unyielding as a moray's jaws: She'd suckered him as he had never been before. If he'd never understood the fury of a woman taken for a ride, he thought, he'd have no trouble now.

He turned back to her, rubbing at the raw skin of his wrists where the tape had been ripped free. "Maybe you should have left me tied up," he said. "We could have tried it that way. It might have been more fun for you."

She colored and moved forward as if to strike him, then stopped herself. She glanced at the tall man with the swept-back hair, who stared back impassively. She turned back to Deal, then, seeming to gather her composure. "I am sorry for what has happened," she said. "I could not have expected you would be brought here by others."

Deal stared back at her in disbelief. His head felt as tenuously attached as some bobble-head doll's. "So Fuentes is in on this?"

Her eyes flashed. "Antonio Fuentes is no friend of ours. It was a coincidence that he brought you to Havana. It simplified my task; that is all."

Deal shook his head. "I'm afraid you've left me way behind, Angie, or whatever your name is. It's probably just jet lag, but maybe you could fill in the blanks."

"That is why we have brought you here," she said.

"You mind if I sit down?" He gestured at one of the wooden chairs by the table, and she nodded.

"Would you like some water?" she asked as he sat.

"Sure," he said, putting a hand to the back of his neck. "Water would be good."

She said something to one of the men, who went to an ancient refrigerator in a corner and brought him a plastic bottle. Deal stared at it. "Evian?" he asked, holding it up.

She gave a humorless laugh. "The long reach of capitalism," she said. "I brought it from Key West, if you want to know."

He nodded, taking a swig of the water. When he put the bottle down, one hand casually brushed the sole of his shoe.

"Maybe you could start by telling me where we are," he said. He'd peeled and pressed one of Vines's listening devices into place. Just a wad of gum stuck in the crevice between sole and heel, he saw with a glance. He was also wondering if Vines's claims about the range of the device had any basis in fact.

"It is unimportant," she said. "More to the point is why you are here."

"I'll settle for that," he said. "The last thing I remember I was on my way to bed in the Santa Isabel."

She stared at him for a moment as if she found the statement odd. He'd have to give up the expository dialogue, he told himself. A chancy device, just like all his English teachers said.

"My name is Angelica Mondescu," she told him. "You have already met Señor Vedetti."

"I thought I had met you, too," he said. "But that must have been someone else. There was this woman in Key West. She told me her name was Angie Marsh."

She closed her eyes momentarily, but whether it was an apologetic gesture or an exasperated one was impossible to tell. "Be patient," she said finally, and Deal nodded in response.

"I am a citizen of Cuba," she told him. "As are all of us here," she added, with a sweep of her arm.

Deal glanced at Vedetti. "Somehow I got a different impression this afternoon," he said.

Vedetti shrugged. "My parents died in the revolution," he said. "I was a child when I was taken to Napoli by relatives. It has been more convenient to live as an Italian citizen."

"I'm sure," Deal said, though he had never felt less sure of things in his life.

"You must understand," Angelica cut in. "We are patriots. We love this country and its people. We are part of a group that has been working quietly to prepare for the inevitable changes Cuba must soon undergo."

"You're ready to put Batista back on the throne?" Deal asked.

"Don't speak foolishness," she said. "We wish to see the emergence of a democratic nation. Most of the people in Cuba want the same. But no one wants another puppet government run by the business interests of the United States. It is as simple as that."

"You'd like to think so, anyway," Deal said.

He wondered if there were gnomes somewhere in the bowels of Vines's listening post taking all this in. Had any alarm been raised? Were sophisticated electronics devices hard at work at this very instant, triangulating his position? Were crack commando units daubing on their camo paint right now, readying for an assault on this remote farmhouse?

Pleasant enough fantasies, of course. But more likely a tape recorder was grinding away in an unmanned basement room laying down the hiss of static from an out-of-range listening device. And even if they could hear him, there would be no assault forces marshaled on Cuban soil. He'd stand a better chance of rescue if he were stashed in an Iraqi cave. Whatever he was up against, he was on his miserable own. For a moment, he felt an almost wistful yearning for the face of Antonio Fuentes.

"Democracy will take told in Cuba," she assured him. "It is the will of our people."

Deal nodded. "I hope you're right," he said, glancing about the room. "Are we getting to the part where I come into all this?"

She nodded, glancing at the tall man behind her before she continued. "When we met in Key West, it was impossible for me to be forthright with you. Once you have heard me out, I hope you will understand."

"Anything's possible," Deal said, though he could not imagine applying logic to what had happened.

"You must understand that ours is a gravely dangerous position," she told him. "There are spies everywhere, men willing to betray our ideals for a scrap . . ." She broke off momentarily, giving an angry toss of her head.

"Many people have already died for what we believe in," she continued. "No one can be trusted implicitly. One day a person is a friend, the next day, everything changes . . ."

"Tell me about it," Deal countered.

"Listen to me," she said, her voice taking on a new urgency. "It was imperative that we learn the truth . . ."

"The truth about what?" Deal cut in.

"About your father," she blurted out.

It was yet another stunner in a night already full of them. Deal stared back, not sure he had heard correctly. "What does my father have to do with this?" He heard the threat in his own voice, saw the tall man take a step forward.

She turned to the tall man. "Give him the package, Victor."

The man glanced at her, then reached for a manila envelope that was lying on a cabinet top. He took another step toward Deal and tossed the envelope on the kitchen table where it landed with a thud.

Deal glanced at the packet, then back at Angelica. "What is it?" he asked.

"Go ahead," she said, "open it."

He glanced again at the packet. Surely nothing explosive inside. They'd all be diving for cover, not staring at him expectantly. Still, something was holding his hand from the packet. Some dread, some uncertainty that had been part of the very fabric of his life for as long as he could remember.

Some kids grow up with ordinary fathers who soldier on through everyday life and everyday jobs with a stop here and there at a baseball game and a birthday party and—so long as fortune smiles—a roof overhead and smiles all around at the evening dinner table. On the other hand, he'd had Barton Deal as his father, and that had been a little like having John Huston drop in from time to time after a hard month's shooting in Zanzibar.

Deal had loved his father—hell, everyone had loved his father—but he had also spent a lifetime trying to crawl out from under the man's enormous shadow. He had no idea what was in that packet lying on the table in front of him, could not fathom what connection a bunch of purported Cuban revolutionaries might be claiming to his old man—but he would lay odds it could only complicate his own life further.

Still, there was no putting it off. He could no more ignore the challenge of that waiting envelope than he could will himself to stop breathing. He glanced up at Victor, the quiet and handsome man with the swept-back hair, then turned his gaze toward Angelica, a woman he might have loved.

He was reaching for the packet when the first volley of gunfire rang out.

21.

THE FIRST BARRAGE tore across the façade of the farmhouse in a snapping of splintered wood. Deal heard an answering burst of fire from outside, followed by a sharp cry and a momentary silence that was broken by shouted commands in Spanish.

Vedetti was running toward the window when the grimy panes disintegrated in a burst of automatic fire that vaporized the glass and blew the curtains to shreds. Vedetti stopped as if he'd hit an invisible wall, then toppled sideways without a sound.

One of the men on the far side of the room was rushing to extinguish the kerosene lantern when a round blew threw the copper tank. The flattened slug cartwheeled on into the man's chest, spraying flaming fuel everywhere. The man who'd been hit was enveloped in flames instantly. He staggered forward, waving his arms like a man just emerged from hell.

Other slugs tore into the wall, some whanging off the front of the ancient refrigerator, others shattering off the porcelain back of the sink. Deal felt shards spray fiery on his cheeks even as he dove beneath the table for cover.

He had hardly hit the floor when he felt a hand dig fiercely into his hair. "Get up," he heard her cry. "This way."

She yanked again, so hard he thought she'd tear his scalp away. Two of her men were at the shattered window frame spraying fire from their own automatic weapons blindly into the night, then ducking away as the answering fusillades came.

He scrambled to his knees, cracking his forehead painfully on the edge of the table as he rose. He made it to his feet, staring dumbly at the flaming man now collapsed across the chair where he'd been sitting. The fire had spread to the cabinets on the opposite wall, flames shooting toward the ceiling.

He heard the clatter of heavier arms from outside and saw the wall beside the window frame erupt inward in a shower of wood fragments and plaster dust. One of the men who'd been crouched there took the last of the volley, the force of it blowing him half a dozen feet across the floor.

"Go!" she shouted, shoving him hard in the back.

He hesitated. Whoever was out there firing, it didn't seem the time to run onto the porch waving a white flag and shouting "Amigo."

He turned and stumbled down a hallway, following after Victor, who turned as he ran, motioning wildly for Deal to follow. Deal assumed they were headed toward some rear exit, when the man came quickly to a halt near the hallway's end and stopped to kick aside a throw rug.

"Here," Victor said, bending to grasp an iron ring set in a recess of the floor. He yanked up, bringing a section of flooring away, and Deal felt a wave of cool air rise up from the yawning hole that had appeared.

"Follow me," Victor said, then lowered himself quickly into the darkness.

Deal didn't hesitate, slipping into the opening the instant the man had disappeared. He gripped the sides of the trapdoor and let himself drop, feeling his feet hit ground just as his fingertips slipped loose. It was utter blackness inside the passage, and he groped about blindly for a moment before he felt a hand on his shirtfront.

"Come," he heard Victor's voice say. At the same time there was the sound of Angelica's feet dropping to the floor of the passage behind him.

Deal tried to gauge their progress as the three of them moved quickly along the narrow passage. He kept one hand up to shield himself from bashing his skull against the roughly chiseled roof, at the same time trying to count his paces. He'd taken maybe forty steps, he thought, possibly a few more, when the man in front of him stopped and placed a hand on his chest to hold him back.

There was an opening just ahead; he saw the outline of an irregular, leaf-strewn opening lit by the glow of moonlight. The sounds of gunfire still echoed in the distance, but in the tangle of underbrush just outside, everything seemed calm.

"Quickly," Victor said. "Stay quiet," he added, then ducked through the opening and into the brush.

Deal felt Angelica's shove at his back and moved out into the night in turn, finding himself wincing at the touch of the dappled moonlight. After the darkness of the passage, it might as well have been a floodlight, he thought. But the only gunshots were those still sounding in the distance.

They were moving down a hillside now, away from the farmhouse that commanded its crest, hurrying along a narrow passage that twisted through the junglelike underbrush in a mazelike fashion. Stubby branches lurked in the shadows at every turn, jabbing at his cheeks and scalp and eyes, and roots reached up for his ankles like clutching hands. None of that was any obstacle for the deer or the wild pigs who had probably cut the trail, he thought, but it was no help for the clumsy humans using it as a lifeline, either.

"Wait here." He heard the quiet command from the tall man who'd been leading the way.

He stopped, grateful for the rest, his breathing harsh in his ears. "Where are we?" he asked, as Angelica came up in the gloom to join him.

"Quiet," she said, peering anxiously into the darkness ahead.

They waited together in a silence that was cut by the occasional rattle of distant gunfire and the gathering whine of insects. After a moment she squeezed past him. "Stay where you are," she commanded. He saw that she carried a pistol in her upraised hand.

"Oh, sure," Deal muttered to himself as she disappeared into the darkness. He waited for a few seconds, then moved after her as quietly as he could.

He had made his way another fifty feet or so without catching so much as a glimpse of her or Victor, the man he took to be her lover. The thought crossed his mind that he could escape them now, but just as quickly he canceled the notion out.

Escape to where? Back to that slaughterhouse on top of the

hill, try to use his fractured Spanish on a band of killers, explain he was just an innocent bystander who had wandered off from a trade mission to Cuba? Not likely.

And as for escaping through this jungle thicket, he could forget it. You couldn't move a D-9 Cat a dozen feet through this stuff. No, there was only one way to go, and that was straight ahead.

In the moment he'd paused to think things through, his eyes had picked up a glimmer just ahead. He slowed his pace, picking his way carefully over the roots that crisscrossed the path, trying to keep his breathing quiet, ignoring the whine and the sting of the insects boring into the flesh of his ears and neck.

A clearing out there, he saw, just visible through the underbrush, perhaps thirty feet ahead, a broad turnout at the end of a narrow graveled road. At one side, he could make out the silhouette of a car, one of the nondescript boxy Ladas that were everywhere on the streets of Havana.

Deal stopped, sensing movement in the shadows near the flank of the Lada. Victor, he realized, as the tall silhouette stole quickly from the shadows. The Lada was their getaway car.

Victor paused, seemingly to make one last check of the surroundings, then moved quickly for the door of the Lada. It was so quiet, Deal could hear the jingling of keys, and the scrape of a lock tumbling open. In the next moment, he caught sight of a second figure entering the clearing in Victor's wake.

Angelica, Deal thought at first, following after her lover to the car. Deal glanced around the darkness where he stood. He could worm his way into a crevice of this tangle; they would never find him. He could hide for as long as it took, then make his way back to civilization once things had died down.

He was still calculating this possibility, and had cast his gaze back to the clearing, when he realized that something was wrong. Victor had just swung open the door of the Lada, and the figure that had followed him into the clearing was running full-tilt now across the gravel, an arm upraised.

Deal saw the glint of steel in the moonlight and realized how wrong he had been. Not Angelica at all. Not a woman, but a man. With the heavy blade of a cane cutter raised and a guttural curse flying from his lips.

Deal heard the cry of warning from his own throat at the same time Victor must have realized what was happening. He spun from the open door of the Lada, flinging up his arm in reflex, but the gesture was useless.

The heavy blade arced down, hardly slowing as it clipped off Victor's forearm and buried itself in his head. The thudding echo reached all the way to Deal's place in the dense grove.

He had begun to run down the path without thinking, when he heard the first explosion from the clearing. It was followed closely by a second, then a third. He burst out from the path to find the man with the cane cutter slumped against the side of the Lada and Angelica bent over Victor's body, the pistol she had used to kill his assailant still in her hand.

She was sobbing when he reached her, her shoulders heaving as she clutched Victor's unresponsive form. "Angelica," Deal called.

Down the narrow lane where the Lada's nose was pointed came the sound of approaching car engines. Headlights waved crazily through the underbrush. Whoever it was would be here in seconds.

"They've heard," he called again, shaking her by the shoulders. She stared up at him in a daze, tears tracing her dark cheeks.

After a moment, she seemed to register the sounds of the approaching engines and rose to her feet.

She paused for one last glance at the tall man who lay crumpled in the gravel at her feet, then turned to Deal. "Come," she said.

And they were hurrying back into the jungle.

22.

THEY WERE no more than a hundred yards back up the hillside when Deal heard the slamming of doors and the shouts from the clearing below. Hellfire ahead of them, doom below, he thought. The men who wanted Angelica and her friends would simply advance from either end of the trail. It was just a matter of time.

He slipped on a knobby root and went down on one knee, feeling the fabric of his khakis give way against something jagged. He felt the warmth of blood down his leg as he rose, but it was nothing compared to what might come. He staggered around a bend in the path, his breath heaving, and found her waiting for him in the darkness.

"This way," she said, dragging him through a screen of brush. No sooner had she pulled him aside than she was off again, hurdling a tangle of roots that rose like nesting snakes across an even narrower track. He went across the tangle on hands and knees, ignoring every scrape and blow.

In seconds, he was on his feet again, a few paces behind her, and realized that the path had dived downhill once more. He couldn't hear anything behind them yet, but he was certain they'd be coming. How long he could keep up this pace he wasn't sure.

"Be careful." He heard Angelica in front of him.

She was stopped again, her foot pressing a string of fence wire to the ground, her hands pulling another high, so that he could duck through. He stopped when he saw the porcelain insulators on a nearby post.

"It's electrified," he said, pointing. "How . . . ?"

"This is Cuba," she said. "Who can afford to electrify a fence?"

Deal didn't stop to argue. He rolled under the upraised wire, then scrambled to his feet as she ducked to join him.

They were standing on cleared ground now, he realized, the outskirts of someone's farm. Just ahead he saw the vague outline of a service building, and beyond that the improbable yawning pit of an empty swimming pool. Not a farm, then, but some secluded estate.

"Where are we?" he asked.

Before she could reply, they heard shouted Spanish from the hillside above. "Quickly," she said, pulling him down the hillside past the looming service building.

They were running down a sanded path beneath towering trees now, an unimpeded, flat-out sprint. Where it would all end, he had no idea, but he knew as well that he'd go until there was nothing left to give.

There was another structure looming up in the gloom ahead,

some oddly shaped building plunked down in the middle of nowhere, he was thinking . . . until his strides brought him closer and he was finally able to see clearly what it was

"A boat?" he called to Angelica in disbelief.

And indeed that is what it was, a forty-foot cabin cruiser mounted on blocks on the side of a mountain, the whole thing surrounded by a raised catwalk with a wooden walkway stretching from the path to join it.

For her part, Angelica never even hesitated. She bounded onto the wooden walkway and in seconds had reached the catwalk that encircled the landlocked yacht.

Deal took one glance back up the way they'd come, another at the path that dwindled to nothing a few feet in front of him, then ran to join her. By the time he'd made it to the catwalk, she was already on the deck of the boat, motioning for him to join her. What were they going to do now, he wondered? Cruise a dry-docked yacht to safety?

By the time he joined her on the deck of the boat, he saw what she had in mind. She'd dug her fingers beneath a crevice in the floorboards of the rear decking, exposing an empty compartment that lay below. "Get in," she commanded, her voice an urgent whisper.

Deal hesitated, glancing back up the hillside. He heard muffled shouts and the tramp of boots. "If they find us in there, we're done," he said.

"There's nowhere else," she said. She showed him her pistol. "I've got three bullets left. Say what you want to do."

He stared at her, saw something in those dark eyes that had held him from the first. Something told him if he suggested it, they'd make a stand there at the railing of the boat. Go up against the men who were coming after them with three shells and a pair of bare hands. Whatever she believed in, he thought, she believed a lot.

He nodded then and jumped down into the compartment. In the next moment, she was beside him, the top of the compartment swinging down like a coffin lid.

"It is the boat of Hemingway," she told him in the darkness. "The *Pilar*. My father once sailed aboard it with the man himself."

If she'd said Hemingway was asleep in the midships cabin, Deal wouldn't have raised an objection. "What's this we're hiding in?" he asked.

"A smuggler's compartment," she said. "According to my father, many things were carried inside here, to and from our country."

"What's Hemingway's boat doing in the middle of the woods?" he asked.

"We are on the grounds of the Finca Vigia," she said. "Hemingway's estate. It is a museum now. They moved the boat here only recently."

"A museum? How about this compartment? Is that part of the tour?"

"My father told me no one knew about it," she said. "You must be quiet now."

He heard the rumble of footsteps on the wooden gangway then, and a few minutes later the thud of boots landing on the deck above. There were muffled conversations in Spanish and the rattling of a locked door that must have led from the yacht's cockpit to the staterooms forward. He heard the creak of the engine-compartment door being raised and saw the glint of a flashlight beam through a crevice in the compartment wall at his side.

He felt Angelica shift silently beside him. She was on her

back now, her shoulders propped against the end of the compartment, poised as calmly as if she had just sat up in bed. If that compartment door came up, he thought, pity the first three men in sight.

After a moment the flashlight winked out and the engine-compartment door slammed down. There was a moment's desultory conversation from above, then a creaking noise from the deck and, finally, the sound of departing footsteps on the gangway.

He turned to whisper something to her but felt her fingertips press against his lips and her head bury itself against his chest.

"Victor," he began. "I'm sorry . . ."

"He was my brother," she managed.

He felt her shoulders begin to quake then, and the heaving of her silent sobs began. It seemed like hours that they lay that way, though it was still well before dawn when she rose to lead him away.

23.

Russell Straight awakened to find himself alone in his bed, a mild headache gnawing at the back of his head. After a moment he swung his feet onto the cool marble tile, then rose and padded to the bathroom, which he found empty. He turned and went down the short hallway to the sitting area and found that empty as well.

It had occurred to him, as he looked about for Delia in his still-groggy state, that he and his brother and his mother—and during rare periods, his father as well—had lived in a house that was no larger than this hotel room he now occupied. His brother, Leon, had escaped all that, of course, no matter how briefly. Leon had gone to college, and though he'd barely learned to read, much less manage to graduate, had gone on to play professional football, until the injuries and the resultant drug habit had caught up with him.

Leon had died where he'd started out early, back in the company of bad people, but at least he'd had a taste of the good life, Russell thought, and who could begrudge him that? For Russell, though, such luxuries as he was enjoying just now seemed manna from heaven itself. He couldn't imagine ever taking such things for granted. In the eyes of the woman he'd been with last night, for instance, he was a man of wealth, a perspective he would strive to be mindful of.

He walked back into the bedroom, then, and though he thought less of himself for doing so, pulled out his wallet and checked the contents. He should have known better than to suspect Delia, but he had spent some years in prison and certain habits died hard.

He went back into the bathroom then and allowed himself the satisfaction of a luxurious whizz with no one on either side of him casting surreptitious glances at the wand he held in his hand. When he was finished, Russell pulled the dangling chain that worked the old-fashioned toilet, and when the cycle was finished, pulled the chain again, just for the hell of it. By the time he had showered and shaved and put on a fresh polo shirt with "DealCo" embroidered in the cloth that strained across his pec, and pulled on a pair of khakis of the sort that his boss had gotten him accustomed to, he was feeling about as good as two or three of himself.

He made his way down the hallway to Deal's room and knocked, and even the fact that there was no answer did not faze him. As he was showering, he had developed an inner certainty that coming to Cuba had been one of the most inspired actions of his relatively short life. He had the sense that Antonio Fuentes, slimeball or not, was going to bring a lot of business down DealCo's lane. And something told him as well that he had not seen the last of the lovely dancer he'd been with last night, and never mind her momentary vanishing act.

Russell strolled toward the elevator doors whistling tunelessly, his only downcast thought having to do with his brother, Leon, and wasn't it a pity they could not share such times together. Though his brother had been drug addled by the time he died, Russell might have been able to turn him around, if he'd been on the outside, anyway, but whose fault was that? He was on the ground floor now.

He pushed sad thoughts aside and stepped out of the elevator and crossed the pristine lobby with its tasteful jungle plants and its squawking, mother-huncher birds and found the entrance to the restaurant that he and Deal had ducked through last night. Fuentes's driver was right there in the reception-area chair he'd parked in last night, another newspaper in his hands. You want to know what's going on in Havana? Russell thought. There is the man to ask.

He walked on inside the restaurant, and sure enough, there was Antonio Fuentes, all right, looking starched and chipper in a fine wool suit, and ready for some kind of business summit meeting, whatever that might turn out to be. Yes indeed, Russell Straight told himself, just one more good day in a long run of them shaping up.

It wasn't until Fuentes glanced at his watch and asked him where John Deal might be that anything like worry shook a finger in Russell Straight's way, but it sure as hell went way downhill from there.

24.

Deal stepped from the tiny shower in the bathroom of the apartment Angelica had brought them to, reaching for the towel she'd left folded neatly on the toilet tank. Hardly the luxurious bathroom of the Santa Isabel, he thought, but then again, it was a decided step up from the grave.

He blotted himself with the thin fabric, then stared at the trousers and shirt she'd left along with the towel. Victor's clothes, he supposed, not surprised when he had to roll the cuffs of the pants up a notch.

On the other hand, he wouldn't cause much of a stir in makeshift dress; he had already learned that much this morning. They'd crawled out of the smuggling compartment into the predawn darkness, then made their way on down the hillside where the Hemingway compound sat, using a path she informed him the museum workers took.

"What if we run into one of them?" he had asked.

"Too early," she'd assured him. "Besides, they are not the ones to worry about," she'd added.

A twenty-minute walk brought them to the side of a dusty highway where a score of people milled around in the gloom, waiting for one of the double-sectioned "camels" to take them into the city. Some of the crowd were wearing what looked like service-staff uniforms, and here and there a woman might be attired in a smart blouse and skirt, but there were more than a few men whose appearance made Deal look like a barely rumpled country squire. In any case, the still-sleep-worn crowd barely noticed the arrival of two more of the downtrodden.

Angelica found a discarded baseball cap trampled beneath a bench at the bus stop and slapped its dust away against her thigh. "Put this on," she said, handing the battered cap his way.

The thing had been black once, he supposed, but had faded to match the color of the concrete curb where they stood. "Havana Club" read the script above a rendering of the Betty Grable–like babe he'd seen on the card yesterday. "Ron" was scripted beneath her heels. He'd seen the same label on rum bottles in his parents' bar.

He took the cap and looked inside it doubtfully, then mashed it down on his head, tugging the bill low over his eyes. "How do I look?" he asked her.

"Like a Russian," she said. She glanced toward the road where one of the massive buses wheezed over a rise and began to slow on its way toward the stop. "Let's go."

Though they were among the first passengers on the dimly lit bus, both compartments were crammed by the time they'd reached the outskirts of the city. Yet somehow more and more people managed to squeeze on board at every stop.

"Aquí," she'd said to him finally, as the bus pulled up before a busy intersection. She'd pulled him through the crowd struggling to get on the bus, then on a dash across a busy street where smoking Fiats jockeyed with smoking Ladas and ancient Chevies and Fords, all of them outdone by scooters darting and whining like motorized wasps.

Once across, she led them off the thoroughfare down a street between two tenements, then stopped to check behind them. Abruptly, she ducked into an unlit building entrance that reeked of a half-century's decay, pulling him in after her. "Up," she said, pointing at a staircase.

Deal glanced at a set of elevator doors set into a rear wall of the gloomy entrance and turned back to her with a questioning expression. "Can't we use that?"

"It hasn't worked in years," she said, and led him to the stairs.

Seven flights up, and at every landing the smell of decades grew one layer thicker: must and mildew and cooking and living and sweating and breathing, he thought, and no crispy air-conditioning to whisk all the evidence away. Meanwhile, Angelica undid two locks on an apartment door and took them inside.

She'd showered first while he lay exhausted on a couch that he remembered vaguely as in the style of Danish Modern, a fad his mother had sniffed at in his youth. He'd noted idly that the listening device he had planted on his shoe last night was gone, probably scuffed off during that struggle over the jungle path.

Maybe they were listening to the sounds of iguanas mating over in the Interests Section right now, he thought, as Angelica emerged from the bathroom in jeans and a bra, toweling her dark wet hair.

When she noticed him staring, she'd shaken her head as if he were an addled child. She pointed at the bathroom. "Don't waste time," she said. "We cannot stay here long."

When he came out, he found her busy in the small kitchen that opened off the living area, pouring coffee into a pair of espresso cups that sat on a two-person table. There was a chunk of thick black bread there, along with a dish of butter and a jar of what looked like jam.

"Feel any better?" she asked, surveying him. He nodded. "Thanks."

"I hope you like Cuban coffee," she said.

"I'm from Miami, remember?" He reached for one of the cups, but she put out a hand to stop him. Even her touch felt different, he thought, glancing at her hand, where it lay on his.

"Please," she said, "sit. For just a moment."

His eyes met hers briefly. She stared back, then seemed to realize her hand was still on his. She lifted her hand and glanced away.

He glanced at the table again, noticing that a gold signet ring lay beside one of the cups. He sat down and lifted it between his fingers. "What is this?"

It was a wasted question, though. Anyone would have known it by the tone of his voice. He was already certain what it was. He'd held it often enough as a boy, slipped it onto his own tiny fingers back and forth, back and forth in one of the idle bedtime games the two of them had invented.

It had felt as heavy as lead on some giant planet then. And so it felt now. BMD still the initials cut into the flat gold face. The facets rounded a bit by time, perhaps, but no mistaking what they stood for: Barton Malory Deal. His father rarely acknowledged his ancient namesake, but he ought to have. If you were Barton Deal, why not call yourself after the man who'd invented the legend of Arthur?

"Where did you get this?" Deal asked. He had slipped the ring onto his own finger without noticing. A perfect fit, some distant part of his brain announced.

She stared back with an expression that suggested she wasn't sure that she should tell. He could understand that, some part of him reasoned. He wasn't certain he really wanted to know.

He saw that there was a packet extended in her hand, the very envelope Victor had tossed to him in the farmhouse the night before, just as the shooting had started. There was a splash of something dark across its face now, along with smudges of what must be dirt.

"Look inside it," she said. "Please."

He took the package from her hand and undid the clasp, then reached inside. A set of photographs, he saw, as he withdrew his hand. He gave her another glance, then pushed his coffee cup aside and spread the images on the table before him.

Four pictures, he saw. An old man in what looked like a jail cell. Curled asleep in a fetal position. Sitting with his head between his hands on the edge of a cot. Lifting food from a tin plate toward his mouth with his fingers. Sitting on the floor of his cell, staring up into the camera with an expression impossible to define.

"So?" he said, looking up at her. His voice sounded dead in his own ears. He thought that a part of him might be closing down, refusing to recognize any more.

"Look more closely," she said.

He turned back to the photos, fighting the certainty that was already seeping into his brain. You can build a concrete roof and make it two feet thick, the odd thought came; if the rain water sits up there long enough, it's going to make its way down through anything.

The shots were grainy, out of focus, poorly lit. And the man's face was hidden or distorted in most of the shots. But the longer he stared at the photographs, the more impossible it was to deny the truth.

"It's my father," he said at last, and stared up at her, his mind strobing through a thousand possibilities at once. He was exhausted, his brain already turned inside out. Whatever notion of reality he'd carried around with him prior to these last few days, that baseline measure had long ago disappeared.

Was this woman friend or foe? Had he once made love to her, or was that all some crazy dream? Impossible to tell. He could have been staring at a sorceress, for all he knew.

She said nothing. Simply stood and nodded in answer to his madman's plaintive stare.

"When were these taken?" he managed. He was already inventing impossible scenarios, none of which presented logical explanations. He'd seen his father's body sprawled in his chair, had mumbled incoherent good-byes at graveside years before. And yet . . .

"Last week," she said, her voice even.

"Bullshit," he said. He swept the photographs off the table, flinging the coffee cups with them. Cups and saucers shattered as he rose to snatch her by her shoulders.

"Tell me the fucking truth," he shouted. "Tell me what's going on or I will kill you. I swear to God I will."

She stared back at him, making no effort to break his hold. This was a woman he'd seen ready to put a bullet in the first three men to cross her path, he reminded himself. "You're going to attract attention," she said to him calmly.

"You're goddamn right I am," he said, shaking her again. "Tell me the truth."

"I *am* telling the truth," she said, staring back at him. "It is your father in those pictures. They were taken last week, inside the Castillo Atares, the headquarters of the National Police here in Havana."

"My father is dead," he told her, shaking his head as if to shed her words. "I saw his body. He blew his brains out with a shotgun in his own goddamned office . . ."

He was still raging when he felt his hands slide away from her shoulders, felt his legs give under him, felt himself slump into the chair where he'd been sitting moments before. His hands were on his face now, trying to stanch the tears.

He felt her hands cradling his head gently as he wept, felt her pull him close. It was all crazy, he understood. It was impossible. It could not be true. He would wake up soon, and with any luck, he would find that the last dozen years of his life had been nothing but a dream.

25.

"No, it wouldn't be like John Deal to just take off without telling anybody," Russell Straight was saying. He and Fuentes were alone in Deal's room now.

It hadn't taken much to make that happen, Russell reflected. His own request hadn't made much headway, but then Fuentes had turned up at the front desk behind him and a moment later they were on their way upstairs with a *pair* of bellhops bowing and scraping all the way. There'd been no sign of Deal inside, of course, and no note either.

"Perhaps he has just gone for a stroll," Fuentes offered.

Russell shook his head. "You said eight-thirty, he would have been Johnny Deal on the spot, downstairs at eight twenty-eight. Even if he had to walk through hellfire. That's the kind of guy he is."

Fuentes nodded, but he didn't look convinced. Russell glanced around the sitting area again, wondering if he might have missed something, a note fallen to the floor maybe. He saw what looked like a quarter on the floor just inside the door, but when he bent to pick it up, he saw it was just a paper disk about that size. He picked the thing up, then turned it over, to find a wad of gum stuck on the other side of the paper disk. He was about to toss the thing away in disgust, when he realized there was something odd here. Way too light to be a wad of gum, for one thing. And there was a little tab sticking out from the paper side, to help to pull something loose.

"What is it?" Fuentes asked. He'd been across the room, standing at the balcony and scanning the streets below.

"Nothing," Russell said, slipping the disk into his pocket. He glanced at the phone in the sitting room and thought for a moment. "You think we could find out if there were any calls in or out of here last night?"

Fuentes's expression suggested that Russell could not have underestimated him more. He picked up the phone and waited for a moment, then spoke in rapid-fire Spanish to whoever answered. There was a pause and then the sound of a voice on the other end. Fuentes listened for a moment, then hung up.

"Mr. Deal attempted to call the United States twice earlier in the evening. Other than that, only one other call, from outside the hotel, shortly after midnight."

Russell nodded. While he had been otherwise engaged. He nodded at the phone. "They say where it came from?"

Fuentes smiled. "We are in Cuba, my friend. Such technology is yet to arrive, although . . ."

"Right," Russell said, cutting him off. "That's what we're

here to accomplish, right? Give you a running start and a couple of good weeks, everything in Havana will be up to speed."

Fuentes gave him a weary look, then glanced at his watch. "We have a bit of a drive before us. I hope Mr. Deal returns soon."

"That makes two of us," Russell said. He reached back into his pocket and withdrew the card that his dancer friend had scrawled her number on.

"How are you supposed to call out?" he said to Fuentes, noting that there was no dial on the phone.

"Just speak the number," he said. "They'll dial it for you at the desk."

Russell nodded, reading off the number when a receptionist answered. After a moment and some odd ringing sounds, he heard the connection make, and, over the crackle of some industrial-strength Spanish, the sound of a male voice speaking in Spanish. "Hold on," Russell called into the phone, then thrust the phone at Fuentes.

"Ask if Delia is there," he told Fuentes. "Say it's me calling."

Fuentes did as he was told, then held the phone away. "He says there is no Delia."

Russell stared. "Ask if it's the dance school. Where they give lessons."

Fuentes rattled off some more Spanish, then gave Russell a look. "It is, how would you call it, an animal-control center. They round up the strays."

"Maybe we got the wrong number," Russell said, handing Fuentes the card. "You try."

Fuentes shrugged and broke the connection, then signaled the hotel receptionist and read off the number carefully. He listened for a moment, then hung up. "The same place," he said to Russell. "With great barking."

"Fucking dog pound," Russell said, snatching the card back from Fuentes. It was Delia's careful script, all right. He'd watched her write the number down. If he ever needed a lesson . . . he recalled. How conveniently she'd come along. Maybe he'd already gotten his lesson.

"Let me ask you something, Fuentes," he said, giving the man a sharp look. "Just on the off chance and all."

"Of course," Fuentes said.

"All this meeting and greeting you have lined up for Deal over here. Say somebody found out about it, didn't want it to happen."

Fuentes gave him a skeptical look. "And who do you think that would be?"

Russell shrugged. "The government, for starters."

Fuentes smiled. "We have nothing to fear from the government. Who do you think greases the gears of this government, now that the Russians have gone?"

"What are you talking about?"

Fuentes shook his head as if Russell were still back in fourth grade, struggling as hard as his brother Leon to get it. "There are *arrangements* everywhere, Mr. Straight, even in a so-called bastion of communism like Cuba. We make our contributions in the right places, and in turn our so-called enemies agree to look the other way at various times. We are permitted a certain latitude. Lines are drawn, boundaries are respected. It is the way of the world. But then I don't have to tell you these things. You are obviously a man of experience."

"You're talking about paying off the man."

"That is a simplified way to put it."

"And that's why nobody's going to fuss with us while we're over here."

"That is one thing you can be sure of."

"You didn't send a hot girl my way last night?"

Fuentes raised his eyebrows. "I did not. Though such an encounter is not unusual in Havana."

"Spare me," Russell said. He glanced at his own watch then. "But here's one thing I'm pretty sure of. You better talk to whoever we were supposed to see this morning. Something tells me there's going to be a delay."

26.

"How long have you known him?" Deal asked her.

She was behind the wheel of a battered Fiat now, inching forward through the maze of early-morning traffic that clogged the streets. A shower had passed while they were still inside the apartment, glazing the sooty roadways to glass and making the drive even more harrowing.

"As long as I can remember," she said. "I was an infant when my own father was killed. The first man I remember in my life was Barton Deal."

She cut a glance across the narrow seat. "I am sorry if this upsets you."

Deal shrugged. "I figured out pretty early on that my mother and father were married in name only. It seemed to be an accepted fact between them."

She gave him a speculative look. "That couldn't have been pleasant for you."

He glanced out the window. "That was the way it was. So far as I could tell, most of their friends lived pretty much the same way."

There was silence then, underscored by the passing of a policeman on a motorcycle threading down the narrow passage between their lane and the curbside traffic. The cop gave the Fiat a glance as he passed, but if he noticed anything from behind his dark sunglasses aside from the attractive woman behind the wheel, it didn't seem so. In a few seconds he was gone, twisting on through the clogged traffic and out of sight.

Deal glanced over, his voice casual. "So, how hard was it for you to sleep with me?"

She hit the brakes with that one, sending them into a slide that stopped just short of an ancient pickup nearly stalled ahead. She dropped the Fiat into gear and gave him a dark look as they started forward again. "It was not my intention," she said. Her tone was a quiet one, he thought.

"What *was* your intention?" he said.

"As I told you," she said, her voice rising. "To be absolutely certain you knew nothing of your father's existence, that there was nothing that might compromise our plans. Some worried that he had already compromised us with the likes of Fuentes and the others jockeying for power, that he would find some way to return to the United States. He was a rich man, after all. If it were true, who would be more likely to know about it than you. And when it was discovered that Antonio Fuentes was trying to contact you . . ."

"You could have just called me and asked."

"It is easy for you to make light of such things," she said.

"You live in a different world." She waved an arm at the smoking wave of traffic about them.

It was like being caught in a traffic jam that had begun sometime before Elvis, he thought. That much he would have to concede. "How much of what we're doing right now has to do with my old man's money?"

The look that crossed her face was dangerous. She yanked the wheel hard, cutting off a produce truck behind them, and slammed to a stop against the curb. "If you think that, then get out. Get out right now. Go back to the criminals who brought you here. They're the ones who care about money, I can assure you."

Deal stared back. If her fury was an act, it was a good one, but then again, she had already proven what she was capable of in that regard. In any case, getting back to Fuentes was the last thing on his mind right now. The trucker behind them had begun to lie on his horn. "Drive on," he said. "I'm sorry."

She shook her head angrily, her foot still on the brake. "I mean it," she told him. "This is the time to leave, right now. Your father is no political man. You of all people should know that. When he came to Cuba, his money was a tool to buy him safe haven from a corrupt regime, nothing more. Over the years, he saw for himself the many wrongs compounded here, all the things my father and so many others had attempted to correct. He cared for me and my mother and my brother because he loved us, and finally he decided to aid our cause as well. For him to jeopardize his safety was an act of great courage and selflessness."

She had seemed formidable enough with a pistol in her hand, Deal thought. Right now she seemed downright scary. The blaring of horns from behind them, in the meantime, had become apocalyptic. "Please, Angelica," he said. "Drive on."

"You are certain?"

"I'm certain I don't want that motorcycle cop to come back here," he said. "Let's get going."

She flashed her gaze at him once more, then jammed the Fiat into gear. A good thing the trucker hadn't made the mistake of climbing out of his cab to confront her, Deal was thinking as they rejoined the river of traffic.

They had gone through some of the explanation before, back at the apartment, talking quickly while she picked up broken crockery and he flipped through the short series of photographs, trying to convince himself that the impossible was indeed true. His father gone for thirteen years now, long presumed dead, turned up like the ghost of Robert Vesco and locked in a Cuban jail.

His suicide had been staged, Angelica had explained, though it had been some years before she had realized that not even Barton Deal's family knew that he was still alive. He had done it to save their lives, she had learned. There were men who would have stopped at nothing if they had learned of Barton Deal's existence. She'd never understood just why, only that Barton Deal had lived with the profound sadness of this truth. Of that much she was certain.

Even if most of what she'd told him had been manufactured for reasons impossible to fathom, Deal could not suppress the sense that at its core the story added up. The more he strained to re-create the events of the night he'd found his father's body, the louder came an insistent voice from somewhere in the recesses of his brain.

"Of course," the knowing voice intoned, *"the perfect Barton Deal exit. Business going south, marriage a sham, a government spook named Talbot Sams breathing down your neck and threatening to put you behind bars, or worse . . . Why not? Why not fake your own death and jump on board the Havana Express? Cut a sweet enough*

deal, so to speak, with El Comandante, you could live out your years in peace and tranquillity . . . minus any bothersome family, of course."

"I don't suppose he ever talked about us," Deal said, as she turned off the major thoroughfare at last, starting down a narrower, tree-shaded street.

"In time I learned things," she said. "His heart was broken to be apart from you, that much I am certain of. He left the money, of course, but that was nothing compared to the guilt . . ."

Deal stifled a bitter laugh. "Money? My old man left us with a bare cupboard, sweetheart. I've been trying to dig DealCo out of that hole ever since."

She turned, a look of surprise on her face. "I am sure of it. It was the one thing that he prided himself on, having left his family well provided for . . ."

"If you bought that, then he's a better actor than you are," Deal said. A flush came to her cheeks and she turned away, at the same time the all-knowing voice returned to insinuate itself into his thoughts:

"And who is to say it wasn't true? Who is to say that Talbot Sams didn't help himself to that supposed pot of cash, Johnny-boy? Or, maybe your old man needed the help of one of his cronies on the force to stage that sudden exit. If there was someone like that involved, someone who knew about a cache of money that could never be claimed . . . Maybe that's why you never got any wind of what happened, everything buried under the wake that stolen money leaves behind . . ."

In any case, it was hardly the thing to dwell upon now. There were far larger issues looming before him.

"Look," he said. "Let's put aside my family problems. It's been a hell of a night and day, that's all."

She gave him a look. "You're not the only one who's mourning, you know. At least your father is alive."

It stopped him like a slap, the terrible image suddenly blooming again in his mind: her brother turning just as the heavy blade swung down, the awful sound that echoed through the trees . . . At least he'd been spared the knowledge of what had happened all these years. Angelica and her family had lived on the brink of calamity all that time and more. Despite everything, he could grant her that much.

She had turned the Fiat off the street they'd been traveling on, and he saw that they had emerged upon the far reaches of a parking lot that seemed to be transforming itself back into the field it had once surely been. Giant potholes dotted the gone-to-gray asphalt, and clumps of sawgrass erupted here and there like nightmare weeds. There were a few cars parked in the lot, but those seemed half a mile away.

In the even farther distance rose a featureless multistoried concrete building, with bulky rounded shoulders and narrow windows like slitted eyes, the thing looming over the flattened landscape like a giant fossilized slug. "What is it?" he asked her.

"The Hospital Nacional," she said. "A gift from the Soviet Socialist Republics."

"It seems in keeping," he said. Just a glance at the place was enough to make you fall ill.

"He is in there," she added. "That is where they have taken him. At the orders of the *comandante* himself. He believes your father may be feigning the injuries he received at the Marina Hemingway. At the very least, he is to have his faculties restored through the miracle of state-run medicine."

Deal gave her a glance, then turned to stare out the grimy

windshield in the direction of the distant place. "It's not a prison hospital?"

She shook her head. "Were he still in the Castillo Atares, it would be a waste of time to even think of freeing him."

He turned back to her and began to speak, not seeking answers so much as reciting what his reasonable self had come to. It seemed ludicrous even to apply such a concept as reason to the events of the past twenty-fours hours, of course; more sensible to dismiss it all as a drug-induced nightmare. But he'd seen half a dozen men die, had watched her brother's head nearly hacked off before his eyes. There was some terrible truth buried in all this, and he would learn what it was; that much he had decided.

"Here's what I think, Angelica, and you can spare me the histrionics, no matter how it sounds to you. The first thing is this. You already have it figured I didn't know anything about my old man being alive. If you told me it was anybody else in the world in there—Judge Crater, Jimmy Hoffa, JFK—I wouldn't believe you, no matter how good you were. But Barton Deal, he's another story altogether. It just might be possible. And maybe you're even telling me the truth about how he got there, and about how selfless and other-directed you and everyone who works with you really are."

He paused for a moment, something in him heartened by the fact that she'd simply sat and listened and hadn't tried to interrupt. "But I also know this much. If my old man *was* on the way out of this country, he was doing it on his own terms, no double-crosses involved, and he would have made sure his money made it out before he did. No matter what he might have told you or anybody else about what he was giving to whom, he'd have seen to it there was only one person who could open the chute where the rat pellets and the coins fall out, and that would be him. So that has to color my thinking, no matter what you say." He saw the color rising in her cheeks again, but he held up a hand to stop her from getting any ideas.

"On the other hand, here you come, telling me you want to give me my father back, so how can I not listen? How can I not find out if it's true? How can I not run this thing out to the end?"

There was a silence then. It was steamy inside the car, he realized . . . no A/C in here either. He could see sweat collecting in the hollow above her breastbone, smell the tang of it, and his own sweat too. It reminded him of something, but he wasn't going to let himself go any further than that.

"Are you finished?" she said, finally.

"For now," he told her.

"Good," she said. "Because all I want for him is to see him out. Out of that place. Out of this country. Off to somewhere he can live his last days in peace and dignity. I love him as if he were my own father. I don't care if you believe me or not. It does not matter."

"You're right," he said. "It doesn't matter."

He stared at her for a moment, her gaze boring back into his. It seemed as if the tiny car were humming, levitating just slightly off the ground. "When you fucked me," he said, "was it like you were fucking him?"

She hit him hard with her fist, not a slap but a straight-out punch that caught him on the cheek and slid across the corner of his mouth. He saw it coming but he didn't dodge the blow.

He felt his lips fatten, and blood begin to flow from the tear a tooth had made inside his cheek. The back of his head bounced off the glass of the passenger door so hard he was surprised it didn't break.

On the rebound, he caught her with a backhand right—the

heavy ring still on his finger there. Her head snapped sharply sideways.

She gasped, but she'd been expecting it—she'd had the pistol leveled at his gut, after all—but she hadn't flinched either. When she turned to face him again, there was a trickle of blood leaking from one nostril.

He saw a quiver in the hand that held the pistol, but he was well past fear. He saw the hand go up and come his way, but there wasn't the hint of a threat.

He felt the press of steel at the back of his neck as she pulled him down. He felt lips and teeth and salty slipperiness. He felt that the little car might have caught on fire.

27.

José Martí Airport
The following day

"Hey, look here," Vernon Driscoll said, as he emerged through the wooden door of Cuban Customs. "This could be an airport."

"You should see the other terminal," Russell Straight said, glancing around the dimly lit, fifties-style lobby of this satellite field. "That's where the real airplanes land. I had to bust my ass getting over to this crop-duster place in time."

"*Two* airports in Havana?" Driscoll said. "Who would have ever thought?"

"It's all domestic out of here," Russell said. He pointed at a family in jeans and rustic peasant wear camped around a stack of crates in which small furred and feathered creatures stirred. "Just that and the puddle jumpers to and from the U.S. and Cancún."

"Puddle jumpers is right," Driscoll said. "But it's American Airlines, you know that? I give the ticket to the clerk and ask her if I'm gonna get frequent flier miles. She tells me it's really a charter and the embargo don't permit it. I say I'm flying American, aren't I, but anyways . . ." He broke off when he saw that Russell wasn't listening.

There was a big man waiting by the glass doors of the low-ceilinged terminal, his hands folded in front of him, glowering like the heavy from a James Bond movie. "That's Tomás," Russell said to Driscoll. "He works for Fuentes."

Driscoll nodded. "Fuentes is a bad actor, all right. I been doing my homework since you called."

"He knows his stuff, though. Got your ass right over here, no questions asked."

Driscoll shrugged. "I didn't say the guy lacked suck. I'm traveling on a research permit, did he tell you? Soon as I get a chance, I need to drop by the government's citrus canker labs." He turned to the big man waiting for them by the doors.

"You're Tomás, right? I'm Driscoll. You speak pretty good English, I'm guessing. All my stuff's in here."

He lifted up a small soft-sided valise that looked like it had been in storage since the Eisenhower era, then thrust his other hand toward Tomás, who caught it as easily as he might a cobra's head coming his way. Russell watched the two men stare each other down, wishing he had a chunk of coal to toss between those two clasped palms. He'd seen Superman squeeze his hands together like that once, afterward handing Lois Lane a diamond.

The two men finally broke, and they all walked outside, the

warm air washing over them like a wave. "Just like Miami," Driscoll said, glancing around. "Only old."

"You haven't seen anything yet," Russell assured him.

"I will bring the car," Tomás said.

"Atta boy," Driscoll said.

"Take it easy," Russell said as Tomás started off.

"Guy liked to break my knuckles," Driscoll said, shaking his free hand. "You see him start to sweat?" he added.

"Maybe I missed it," Russell said. "In case you haven't noticed it yet, we're not exactly in the hood. We need all the help we can get."

"Don't put your faith in scumbags, Russell. That's rule number one. Where's that bug you were telling me about?'

Russell glanced around in disbelief. "You want to look at it right here?"

Driscoll followed his gaze. Twenty feet away there was a taxi driver nodding off while he slouched against his ancient hack, and a few yards farther along the shattered sidewalk was a gnarled-up guy in a ragged woven hat vending oddly colored drinks from big jugs on a rolling cart. "You're right to suspect these men," he said to Russell. "Now give me the fucking thing."

Russell reached into his pocket and opened his fist over Driscoll's outstretched palm. The thing landed gum-side up.

"Looks tasty," Driscoll said. He snapped his wrist and the thing flipped over, exposing its paper backing. "These things activate when you peel the paper off," he said, glancing up at Russell. "Wonder who's listening."

"You mean now?" Russell said, his voice rising.

"I mean when you take the paper off," Driscoll said.

"How do you know all this?" Russell's tone was doubtful.

"A pal of mine runs an outfit up in Boca," Driscoll said. "He contracts out, listens to what the government can't. He showed me some things like these a couple of months ago. I'm not sure what the range is, though." He glanced around at the dusty hills surrounding the airport.

"You found this in Deal's hotel room, you say?"

"On the floor," Russell said. "Could have been someone in the Cuban government trying to listen to him, I guess."

Driscoll lifted a skeptical eyebrow. "This gizmo right here is pretty high-tech stuff," he said to Russell. "The way I get it, since the Ruskies pulled out, this outfit's been having a hard time keeping the lightbulbs lit, never mind keeping up with this kind of thing."

"Where'd it come from, then?"

Driscoll shrugged. "Maybe the last guy who stayed there dropped it."

Russell shook his head. "Get real."

"Or maybe it was your buddy Fuentes, wanting to keep an eye out on Deal."

"For what?"

"Hey, paranoia runs deep. Particularly when you run in the circles Fuentes does. Maybe you and I know Deal's Mr. Straight Arrow, but how can a scumsucker like Fuentes be sure?"

"I suppose . . ." Russell said, but his tone was skeptical.

"Did you check your own room for one of these?"

Russell gave him a blank look. He hadn't, of course. The thought of Fuentes, or anyone else for that matter, listening in to what had been going on in his room two nights before froze him in place.

"Why the guilty look, Russell?" Driscoll asked.

"Nothing," Russell said. "Don't lay that cop shit on *me*, now. That's not what you came here for."

Driscoll shrugged. "Old habits die hard. We'll take a look around your room later on."

Russell nodded, feeling vaguely like a schoolboy. Why hadn't he thought to check out his own room, anyway? And what was it about Driscoll that always made him feel so uncertain of himself? If this old tub of guts thought Tomás had a grip . . .

He shook his head then, forcing such thoughts away. There were far more important matters to attend to. Driscoll had been a cop, a good one by all accounts. He was happy to have him here, he told himself. He would have to be.

"The other thing to consider," Driscoll was going on, "maybe there's a party involved we're not even thinking about."

"If not the Cubans and not Fuentes, then who?"

Driscoll gave his characteristic, all-purpose shrug that seemed to implicate just about everyone still drawing breath. "You mentioned that squeeze who worked downstairs from Deal's Key West office, for instance."

Russell glanced up. "What about her?"

"I stopped in Key West to have a word with her."

"And . . ."

"She's gone. Her place cleared out. Nobody's seen her in days. The landlord says she first showed up two weeks ago, paid first and last month, that's all he knows about her." He registered Russell staring at him and shrugged again. "It's Key West, okay?"

"How about the people she works for?"

"What people?" Driscoll said. "That title company's been out of business for six months."

"There was some guy named Rayfield or Ray Bob . . ."

"That's right, Ray Bob Watkins, current address Starke, Florida. Oldest living marijuana smuggler in state custody."

"Oldest?"

"He's seventy-four."

"This woman said she was going with him."

"She'd be the first in quite a while. Ray Bob is gay."

"Damn," Russell said. "You think she was setting Deal up for something?"

"I try to keep my speculations to a minimum, Russell."

"Who could she be working for . . . ?"

"Like I say," Driscoll told him, raising a warning finger.

"So what's next? Check out the hotel?"

"In due time," Driscoll said. "There's someplace we need to stop at first."

"As in where?" Russell asked, but Driscoll's gaze had traveled over his shoulder. It was clear he'd stopped paying attention.

A smile had taken over the ex-cop's features, and he seemed almost transported as he stepped down off the curb in the direction of the approaching Cadillac. "Mother of Mary, would you look at this?"

He reached for the door handle before the car had quite halted and slid into the front seat alongside Tomás. "Hot damn, Tomás, I do admire your taste in cars." He glanced back at the curb where Russell still stood.

"What are you waiting for?" he called, then turned back to Tomás. "We need to go to the American embassy," Driscoll said.

Tomás gave him a stony stare. "There is no American embassy in Havana," he said.

Driscoll snapped his fingers. "My mistake. Let's go to the Interests Section, then."

Russell had climbed into the backseat by now, and Tomás

turned to give him a questioning look. "It is very difficult to get inside there," Tomás said, as much to Russell as to Driscoll.

"Yeah, well you can leave that part to me," Driscoll said.

Tomás turned his gaze back to the front seat. He seemed about to say something, then changed his mind. He gave a shrug of his massive shoulders then, and off they went.

28.

Later that evening

"This is Jorge Pozzo," Angelica said, ushering a heavyset man in what looked like a work uniform into the dimly lit living room where Deal had been waiting. It was another walk-up apartment she had taken them to, this one somewhere deep within the vast sprawl of Centro Habana, the district where, once upon a time, he and Russell had eaten a pleasant dinner. Only a couple of nights before, he knew, but it seemed like the stuff of a distant dream.

Several floors below where he now sat, there had been a young man to swing open a wooden door set in the building's façade the moment they'd arrived. In seconds the tiny car was parked inside the building's courtyard, the door swung shut and locked in their wake. Only four or five flights up this time, though, and apparently safe enough. They'd spent their time there since, a good portion of it continuing what had started inside that tiny car in a ruined parking lot on what he had since learned were the outskirts of Vedado, the neighboring district where a fair amount of construction had gone on when the Russians were still handing out largesse.

What had passed between them, though, was more like combat than sex, as much flat-out aggression as tenderness. Nothing they'd be touting in *Cosmo* any time soon, he supposed, but nonetheless it had boiled up out of them both like lava, just as dangerous, just as impossible to stop.

Nor did the concept of stopping seem to have much currency in his mind any longer. He had given himself over to this course of action, mind and body, along with whatever he had left of a soul. This was what he was now. This series of actions, which he would continue until the intended conclusion, or until something cut him down.

There'd been more, of course, including considerable time devoted to their planning. Furtive phone calls made by Angelica from neighboring apartments, a series of visitors in and out, translated versions of the conversations to follow for Deal's benefit.

"Jorge is the one who took the pictures," Angelica said, guiding Jorge Pozzo to a seat in the tiny living room. "Your father entrusted his ring to Jorge's care."

Her gaze held Deal's for a moment. He wasn't sure what to read there, but it didn't matter. He'd given up trying to read her some time back. He glanced down, saw he'd been twisting the heavy gold signet around and around on the ring finger of his hand and forced himself to stop.

"I speak some little English," the fiftyish man before him said. He cast his gaze down for a moment, then regained himself. "You are the son, they say."

"I am the son." Deal nodded.

"Your father is a good man. I know him from before, many years ago when I was still a fisherman." He cast a sidelong glance at Angelica, then continued. "A very strong man, still."

Deal said nothing. What was there to say? The man before him was the one with the information to be heard.

Pozzo leaned forward, his hands clasped. "They are not so good to him in there in the Castillo Atares. Not to anybody." He paused, as if deciding something, then pulled himself up. "The one they call Machado is the worst. He is the one there to make you talk, you understand?"

Deal nodded again. "Perfectly," he said. There was something stinging his eyes, but he ignored it. Bad light. Too little sleep. He'd have to do something about all of it, soon.

"I do what is possible, you know?" Pozzo continued. "Maybe a little extra water now and then. Or I pretend I forget to keep the light on. But I must be careful. Everyone is watching. You understand. I am just to clean there."

"Of course," Deal said. He glanced at Angelica, who took a look at his face, then hurried to the kitchen for water. She came back with a glass for each of them. Pozzo drank his gratefully. Deal watched him, then followed suit.

"This one time Machado had come down early," Pozzo said. "By himself he went in, which is not supposed."

Deal nodded, glancing away momentarily. Machado, he was thinking. A poetic name. He heard Pozzo's voice continuing, but it seemed strangely far away.

"I was the only one, because it was so early, you know. So I saw what happened."

Deal heard something in that distant voice and blinked himself away from the precipice where he'd just found himself. "What was that?" he managed.

Pozzo nodded, eager to tell this tale. "There was something first, I don't know, maybe Machado making noise to wake your father up or something, but anyway he is not looking when it happens."

"When what happens?"

A smile crossed Pozzo's broad features suddenly. "*I* saw it, though. It was like *this*," he said, thrusting his hand upward suddenly, like a man snatching a bundle of grapes. His eyes danced as he made a savage wrenching motion with his hand.

"The other guards heard Machado all the way in the other place. Screams like a bull. They come to help, but somehow the door to the cell got closed." Pozzo shrugged. "It was a long time for them to find some keys." He smiled again. "Your father squeezing all the time."

Deal glanced up at Angelica, who stood watching, her face impassive. Deal turned back to Pozzo, allowing himself a smile. "It must have cost him," he said.

Pozzo gave a little shrug. "Maybe. But then is when the *comandante* himself started coming. Things got a little better after that." Pozzo shook his head. "That Machado, he is an evil man." He turned to Angelica then. "*¿Señorita? ¿Poquito más agua, por favor?*"

She picked up both glasses and went into the kitchen. Deal leaned back in the chair where he'd been sitting, his gaze on Pozzo. "I appreciate your telling me these things," he said. "I am very grateful for what you did for my father."

"De nada," the man said with a dismissive gesture.

Angelica was back, then, with the water. "Jorge is the one who overheard where they were taking him as well," she said to Deal. "He has cousins who work in the Hospital Nacional."

"Six cousins," Pozzo nodded proudly. "One is a doctor. She studied in Russia."

Deal glanced up at Angelica, who gave a quiet nod in return. Pozzo drained his second glass of water, then stood to extend his hand to Deal. "I am wanting to help," he said. "It is good to meet you."

Deal rose to grasp Pozzo's hand. Thick and callused, as he knew it would be. "I am glad to meet you," he said. "You have already been a great help."

Angelica showed Pozzo to the door at the rear of the apartment then, the two of them conversing in quiet Spanish as they went. Deal reached for a drink of his own water then, fixing hard on that image of his father's steely grip crushing the balls of a man named Machado. He'd hold fast to that from now on, he thought. It seemed right for what lay ahead.

29.

"INTERESTING," the man behind the desk, said. He'd told them his name was Markson. He wore dark glasses of the horn-rimmed variety. His black suit was a size too small, the lapels too narrow, the featureless tie too thin. He looked like he'd been dressed by a sitcom writer for a sixties show.

He was turning the listening device Driscoll had given him around and about in his fingers like a none-too-bright high school science teacher examining an insect casing or a seed pod one of his eager students had brought in.

"What is it supposed to be?" he said, glancing brightly up at Driscoll and Leon.

This was the second guy they'd talked to. The third, if you wanted to count the surly young jarhead in the guard booth outside. How did they treat the people they *wanted* to see, Driscoll wondered idly. Then he corrected himself. There was no one who fell into *that* category.

They were on the second floor of the building, however. Making progress. He pointed to the phone on the man's desk. A couple of decades less antiquated, but still oddly out of time.

"Let's get Vines in here, let him explain it to you."

The man cocked his head in a mantislike way. "Vines?" he asked. "I'm afraid we have no one here by that name."

"Maybe he's calling himself John F. Kennedy, now," Driscoll said. "I'm talking about the guy who walked into Belfry Associates in Boca Raton, Florida, twelve days ago . . ."

He broke off to consult a tiny spiral-bound notepad he'd pulled from his shirt. ". . . And purchased two dozen of those clever little wads of gum you're holding in your hand. He was using the name Vines at the time. Five days ago he checked into the Key West Hyatt under the name of Paul Fisher." Driscoll reached into his pocket, replacing the pad, then tossed a grainy photograph down on the blotter in front of Markson. "That came off the hotel's surveillance camera. Even spooks show up on video."

"I don't know how or where you got your information, Mr. Driscoll . . ." Markson began, in a been-there, heard-that tone.

But Driscoll didn't pause. "A night or two later, there's an old fart named Lennie Markowitz who lives in the Sea View Condominiums on Roosevelt Boulevard in Key West. Couldn't sleep because he heard noises, so he got up to take several photographs of a prowler beneath his balcony. He didn't want to use a flash because that would have tipped the prowlers off, right? But he got a couple that actually came out when Vines followed John Deal into the next-door apartment. This Markowitz is bat-shit, but he owns a pretty good camera." Driscoll fanned some snapshots like a three-card monte dealer, then dropped them deftly back in his pocket.

"I don't see what any of this has to do with this office . . ." Markson tried, but Driscoll wasn't listening.

"Copies of all this and more are in the possession of Ellis Dobbins as we speak," Driscoll said, tapping his shirt pocket. "You probably never heard of Mr. Dobbins, since it looks like you live in some other dimension, but Dobbins happens to be the most mad-dog, publicity-hungry attorney to walk the planet. He makes Al Sharpton seem levelheaded. Even if you kill him, he'll find a way to get you."

Driscoll cut a glance at Russell Straight and seemed satisfied with the glowering gaze he was sending Markson's way. "The fact is this: If I do not return to Miami, along with my clients Russell Straight and John Deal, within a reasonable time, Ellis Dobbins will build a pile of stink so big it will bury every spook in South Florida. It'll be years before you're able to conduct normal business again."

There was a pause as Markson tented his fingers and stared up in a thoughtful way. "What would constitute a reasonable time, Mr. Driscoll?" he asked.

Driscoll turned to Russell with a see-there look. "You're something else, Driscoll," Russell said.

"It's a gift," Driscoll told him.

A buzzing sound emanated from the phone on Markson's desk, and the man turned to press a button. "All right, Markson, I'm coming in now," a voice sounded over a tinny intercom.

"Yes, Mr. Vines," Markson replied.

And soon enough, he was there.

30.

"HIS NAME is not really Machado," she told Deal as they waited across the boulevard from the Hospital Nacional for the light to change.

"I didn't think so," Deal said. He picked up the identification tag that had been brought to the apartment, along with the lab coats and scrubs they now wore. The picture of himself was little more than a dark smudge above the Russian name they'd given him.

"Don't worry," she said. "Everyone's ID looks like that. If the quality were any better, they would most certainly be fakes."

"What if someone speaks to me in Russian?" he asked.

She lifted an eyebrow. "You're a doctor. You don't have to answer." She gave him a wan smile. "Just because they're not paid anything over here, it doesn't mean everything is different, you know."

Deal nodded, but he wasn't so sure. They'd come this far on the back of a pair of Vespa motor scooters driven by two young men whose names he had never learned. A few blocks before they'd been dropped off, he'd seen a young man dressed much like himself standing at the curbside, trying to hitch a ride from the river of passing traffic. He'd been trying to imagine a hitchhiking M.D. in the States ever since.

"His real name is Zeneas," she said, stepping down from the curb as the light changed. "José-María Zeneas. He is the head of the secret police and a man who very much enjoys his work."

Deal was at her shoulder, nodding, feeling the wash of headlights across his face as they walked before the lanes of waiting vehicles. Was it strange that the lights seemed hot, he wondered? The two of them made it as far as the center island before the light changed and the traffic began to flow again.

"The names change but nothing else seems to," she said, staring into the darkness above the passing cars. "The real Machado ruled in the 1920s. His death squads killed so many they had to close the harbor to the fishermen." She waved her hand in the vague direction of the distant headlands. "They liked to throw their victims from the walls of Morro Castle. There were even women who did such things for La Porra."

"La Porra?"

"It means 'the truncheon,'" she told him, her eyes fixed ahead. "You still hear the term used."

He nodded, staring back at her chiseled profile, the resolute jut of her jaw. Perhaps her morals were opposed to those of the women she referred to, but he knew where the genes had come from.

She reached to take his hand as the light changed, and he glanced down at where their fingers touched. "Perhaps you should give me the ring," she added, as they stepped down from the curb.

"Why?" he asked, puzzled.

"It is very noticeable," she said, "and unusual, even for a doctor."

He nodded then and slipped the ring off his finger, handing it over to her. "I'll see that you get it back," she said, and touched his cheek briefly. In any other world, he thought, it might have seemed a gesture of tenderness.

"It is not normally your assignment, then?" Angelica was saying. Deal thought her voice was a bit loud, but maybe it was just his nerves. He'd been fine out on the street, had barely wasted a supercilious glance on the bored guards in the hospital lobby. But here, in the cramped confines of the staffing lounge, he had begun to feel closed in, the seriousness of the situation suddenly magnified.

The young woman Angelica had been speaking to—Dr. Cristina Aponte, according to her name tag—shook her head. Deal sought some resemblance to Jorge Pozzo in her fine features, but it was like comparing a teacup to a bowling ball. This woman might have weighed a hundred pounds. Her eyes were pale blue, her hair light brown, almost blond, her cheekbones painfully thin beneath pellucid skin. She'd studied in Russia, Deal recalled. One of her parents must have been part of that bridge.

She gave a faint smile. "I am a gynecologist," she said. "My path and that of *neurológico* rarely cross."

"Is that going to be a problem?" Deal asked.

"I think it is a general oversight of medicine," the young woman said. "But as to the matter at hand, the hospitals and the schools work because they leave us alone, Mr. Deal. It is late and the staff reduced. I can assure you. No one will question my appearance on the floor, nor will they question anyone with me, for that matter."

There was a hulking young man wearing green scrubs and with a surgical cap wrapped about his bushy head of hair, watching from a corner. That one, with his broad shoulders and thick arms folded before him, seemed more the stuff of the Pozzo clan. In any case, he'd be handy to have along if anything went wrong.

"How's my father doing, Doctor?" Deal asked. "Do you think he's up to this?"

She gave him a frank look. "As I say, neurology is not my specialty. And it would not have been wise to have expressed an inordinate interest in the case." She shrugged. "Some of my colleagues may profess a greater degree of loyalty to the current regime than I." She paused, sharing a brief glance with Angelica.

"I have managed a look at the charts, but without a closer observation and further testing, who can say?" Her gaze softened at the expression on his face. "It would seem that your father is suffering the effects of some major trauma, but this is only guessing. It is also possible that he may simply be a very cagey man."

"*That's* something he always was," Deal said.

"We have to get him out of here," Angelica said.

Aponte nodded. "And then?"

Deal said. "Leave that to me," he said. He thought it sounded authoritative. He hoped he could be as good in the doing.

"No one has said anything to him of what we intend?" Angelica cut in.

The doctor gave her a helpless look. "How could we? If he lacks the command of his faculties, he might blurt out anything, at any time."

Deal nodded. "There's a nurses' station up there?"

"Yes, but the cousin of Miguel is tonight in charge there." She glanced at the hulking young man in the corner. "There will be no questions there."

"And there are guards?"

"Two," the doctor said. "One approaches competence, but he is afflicted with a weakness of the flesh. There is an aide on the floor in whom this man has shown a particular interest." She broke off to glance at her watch. "It will not be long before his fondest fantasies begin to take their shape."

"And the other?" Angelica asked.

The doctor shrugged. "He is a fool who would likely be asleep in any case. Tonight he will drink the tea that is brought to him, then dream like a child."

Deal glanced at his own watch. "I guess we're just about ready, then."

Dr. Aponte nodded. "I will make the call," she said. Her gaze met Deal's steadily, then swung with the same assurance toward Angelica.

"We are ever indebted to you," Angelica said.

Deal nodded his agreement.

"It is nothing," the doctor said. "We do what must be done."

31.

"I WISH I could be of help, gentlemen," Fuentes was saying. He raised his hands in a gesture of helplessness. "Whatever has happened to John Deal, I can assure you that none of it is my doing."

He gave Vines a mild look from across the stateroom of the *Bellísima.* He had perched himself on the edge of the big table where Russell had grazed a groaning buffet only days before. Now it had been set up as a conference table, with notepads and pens laid out in readiness for a meeting of seven or eight.

Fuentes glanced about the empty places at the table, then back at Vines, who stood just inside the doorway that led out to the darkened decks. He crossed a leg and plucked at the razored crease of his slacks before continuing.

"My sources report no knowledge of this disappearance, no alarm raised within the government, nothing. But then again, I am sure you already know as much." He gave Vines another glance.

"I don't know what you're talking about, Fuentes," Vines responded. "I'm just tagging along, trying to lend a hand to some fellow citizens."

"Spare me, Mr. Vines," Fuentes said. He turned to Driscoll and Russell Straight, who were standing together near a teak-faced bar that took up most of one wall of the room. "Your helpmate maintains a network of well-paid informants within this country. Some of them are double agents. Others are schemers who would say anything so long as they are paid. A few might provide useful information, but they tend to be so addled by their rancor toward the current regime that it is difficult to sort the wheat from the chaff, wouldn't you agree, Mr. Vines?"

"Why don't you tell us about your own sources, Fuentes?" Vines responded.

Fuentes smiled. "I consult with certain business interests within Cuba, that is all. These men rely upon my discretion, of course. That is why we are able to do business together."

"Why don't we cut the Spy versus Spy crap, gentlemen," Driscoll cut in. He put the glass of soda water he'd been toying with down and stepped away from the marble bar top.

"Russell's already made it clear why Fuentes brought Deal over here." Driscoll glanced at the man, then turned back to Vines. "And my guess is that you'd do just about anything to find out the names of the ghosts who are supposed to be sitting around this table right now." He picked up one of the notepads, glanced at its blank face, then tossed it back on the table.

"None of that is my concern, though. I want to know where John Deal is, that's all."

He paused, fixing them in turn with his no-nonsense stare.

"Let's just assume for a second that both of you are telling the truth, so far as that's constitutionally possible. If neither one of you knows what's happened to him, and if it's true that he's not on the government's radar screen, then who the hell does know?"

"Deal could have simply gone off on his own for some reason," Vines said. He checked his watch. "If we were in the States he wouldn't have been gone long enough to warrant an official investigation."

Russell started forward at that, but Driscoll held him back. "Yeah, and pigs are dive-bombing Guantánamo while we speak," Driscoll told Vines.

He turned to Fuentes. "Who else might want to get their hooks into Deal over here?"

Fuentes shook his head. "If we were in Mexico or Guatemala, I might theorize the possibility of a kidnapping ring, but that sort of thing is unheard-of in Cuba."

Driscoll glanced at Vines, who nodded corroboration. "Say what you will about the current regime, domestic crime and terrorism are not issues."

"There is the Vedado Project," Fuentes offered.

"The what?" Driscoll said, turning to him.

Fuentes made a gesture with his hands. "Nothing the current regime is proud of. It is a loosely knit group dedicated to the eventual formation of a democratic government in Cuba."

"University professors, disgruntled ideologues, workers' groups and other grassroots organizations," Vines chimed in. The disdain in his voice was palpable.

"Real people, huh?" Driscoll said to Vines. "What's your beef with them?"

"This is hardly a group poised to help the country with the massive task of rebuilding itself," Fuentes said.

Driscoll nodded. "No fat cats, in other words."

Fuentes shrugged, and Driscoll turned back to Vines. "Let me guess. This is just a bunch of annoying people who'll probably demand a say in how things go down here once El Jefe gets the heave-ho."

Vines stared, apparently stumped for a comeback. Fuentes glanced away, as if impatient for this to end.

Driscoll regarded them in silence for a moment, then finally shook his head. "Whoever these people are, they must be doing something right."

"What makes you say that?" Vines asked.

Driscoll shrugged. "Because there're three groups of assholes they already managed to piss off." He ticked off the count on his fingers. "So tell me, who's in charge of this bunch you're talking about? Who keeps tabs on what they're up to?"

"Don't ask *him*," Fuentes said, glancing at Vines. "He couldn't tell you what house Castro was sleeping in tonight."

Vines shrugged. "These are not kidnappers, Driscoll. These are people who have meetings and *talk* about things. They circulate *petitions*."

"They sound like idiots, all right," Driscoll said. "Tell me, does anybody get in trouble for any of this?"

"Any number have been imprisoned," Fuentes said. He lifted his palms upward. "Deaths have been rumored, but who can say?"

"Not the ones who are dead, that's for sure," Driscoll said. And yet for all his disdain for the two men in front of him, he couldn't fathom what interest such a group as they had told him about might have in Deal, or vice versa. He broke off, glancing at his watch.

"There're a couple of places Russell and I want to check out yet this evening, Fuentes. You mind if we make use of the car?"

"Tomás is at your service," Fuentes said.

"I'll be glad to come along," Vines added, pushing away from the door where he'd been leaning.

"That's all right," Driscoll said. "Russell's kept his eyes open. We'll be just fine on our own."

He gestured to the big man at his side then, and the two of them were out into the night.

32.

"MA-TAN-ZA!"

Barton Deal had drifted off to sleep, he realized. He blinked awake at the sound of the crooning voice from the bed next to his and saw that the lunatic next door had somehow managed to work one hand loose from his leather restraints again. The last time, the guy had simply taken the opportunity to masturbate violently for the hour or so it took a nurse to wander in and discover what had happened. It was a little different this time.

"*Ma-tan*-za!" the man repeated and jabbed himself again with the shard of broken water pitcher he was holding in his hand. The handle was all there was left of the pitcher, really. He must have shattered the rest away by banging it against the heavy steel side table that separated their beds.

Barton Deal wondered why he hadn't been awakened by the

crash. Maybe it was the good drugs, he told himself. One benefit of the current system.

His neighbor had left himself a nice pointed edge to work with, though, Barton Deal saw. The man had traced a fine network of lines on his chest and stomach, delicate scrimshaw work that created an oozing outline of what must have been some hellish country. *Matanza* meant "killing place." That's what the guy seemed to be adding to his map right now.

*"Ma-tan-*za!*"* the guy called again, and jabbed himself just beside one nipple. A bubble of blood rose obligingly up.

Barton Deal turned his head in the other direction, to the place where there might have been others in their ward. There was a third bed, unoccupied, shoved into a corner against the far wall. In the space where a fourth bed might have been placed were two folding chairs and a small table where the guards usually sat.

One of the guards seemed to be missing just now. The other, the fat one, was asleep, his head thrown back over his chair, his snores ratcheting off the high ceiling. It sounded like two mismatched sprockets trying to mesh, Barton Deal thought, steel teeth snapping, pieces flying everywhere. The guard must have slept through the shattering of the water pitcher, too.

There was another cry from the bed to his right and Barton Deal turned in time to see the next "killing place" marked out, a dot about halfway between the man's navel and his groin. "I'd take it easy, pal," he said. "You're gonna go nuts."

The man's head snapped up. He stared at Barton Deal as if he hadn't been aware there was anyone else in the room. "Mmmmmmmmm," he murmured, waving the bloody glass handle between them. "Mmmmmmmmmmmm."

Barton Deal had another look at the restraints over there.

What if the guy ran out of the room on his own map, managed to wiggle all the way loose?

He glanced next at the door to the ward. Closed, closed, closed. Time had become a rather fluid concept, and without any notion as to when the other guard had left the room, it was hard to say when he might return. Pee-pee, smoke or number two, Barton Deal wondered. If it were the latter, it could take forever.

There were no call buttons in the ward. Lunatics always using them for hangman's nooses, he supposed. Or clogging the lines, trying to get in touch with God.

You could try screaming, but he had noticed that it didn't cut a lot of ice in the nut hatch. He could always try just getting up to run, but there was the small matter of the manacle clamping his leg to the bedpost.

What the hell, he was thinking. He shouldn't distract the guy from his work. With any luck maybe he'd bleed to death before he worked his way out of Camagüey Province or wherever he thought he was.

In point of fact, the guy had left off his dark stare and returned to the examination of his grisly map. There must have been something missing, because he bent and began to trace a bright, bubbling line that rippled over his ribcage and out of sight.

Nothing to soothe the savage breast like art, the old man was thinking, and that is when he saw the door to the ward swing inward. He thought it would be the hawk-faced guard, back from his sally to the crapper, but it wasn't him at all, but doctors, doctors, doctors, come to see him, he thought, and maybe a nurse or two as well.

Big burly fellow leading the way, and if he was bothered by what was going on in the bed next door, he didn't show it. There was a dark-haired Latin lovely following close on the big guy's heels, and she never took her eyes off his. This was what you wanted in a health-care professional, he thought. A good-looking woman who cared about her patients. An odd expression on her face, though, or was it just that she seemed familiar?

Right behind her was a woman he knew he had never seen, one with a pale complexion and a pinched face. If you need to know something, ask her, he thought. She knew it all and it was killing her. She hadn't seen the loony with the self-service tattoo yet either, but when she did, everyone look out.

And this last one, maybe the chief cook and bottle washer. Mr. Sawbones, everyone else out of the way, himself. Not a brain surgeon, you could tell. Wouldn't have the patience for it. But a no-bullshit kind of guy, clear enough to see. He liked the cut of this one's jib. He'd seen his type before.

Not really a man so much as a boy in a man's body, the old man was thinking. And a good boy, he thought, wondering why his vision was blurring up. Mr. Sawbones was shoving past the rest of them, headed toward him now. His mouth was moving, saying things. Things that were hard to understand.

"Dad" he thought was one of them. He could have sworn that was the word he'd heard.

33.

SHE HAD peeled away her clothing expertly, he thought, first her own—smock, white uniform slacks, and nothing but a camisole beneath—then his. She had lingered at his pistol belt, a hand upon that weapon, another clasping his own, a wicked smile on her lips all the while.

She'd approached while he was smoking—he'd been certain she would, eventually—had met his own gaze brazenly, asked for a cigarette, brushed his hand as she accepted his light, allowed herself to stand too close as they lingered at the end of the dimly lit hallway. In moments, it had unfolded as he had known it would.

After all, his was an important position, and he had discovered its aphrodisiacal powers long ago. As to whether women were excited by his authority or were simply too fearful not to submit, he neither knew nor cared. What was important was the bliss itself. And there had been a great deal of that over the years. An apparently inexhaustible supply.

There seemed little doubt about what had drawn this vixen to him, however. She'd raised her cigarette in such a way, had touched it to her lips, her tongue, had watched him all the while. . . .

In moments, smoking had been forgotten, there had been a moment's frenzied embrace, and she had led him to this unused room, this unused bed.

Most glorious of all had been her body's gradual coming into view, bronzed and robust, just as he'd envisioned it. *Voluptuous*, he thought, as she positioned herself above him. But not one ounce of unnecessary flesh beyond that. Perfect, he thought, as she settled silkily down upon him. Absolutely perfect.

Of course, a fool might have taken her for overweight, he thought, as she began to move. But it would have been an illusion cast by the mounding of those magnificent breasts on an otherwise slender body. They had burst from beneath her smock, erupted from the filmy fabric of her undergarment, tumbled free to surpass all his imaginings.

And she had so eagerly pulled him to her, buried him between those wondrous mounds. *Madre de Dios.*

Dark aureoles the size of saucers, budded nipples erupting at their centers like berries from dreams. He'd suckled there like a man found dying in the desert.

Would suckle more, he thought, pulling her down to him as she groaned and twisted atop him. She held fast to the rails of the bed as she writhed and bucked, and it occurred to him just how perfect such a bed was for these purposes. Good for sickness, too, certainly. But just as useful to keep from being flung off the present course. He felt her pubic bone grind against his—a cruel blow that only excited him the more—heard a sigh from somewhere that was as thrilling as a sob.

He clutched the rails of the bed himself and thrust up, yearning for more violent collision, when he heard the cry from down the hall. Curses, he thought, and in an unfamiliar tongue. He stopped, his hands frozen on the bedrails, understanding finally it was the raspy voice of the one he'd been brought to guard.

"Hallelujah! The gang's all here. Sonofabitch. Come the cavalry to the rescue!"

None of the words were clear to him, but the import was. He tried to swing his legs out from under the writhing woman atop him, but if she had heard the commotion outside, there was no sign.

"My god, my god," she moaned. "It is a monster. It is magnificent. Give me, give me, give me more." Her head was thrown back, her hands clamped to the bedrails in a death's grip.

He rose on one arm and drove the flat of his hand against her breastbone. She flew backward like a doll.

More shouts sounded from the ward he'd deserted. And there came the sounds of a clattering tray.

He swung his feet to the cool tiles of the floor and groped in the dim light for his trousers. There was no time for anything more.

He'd begun to understand some things by now, and the notion that it was his undeniable power that had swept this woman from her own post and to this bed was undergoing great revision, moment by fleeting moment. She had lured him to this place, he thought, and the thought was enough to enrage him.

Once the truth had dawned, he did not hesitate an instant. There was no need to hesitate. Whatever he did could not be questioned, no matter the magnitude of the deed. It never had been; it never would be. One instant's business here, then out into the hallway to see what came next. And what was Hector's part in all this, he wondered, a partner so stupid he would rather sleep or eat than fornicate.

He turned to her with his pistol raised, one knee braced at the side of the bed. He aimed between those perfect breasts, and squeezed. He was astonished when nothing happened. The pistol required the slightest touch. It was a fact he knew quite well.

He squeezed again, but still no explosion came. It was his surprise and agitation that kept him from realizing for so long.

He saw it all in a flash, though, in his mind's eye, one of her wretched hands upon his member, the other on the pistol. *The safety*, you idiot, *she's thrown the safety on.*

He glanced down at the weapon dumbly, his finger fumbling for the catch. Anger and confusion were being slowly eroded by some new emotion, but not rapidly enough.

He should have had the foresight to fear this woman, he was thinking as he glanced back up. It had taken only seconds to understand, but seconds could sometimes take too long.

He heard the whisking sound of the scalpel blade as it passed on by his ear, but that was too late as well. In the next moment he felt the searing sensation and a sudden rush of something warm and liquid pouring down his throat.

He had thrown off the safety, had meant to pull the trigger of his weapon by this time, but whether he had or not was impossible to tell. He was on his hands and knees on the hospital bed now.

He was coughing and retching, great heaves that shook his body and which he had no power to contain.

And with every heave came a great warm splash about his

hands and knees. He felt his head droop between his shoulders. His trousers were bunched about his knees. His member drooped like a forlorn stalk. And there was a deep, dark pool that had formed in the cavity of the bed below.

A woman by the bed stood calmly dressing, a surreal rewinding of a film he'd helped to make. She stared at him without expression, then shrugged into her smock and turned to go.

The sliver of light that fell into the room illuminated the pool above which he hovered briefly, a bright glint in an otherwise dark place. This fountain that fed it seemed impossible to stop, he thought. And then it abruptly did.

He stared at the pool for a moment, a man so greedy he had grown two mouths. And finally he dove, facedown.

34.

"Could you hear the shot?" the young woman who had joined them asked Angelica. Her dark-skinned brow was furrowed in concern.

"A little," Angelica said. "Maybe. It doesn't matter now."

The doors to the big elevator were closing behind them. They'd sedated Barton Deal before they'd moved him to the gurney, but he was still flailing in his restraints.

"Remember San Juan Hill," he said, clutching at John Deal's arm. "Carry a big goddamned stick."

"Take it easy," Deal said, a hand on his father's shoulder. "Just try to rest for now." Maybe Dr. Aponte should have given more sedative. In the next moment, the old man's eyes closed and his grip relaxed from fierce to firm.

"I pressed the pillow over his hand," the young woman said. "It was all that I could do."

"You did much more," Angelica told the young woman.

The woman shook her head. "He was a pig," she said. "He would have killed me without a thought."

Deal watched the numbers tick off on the elevator. Dr. Aponte had inserted her key into the emergency lock. The car would bypass calls from any other floor, even the normal lobby stop. Emergency Receiving was situated on the basement level. The opposite set of doors would open, they'd rush their patient to a waiting ambulance.

Four more floors, then fifty giant steps to freedom, he thought. He and Angelica had met Aponte in the emergency waiting room what seemed like ages earlier. He'd marked every stride from the swinging doors to the elevator.

Four, then three, then two clicked off the elevator's gauge. All of them watched the numbers fall. They passed the lobby with a ping, and Deal felt himself tense as the heavy car began to slow.

There came a hydraulic sigh as the car shuddered into place, then a slight sucking sound as the doors slid slowly open. There was a man in a dark suit standing at the gradually widening opening. He seemed to be thinking about something else as the scene in the car unfolded before him. His distraction might have saved their lives.

"Machado," Angelica breathed. Dr. Aponte's face was ashen.

Machado's face had undergone several transformations in the few moments the elevator doors were open. As his gaze locked onto the form of Barton Deal, puzzlement was giving way to concern.

He glanced at the younger Deal's name tag and mumbled

something in Russian. "He wants to know where you are taking the patient," Dr. Aponte said.

Machado's expression had found its way to outright suspicion. He was reaching for something inside his jacket when Deal strode forward and caught him by his tie. "Why don't you join us, comrade," Deal said, jerking him inside the car.

"Close the doors," he called to Miguel, as he drove his fist into the side of Machado's jaw.

The man went down and Deal kicked the hand that had emerged with a pistol upheld. The gun flew away, clattering across the steel floor like a metal crab. Angelica bent for the weapon, but it skittered out a gap in the closing doors.

Machado rolled over catlike, came up on his hands and knees, and a slender, spring-loaded knife appeared in his hands from somewhere. He rose up slowly, his eyes on Deal, muttering something in Spanish.

"He says you are under arrest," Angelica said. "He says to put up your hands and submit."

Deal nodded, staring at the waving knife. "Submit to what?" he said to Angelica, edging away. Miguel was pinned in a corner behind the gurney. Neither he nor Angelica was armed.

Machado gave Angelica a warning look and rattled off something else. "He says to turn around and place your hands against the side of the car."

Deal had missed the Spanish, but he could read the glitter in the man's eyes. "Tell him he can go fuck his mother," Deal said.

Whatever she said made Machado blink before he came in. The hesitation was enough for Deal to dodge the swipe of the knife. The blade clattered against the steel side of the car, but Machado managed to hang on.

He was moving in again, eyes dancing now, all pretense of arrest out the window. "Maybe open those doors again, Miguel," Deal called, edging away from the blade. He heard Angelica echo the command.

Machado wasn't waiting, though. He strode forward, the knife swinging back, poised for a low strike this time—*disembowelment,* Deal was thinking . . .

. . . when he saw a flash of something at Machado's back, and the man stagger sideways with a groan. He was swatting at something at the side of his head, like a man bothered by a stinging insect.

Dr. Aponte danced away from the aimless slashing of Machado's blade, her eyes fixed on the gleaming hypodermic that she'd jammed in his ear. Machado hesitated, trying to get his feet steady beneath him, a glare of hatred directed her way.

It seemed as if he might be about to make a charge for her, and Deal readied himself for a tackle. Then Machado seemed to wilt like a blow-up doll suddenly relieved of his air. He collapsed without a word, his head bouncing off the wall of the elevator car, then settling to the floor.

Deal felt a draft at his back and turned to see that the doors of the car were open again. A doctor with a stethoscope dangling around his neck stood staring at a pistol that he held gingerly in his hands. A female nurse stood by, equally amazed.

Deal reached to pluck the pistol from the doctor's hands with one hand and with the other pointed at Machado's inert form. "This man needs help," he said to the thunderstruck doctor. Then he motioned the others out the door.

35.

When Valdés came awake, he thought at first it was simply more of his troublesome dreams. The bed beside him, where the old man had lain, was empty. A food tray lay tumbled to the floor, and Valdés wondered if that was the sound that had wakened him after all. How could he have slept through such a thing?

In the other bed, where the lunatic normally lay bound and often gagged, the news was worse. Truly the stuff of nightmares, Valdés thought, as he stood uncertainly, trying to steady himself with a grip on his folding chair.

The lunatic was naked, his body covered with blood—face, chest and legs—his bedclothes drenched in it. The man had managed to work himself loose from his heavy restraints and was sitting with his legs tucked under him, holding something in his hands to which he crooned an unbroken litany.

"Matanza," Valdés heard. And other, even more troubling things as well.

Valdés reached for the pistol at his belt and groped about for a moment before he realized that his weapon had disappeared. He glanced up quickly, reassuring himself that it was not his pistol that the madman held.

After a moment, Valdés stole closer to the lunatic's bed, close enough now to see what it was that he held. The realization sent an icy shock through him. Valdés clutched at his own groin in reflex and fought to repress the pressure that rose in his throat.

Lunacy incarnate. A man talking to his own dismembered manhood, Valdés thought, his mind reeling. How could he remain upright?

And what had become of Diaz? he wondered, staggering away toward the nurses' station. He felt glass crackle beneath his shoes. Something else broken, he thought. Something else he should have heard.

He found the nurses' station empty, the nearby lounge deserted as well. He snatched up the phone but found it dead. It took him a moment to register the slashed and dangling line.

He dropped the phone and hurried back down the hallway toward the elevators. Fear had enveloped him by now, and he glanced over his shoulder repeatedly, certain that someone was about to burst from one of the darkened doorways to snatch at him without warning.

He was so distracted that he missed the inert form that lay sprawled across the hallway in front of him. He felt his feet tangle and slide out from under him, felt himself go down so hard his breath left him momentarily.

He was pushing himself up from the floor when he saw what it was that had brought him down. Diaz's body, an awful trail of blood behind it. He took in the awful slit at Diaz's throat, then his eyes drifted down to an even worse defilement.

The lunatic, Valdés thought, scrambling to his feet, his hands slick with gore. He rushed to the elevators, slamming his bloody palm against the call button repeatedly, whimpers escaping his throat. At any moment, the lunatic would appear in the corridor behind him, and what had befallen Diaz could befall him as well.

His fear was pathetic, but he did not care. All he wanted was escape.

He heard the approach of the elevator then, and turned, tears of relief and gratitude beginning to brim at his eyes. The doors slid open—maddening in their pace, easily long enough for a madman to come bounding down that hallway—and he leaped inside, jabbing wildly at the buttons. Any floor, he thought. Anywhere but here.

The doors closed—no gory claw reaching in to snatch at him—and Valdés slumped back against the side of the compartment, breathing a sigh of relief as the car began to descend. Safe, he thought. Safe at last.

And that is when he noticed the others in there with him: the doctor and the nurse bound and gagged in one corner. And worse yet, the man they called Machado, hands tied behind him, feet bound. Gagged. His gaze burning up at Valdés in a way that made him understand that *safety* was a word that no longer had meaning, not in this world at least.

36.

"HATE TO do this every day," Russell said, cutting a quick glance at Driscoll. He was at the wheel of the Caddy, inching down one of the narrow cobblestone streets of the old city, Driscoll poring over a street map with a penlight clutched between his teeth.

"Take the next left," Driscoll said, glancing up from the map. He craned his neck out the passenger window as Russell made the turn. "Okay," he added, "stop here."

Russell switched off the engine and doused the lights. Squirreling down these narrow streets was no picnic, but driving this machine reminded him of being back home in Georgia. He'd had a great-grandfather owned an old Buick nearly of the Cadillac's vintage. He'd played at driving in the springy seat of that old car. That was back in the days when the purpose of life was enjoyment, he thought. He wondered just when everything had begun to change.

"About a block down that way, if this map's right," Driscoll said at his side.

"Looks like it," Russell said. He noted an open courtyard on their left. It seemed like the one they had passed a few days before. He turned back to Driscoll. "I still don't see why we're doing this."

Driscoll stared at him, exasperation evident even in the moonlight. "Because that's what you do, Russell. You knock on all the doors, you rattle every single chain. You hope something leads to something. Right now, let's have a look at Vedetti's."

Russell gave him a grudging nod and opened the door of the Caddy, then closed it softly. With this beast in the way, there wouldn't be anyone coming or going along this path, he thought. Barely enough room for the two of them to squeeze between the car's bulk and the chiseled walls on either side.

As they made their way along the passage, he could see that this was indeed the route they'd used to approach Vedetti's gallery earlier. Up ahead was the old-timey drugstore he'd marveled at the first time. The shop was closed now, of course, steel grates pulled down over the broad windows, but the big urns of green and red and amber liquids were illuminated, glowing in the darkness like giant night-lights.

"The back entrance is right over there," Russell said quietly to Driscoll. "Maybe we ought to go around front . . ."

"Maybe," Driscoll said. He put his hand out to try to the door, then turned back, surprised. "It's open," he said.

They stared at each other for a moment, then Driscoll eased the door open wider. "You know the way," he said to Russell. "Lead on."

Russell nodded and stepped past him into the darkness, Driscoll close on his heels. They paused, listening intently. The sounds of rustling footsteps and vague conversation drifted down the passageway toward them, muffled by the heavy curtains that masked the entrance to the gallery itself.

Russell glanced at Driscoll, then started forward. Halfway down the narrow hall, he caught sight of a flashlight beam sweeping across a void where the heavy curtains joined. He flattened himself against one wall, holding Driscoll still with one arm. The beam of the light sliced across the face of the opposite wall, then disappeared.

Russell was about to move again when there came the sound of something falling to the floor, the crack of wood, and a faint curse. He took advantage of the commotion to move quickly toward the curtains, vaguely outlined by the glow of the flashlight on the other side. He paused at the gap in the curtains, peering out into the gallery space.

He saw a smallish Latino man bent over the shattered frame of one of the architectural drawings that had tumbled from the wall. He seemed to be examining something in the beam of his flashlight. Something familiar about the guy's wizened face, Russell thought . . . then realized it was the street hustler who'd tried to sell Deal cigars and rum and women. So he was a sneak thief, too? Somehow it didn't add up.

He felt Driscoll at his back, edging up for a look of his own. The little guy had bent now over the fallen drawing, reaching for something, his face glowing eerily in the reflection of the flashlight beam.

"¡Mira!" the old man said softly to someone in the darkness nearby. *"¿Qué es esto?"*

The man plucked whatever it was from the shards of wood

at his feet and held it up to the light, turning it over in his hands. Russell moved closer, straining to see, his shoulders brushing the curtains now, his face surely visible should anyone turn his way: The little guy was holding up a wad of gum with an adhesive backing, Russell saw. The same device that he'd found in Deal's hotel room.

Another shadowy figure stepped closer to the pool of light spread by the flashlight beam and extended a hand. The little guy handed the device over. Russell heard a muttered curse and a command barked out in Spanish. A woman's voice, he realized—something familiar about it, as well. Then he realized there were footsteps hurrying toward him.

He ducked back, pulling Driscoll with him. In the next moment, he felt the curtain fly back and saw her shadow appear, silhouetted by the glow of her companion's light. Driscoll's own penlight popped on behind him and the woman stopped short with a gasp. She was frozen, momentarily, one hand thrust up against the sudden glare, her mouth a grimace of surprise. Still, there was no mistaking who it was.

"Delia?" Russell said, hearing the astonishment in his own voice. He saw that under one arm she had tucked a box crammed with folders and paperwork. She blinked, trying to see past the glare, at the same time calling out some command in Spanish over her shoulder. At the sound of her voice, the little guy's flashlight winked out. Russell heard the sounds of footsteps crunching away through broken glass.

Delia tried to backpedal in the same direction, but Russell caught her by the arm.

"Let me go," she said. "You don't know what you're doing."

"You're goddamned right, I don't," he said. "But you're going to explain it to me."

He turned to Driscoll. "Get the little guy," he called, but it was a waste of breath. Driscoll was already pawing through the heavy curtains, his heavy shoes crashing through the mess on the floor.

"Please," Delia said, twisting in Russell's grasp. "It is dangerous. You must let me go."

The familiar tang of her sweat rose in his nostrils, her hand came to press hard against his chest. What a difference a couple of days make, he thought. Same woman, same frenzied actions, slightly different results.

"Are you part of this Vedado Project? Is that what this is all about?"

"What do you know of it?" she spat back.

"It must have been important, what you were willing to do with me."

"It is a job," she said, still writhing. He'd seen how nimbly she could move. He didn't remember that she'd been quite so strong as well.

"Where's Deal?" Russell said. "Who the hell's got him?"

"He is with friends," she said. He heard something soften in her tone, and she seemed to relax for a moment in his grip.

That sudden shift of body language should have told him something, but he missed it. It was dark, he was distracted by the clamor of Driscoll's pursuit, he'd felt the weight of her body go slack against him, had even had a moment's flash of the first night they'd met, her head thrown back, her neck arched, as she had moved above him . . .

Whatever the reason, he never saw the kick coming, though he certainly felt it. As her knee drove up between his legs, he felt his grip loosen, his arms fold in reflex over his gut. The cruelest blow of all, he was thinking, as he doubled over. Her footsteps were already receding down the hall.

"Driscoll . . ." he managed. He heard a groaning noise, saw the gallery's front door swing open and the silhouette of the little man dash outside into the street. A bulky shadow cut across the newly entered slice of moonlight—Driscoll in thundering pursuit.

Russell might have called out something more, but the sudden explosions from the street outside stopped him. One of the front windows of the place dissolved in a shower of glass. There were more shots and he saw a shadow spin about on the sidewalk outside, then tumble in through the shattered frame. The man's body lay inert, one hand upflung, still clutching a pistol.

"Fucking-A," he heard from Driscoll as another volley of shots chewed across the front of the gallery. The big man dove for cover between the edge of the door frame and the blasted window, his head tucked as more shots blasted through the open doorway where he'd nearly run.

Russell gave one longing glance back down the hallway where Delia had disappeared but knew he couldn't do it. He cursed softly to himself, then ducked through the gap in the curtains and rolled across the moon-striped floor of the gallery, coming up with his hand clutching that of the little man who'd been blown in through the shattered window.

He did his best to ignore the whine of shots that cut the air above his head, prying the pistol from the dead man's hand. With the grip finally clutched firmly, he scrambled toward the far end of the window, then popped up and emptied the pistol in one rapid volley, spraying the second-floor balcony across the narrow street where he'd seen a series of muzzle flashes.

There was a cry, and a form toppled over a railing, then crashed to the cobblestone street. Russell heard the clatter of a weapon on the stones and thought briefly of diving out after it, but Driscoll was on him then, pulling him roughly toward the thick curtains.

"Out the back," Driscoll growled, as shouts echoed in the darkened street outside.

Russell didn't have to be told twice. In seconds he was up and through the curtains, leading the way back down the narrow hallway.

More shouts echoed behind them, along with probing gunfire. Russell, the sick pain in his groin long forgotten, hit the back door with barely a pause, his shoulder slamming the heavy steel aside as if it were made of balsa. Driscoll was on his heels as they flew out into the street, a figure backpedaling away from the two of them in surprise.

"What the hell?" a familiar voice called.

"Vines?" Russell said. He caught the man before he'd steadied himself, jerked him close by the lapels of his coat. "Is that your guys firing out front?"

"Let him go," Russell heard from behind him, then felt the press of steel at his cheek.

He released Vines, kept his hands frozen high.

"It's not us," Vines said. He turned to the man who held the pistol beneath Russell's ear. "It's all right, Belsen."

Russell felt the pressure release from his ear, had to restrain himself from striding forward, dropping Vines with a shot. There was another muffled gunshot from the far side of the building, then a second.

"Who is it, then?" Russell said. He glanced over his shoulder, saw that Belsen still had a pistol leveled his way. A second shadowy figure stood with a pistol trained on Driscoll.

"Our Cuban friends, I'm afraid," Vines said. "That's not good news."

"No shit," Russell said, glancing back the way they'd come.

"See if you can get that door locked," Vines said to the man who'd been covering Russell. "Jam it if you have to." The man nodded and went to work.

Vines turned back to the two of them. "Command has had a fix on the bug in Vedetti's gallery for a few days now," he said. "When they picked up signals from a transmitter that was moving and seemed to be approaching this place, I got the alert. I decided we'd come have a look, in case Deal showed up." He jerked his thumb in the direction of the Cadillac. "We just got here, and realized the bug was in Fuentes's car. It was jammed beneath the rear seat cushions. That's why it wasn't picking up audio."

Another shot rang out in the darkness. "So maybe you're not the only ones picking up signals from those transmitters," Driscoll said. "Maybe El Comandante has more electronics capability than you give him credit for."

"So it would seem," Vines said. There was a grinding noise from behind them as the door to the rear entrance of the gallery slammed shut.

"It's locked," Vines's man called.

"Time to go," Vines said. He turned away as though they'd just had a casual meeting during an evening's stroll.

"That's it?" Russell said, glancing around the narrow street. "There's a guy shot dead in there. And what about the girl?"

"What girl would that be?"

Russell glanced around the darkened street. "Delia, she called herself. She came out just ahead of us, a bunch of papers under her arm."

"We didn't see anyone," Vines told him, starting away. "And we're out of here. Direct engagement with our Cuban friends is way up on the no-no list."

He waved the two men with him back down the alleyway and had turned to go, when a strange chirping noise arose from somewhere. Vines thrust his hand inside his coat and came out with a satellite phone. He was still hurrying back down the alleyway, phone to one ear, his hand against the other, when suddenly he stopped.

"You're sure?" he said, his voice rising in the darkness. He cursed and jammed the phone back into his pocket, then broke into a sprint.

"What is it?" Russell called, snatching at Vines's arm. Vines shook him off, ducking sideways past the hulking Cadillac.

"Fuentes's boat," he said. "They think they heard John Deal come on board."

At that moment a car engine roared into life just across the narrow intersection where the Caddy was parked, and a pair of headlights blossomed, filling the passage with light. Russell threw up his arm to shield himself from the glare.

"Is that someone with you?" Russell called to Vines.

"I'm afraid not," Vines said.

"Everybody in the Cadillac," Driscoll called. "Show us your stuff, Russell."

He flung open the passenger's door of the Cadillac and slid inside, just as Russell mirrored his actions on the opposite side, Vines and his men piling into the back.

Russell jammed the key into the ignition, pressed the starter button and felt the big engines surge when he hit the accelerator.

He levered the Caddy into reverse and floored it, disregarding the tinny sound of the horn behind them and the frantic flashing of headlights from dim to bright and back again.

"Hang on," he called, his hands clamped to the wheel.

There was a crash then, and an impact that sent all of them rocking wildly in the deep-cushioned seats. Russell jerked the transmission into drive without missing a beat. There was a rending shriek of metal, then the Caddy lurched free. He twisted hard on the wheel and the Caddy bounded up over a curb, starting away down a lane that ran perpendicular to the intersection.

"That'll teach them to tailgate," Driscoll said, casting a glance through the rear window.

Russell checked his rearview mirror. A man struggled out from the driver's seat of a greatly foreshortened and steaming Fiat, its front bumper torn loose, and tumbled to the pavement. He saw muzzle flashes and heard the explosion of shots, but the Caddy was well away by now, swinging out onto the broad avenue that led back toward the Malecón. Russell pressed down even harder on the Caddy's accelerator and gave the big car its head.

37.

"How fast are we going?" Driscoll said. He had one arm across the top of the seat between them, his other folded with his elbow out the window. Maybe he was trying to look casual, Russell thought, but his voice gave him away.

"You worried?" Russell asked above the groan of the Cadillac's mighty engine.

"No," Driscoll said. "I figure you for at least half a dozen instances of grand-theft-auto."

"You've seen my sheet," Russell countered. "There's no such entry on there."

"And now I know why," Driscoll said. He was trying to keep himself from leaning as they blew around the big curve just past the U.S. Interests Section.

"You want to stop and pick up reinforcements?" Russell called into the back, where Vines and his men sat silently.

"You can forget that," Vines called. "So far as the Section's concerned, none of us even exist."

"That's a comfort," Russell said. He glanced down at the Caddy's speedometer. Eighty-five, it said, but the heavy car gripped the pavement like a freight train.

"You're not worried about getting us picked up?" Driscoll asked.

"Not in *this* car," Russell said. They were approaching the tunnel that ducked under the river to the suburb of Miramar. There was a flashy restaurant just on the other end, and he slowed a bit as they emerged just in case a carload of drunken diplomats might be pulling out in front of them.

He needn't have worried about drunken patrons. It was past midnight, and the restaurant's parking lot was virtually empty.

There did happen to be a motorcycle cop there, though. The guy was leaning against the seat of his bike, his arms folded, his chin on his chest. He glanced up when he heard the Caddy's approach, had a closer look, then turned away as they sped past.

"What'd I tell you?" Russell said.

"I'm just glad we didn't have to run over him," Driscoll said.

They were approaching the entrance to the Marina Hemingway now, and Russell brought the Caddy down to a speed approaching normal as he prepared to turn.

"What the hell is that?" Vines called from the backseat. He leaned forward to point at something approaching from the direction of the guard's shack.

Russell slowed even further, staring in disbelief. It was a guy in khakis who'd been gagged and bound to a wheeled office chair, he realized. The guy was pretty well taped up, but he had managed to work one leg free and must have pushed himself out from the guard shack and down the little concrete ramp that led from its open doorway. Now he was kicking himself frantically along the rough asphalt pavement of the access road, desperate to make the highway, Russell supposed.

It looked like the process would have taken a while, even if they hadn't come along. Every kick sent him in a spiraling turn that lost him almost as much yardage as he gained.

When the guy saw the lights of the Caddy, his eyes bugged and his checks bulged as if he were trying to call out to them. "He probably thinks we're Tomás," Russell observed.

"I'll bet he does," Driscoll said.

Russell eased the Caddy up to a near crawl as they approached the man in the lurching chair. "Hold on tight," he called out the window, then gunned the engine.

The Caddy bumped into the guy and his chair and began to push him forward. The guy was staring at them in disbelief, his eyes going frantic as the Caddy picked up speed.

"You really going to do it?" Driscoll asked, as the edge of the seawall loomed up ahead.

"Why not?" Russell asked.

"He's just a slob like you and me," Driscoll said.

"I know," Russell said. "I couldn't do a thing like that."

He swung the wheel away from the water, and the guy in the chair shot away from the front of the Caddy like a puck from a mechanized stick. The wheels of the chair hit a tangle of cable beside a remote storage building, then went over sideways with a crash. Even if the guy got himself upright, he was looking at maybe a year's worth of circling back out to the highway.

Meanwhile, Russell was scanning the far reaches of the marina, his eyes searching for the distant slip where the *Bellísima* had tied up. He hadn't paid all that much attention when they'd left the place. He never did when someone else was driving. A bad habit, he was thinking. Something he would have to work on.

They approached a fork in the narrow service road, and Russell chose the path where the weeds poked up heaviest from the gaps in the cracked pavement. The road made a sharp left between a set of pillars where there might have been a chain stretched once, then hooked back right to run alongside an oily looking channel where trash bobbed up thickly at a dead end.

"Look out!" Driscoll called at his side, and Russell slammed on the brakes as three figures emerged from behind a stacked pile of conduit and hawser rope on the opposite side of the narrow road.

"Sonofabitch!" Russell said, rocking backward as the Caddy stalled and slid to a halt.

"Jesus, Mary and Joseph," Vines said, staring out at the two women and the big man in hospital scrubs, caught there in the Caddy's headlights.

"Not exactly," Russell said.

His hand was already clawing at the Caddy's door. In the next moment, they were out into the muggy night at the side of a sloshing boat slip where the *Bellísima* had once been berthed, listening as the throbbing of heavy boat engines receded in the distance, a sound that battered at them all.

38.

"STEADY AS she goes, Fuentes," Deal said. He had the pistol leveled on his former host, who stood now at the wheel in the pilothouse of the *Bellísima*, all his practiced bonhomie vanished. They were well past the end of the breakwater now, the boat beginning to pitch as it hit the swells of the open sea. Maybe ten more miles to international waters, Deal thought, with a glance at the rapidly receding lights on shore. Less than a hundred to Key West.

"I can assure you that your weapon is not necessary," Fuentes said, glancing nervously at him.

"You've been assuring me of a lot of things," Deal said, holding the pistol steady. "Let's just say I'm more comfortable this way."

"I myself am not," Fuentes replied, giving him a sour look. "Accidents are always happening where guns are concerned."

"That's something you should keep in mind," Deal said. "For every second we're still in Cuban waters."

Fuentes might have been tempted to say something else, but Deal gave him a look that stopped him. He would have preferred to be at the helm himself, of course, but he hadn't had much choice while they were busy casting off. Now, of course, Fuentes was theoretically dispensable, a fact that had surely not eluded the old con artist.

Deal took a glance at his still-sleeping father curled up on a stack of deck cushions at the rear of the compartment. At that moment, the old man's eyes fluttered open and he croaked something that Deal couldn't quite catch over the rumbling of the engines.

"What?" he said. He bent down close to his father, his eyes still on Fuentes.

". . . give a sucker . . . an even . . . break," his old man said, the words coming in fits and starts.

Deal turned at the last, found his father's eyes closed once again. Dr. Aponte had assured him the drugs she'd administered would wear off soon enough, but there was no way of telling just when that would happen or how he'd behave when it did. That outburst in the hospital could have gotten them all killed, and even though there were none of Fuentes's henchmen left on board, Deal wasn't sure what he'd be faced with when the old man came around again.

A pretty cruel joke, he thought. Get your father handed back after all these years, but look what shape he comes in.

"Who *is* this man?" Fuentes asked, his tone slightly aggrieved. As if he might not otherwise have been kidnapped and forced to pilot his boat out of the Marina Hemingway at gunpoint.

Deal glanced up, his finger tracing the edge of the trigger guard. One little flick of the finger, he was thinking; that's all it would take. Toss what was left of Fuentes to the fishes, hope his father slept through the ride across the Straits.

"I am sorry," Fuentes added hastily. Perhaps he had read his mind, Deal thought. Maybe that's how Fuentes had lived as long as he had in the company he kept. "I was only wondering. In actuality, I do not care who it is."

Deal nodded, his eyes on Fuentes, his pistol still ready. "This is John F. Kennedy," he said, after a moment. "He never died that day in Dallas. He's been in Castro's prison all this time."

Fuentes gave him an uncertain look. "Please," he said. "I was only making conversation."

"Make some up in your own head," Deal said. "Do a little life review. You might be finding it useful soon."

Fuentes nodded, though it didn't look like he welcomed the prospect. Deal saw that sweat had come to bead on that normally unruffled brow. Good. It was about time someone else felt pressure.

"What's this thing make, flat out—about twenty knots?"

Fuentes nodded, his eyes fixed ahead. "Twenty-two, perhaps."

"Good." Deal glanced at his watch. "We'll be out of Cuban waters in a few minutes. We can make Key West before morning."

"If all goes well," Fuentes said.

"It's going to go well," Deal said. "It is going to go unbelievably well."

Deal turned to glance at his father. It *would* go well, he told himself. There was no reason to think otherwise. Boats plied the route with impunity every day. They might run the risk of being stopped by a Coast Guard cutter close to the U.S. mainland, or find themselves approached by Customs or INS at the Key West docks, but certainly they had little to fear from Cuban officials now that they were out of port. Pleasure boats came and went from the Marina Hemingway by the score, their captains encouraged to come and scatter their tourist dollars like bread crumbs, no way to keep track of comings and goings . . .

Fuentes's eyes darted toward him, then skipped quickly away. "You are making a huge mistake, you know. No matter what happened back there on land, it can be dealt with. Nothing has to change, as regards our plans . . ."

"You can save all that," Deal told him, waving the pistol. "You get us to Key West, then you're on your own. Bring someone else back to Cuba. I know plenty of builders who'll be happy for the chance."

"DealCo," Deal heard the booming voice behind him, then. He turned to see his father pushing himself up from the cushions, his eyes vacuous but suddenly owl-wide, a loopy salesman's smile on his grizzled face. It was that same manic energy that had emanated from him back in the hospital. "DealCo's who you want," he proclaimed.

"Dad . . ." Deal said. He'd noted the look in those eyes. Whomever the words were directed toward stood in some other dimension.

"I know the top dog over there," the old man bellowed in the general direction of Fuentes. "There's nothing they can't handle. Let me make a few calls . . ."

His father pushed himself up from the cushions just as the prow of the *Bellísima* dropped into a trough, then cleaved a following swell. The old man lost his balance and toppled sideways. As Deal lunged for him, he caught sight of Fuentes, clinging to the wheel with one hand, rummaging for something in a cockpit compartment with the other.

Fuentes came out with a flare pistol and was just bringing it around when Deal let his father go and strode forward, swinging his arm in a broad arc. The pistol he was holding cracked into Fuentes's arm near the wrist. There was a snapping sound that might have been a bone breaking, and a cry, followed by a muffled explosion and a jolt of sulfurous flame as the flare burst from the stubby barrel and began to careen about the closed pilothouse like some hissing, insane creature.

Deal threw one arm up over his face and bent to snatch his father by the collar. He had just dragged the old man through the pilothouse door when the flare finally burst, filling the cockpit with a blossom of brilliant red and gold. The windowpane in the door blew out in a shower of superheated glass pellets, and the force sent Deal tumbling across the deck, all the way to the transom.

Deal struggled groggily to his feet, his ears ringing from the explosion. His old man stood nearby, bent at the waist, his hands propped on his thighs, peering down at him in concern.

"How you fixed, there, son?" the old man asked.

"I'm all right," Deal said. There'd been nothing familiar in the question. Just the idle curiosity of a man who didn't know he'd damned near died.

Flames danced inside the pilothouse now, he saw. Fuentes's body had been blown halfway out one side window. The man lay motionless, head and hands dangling down as if in an endless dive.

The engines of the *Bellísima* were still laboring, he realized, though the boat had its heading and was now wallowing in the swells. "Stay right here," he said.

He pushed past his bewildered father and snatched a fire extinguisher mounted by the pilothouse door. He shoved his way inside past the inert body of Fuentes, coughing in the acrid smoke as he doused the burning boat cushions with CO_2, then kicked the smoldering remains out onto the deck and over the side.

He tossed the canister onto the deck, then hurried back into the pilothouse, tearing off his shirt and using it to clutch the blackened and smoking wheel.

The instrument panels were blank, the radio controls a melted mass. He'd expected nothing as he clutched the scorching wheel, but amazingly, the *Bellísima*'s rudder responded to his touch. In moments, he had turned the boat's prow back into the swells. He felt the engines shudder, but hold.

He glanced at his watch. Out of Cuban waters by now, he thought; they had to be. That much was good news. But how much damage had the boat received? He could smell burned plastic and rubber, but whether it was the wiring eating itself up as he stared or simply the remnants of the melted cushions was impossible to tell. Electrical fires could smolder for a long time before they blew back up full force. Little currents of flame could be burrowing down every conduit in the ship at this very moment.

He turned loose of the wheel for a second and hurried outside, searching about the decks for the fire extinguisher he'd tossed aside. He'd intended to take the canister in and give the instruments a good dousing, when he heard his father's voice.

"I'll bet this here is trouble," the old man called, his tone jolly. He was pointing back in the direction they'd come, toward a set of running lights that was rapidly closing toward them. A cutter with a searchlight sweeping the heaving waters before it, Deal saw, and at the same time he remembered something.

"Come in here and hold this wheel," he called to the old man. "Do you think you can do that?"

The old man stared at him, offended. "Of course I can. Just who the hell do you think you're talking to?"

"I wish I knew," Deal said. Then he was off and running toward the saloon and the heavy teak table where he'd planted that listening device on a day that seemed to have existed about a hundred years ago.

39.

"The signal's gone," the technician at the console said, glancing up at Vines.

Vines pointed at the man's earphones. "You mean the audio's out?"

The man stared back at him patiently. "I mean we've lost the signal altogether."

Vines glanced at Russell Straight and Driscoll, who stood nearby in the cramped control room, then turned back to his technician. It could have been a recording studio or command central for a radio station, but they were an unlikely-looking foursome for the entertainment field.

"Maybe they're out of range," Vines said.

The technician stared his patient stare. "They're out of Cuban waters," he said. "They're not out of range."

"Then what's wrong?" Russell said.

"Maybe nothing," Driscoll said. His expression suggested otherwise.

"Give me those coordinates," Vines said.

The technician nodded and punched a series of buttons on his console. In moments a sheet chunked up from a clattering printer. The technician glanced at the sheet, then handed it over to Vines.

Vines studied it briefly, then offered something like a smile as he pushed by Driscoll and Russell Straight.

"Hey," Russell called as Vines headed off down a narrow hallway. "What about Deal? Where are you going?"

"To start World War Three," Vines called back. And then he was gone.

40.

"We must turn back," the captain of the Cuban vessel said. "We are no longer in Cuban waters."

"We will turn back soon," Zeneas told him, his expression resolute. He put his finger on the blip that formed at ten o'clock when the cutter's radar made its sweep. "When we complete our business."

The captain shook his head, tracing an imaginary line between the cutter and the motor yacht they had pursued. "It is impossible," the Captain said. "The Americans . . ."

Zeneas pressed his hand down atop the captain's. The man caught his breath, suddenly unable to speak. There came the faint sound of cracking glass, and a bubble of blood oozed slowly down the broken face of the radar screen.

"The Americans are not here to bother us," Zeneas said. "Do you see any Americans out there? Do you see a sign that says 'Turn Back'?"

The captain's face was ashen, but he managed to shake his head. "Nor do I," Zeneas said. "Let us complete our mission and then go home."

He withdrew his hand from atop the captain's and stood staring. "Call your weapons room, Captain. I won't waste another instant with you."

The captain stared down at his bleeding hand, then back at Zeneas. He glanced at the door that led from the command bridge. Zeneas could see the thoughts that paraded behind the man's eyes as if he were inside his brain. He had heard the stories. They all had.

The captain nodded curtly, then picked up the intercom. "Lock torpedoes on target," he said.

Something was spoken on the other end, and the captain repeated his command. Zeneas listened for a moment, then gave a final nod.

The captain depressed the key with a finger of his good hand and gave the command. There was a faint shudder and a burst of flame as the first of the deck-mounted torpedoes left the cutter and splashed down into the water, followed closely by a second.

"Take no chances, Captain," Zeneas said, his eyes fixed on a point in the darkness before them. The motor yacht had ceased to send its homing signal and had doused its running lights, but that had come too late. It would make no difference now.

The captain spoke again into his microphone. A third shudder moved through the steel superstructure beneath Zeneas's feet, and then a fourth. Zeneas smiled, watching the faintly phosphorescent trails unfurl out into the darkness. It only pained him that he would not be there to see the expression on the old man's face.

41.

THE PILOT of the F-16 was screaming just above the wavetops of the Florida Straits at less than fifty feet, not all that unusual when skirting this close to Cuban waters. Normally, they held their runs thirty miles or so out from shore, but these were not normal circumstances.

In any event, his altitude might not necessarily keep him off the enemy's radar screens, but it wouldn't make things any easier for them, either. Less than ten minutes before, he'd been sitting in the ready room of the Noble Eagle Alert Facility on the grounds of Homestead Air Reserve Base at the southern tip of the Florida mainland, whiling away his duty stretch by watching a Clancy film on DVD. It had just gotten to the part where the Nazi who'd blown up the Super Bowl was about to climb into his sedan and turn the key that would splatter his body parts across a goodly portion of Munich when the call came in.

The pilot was airborne inside of four minutes, and less than five minutes after that had picked up the two blips now displayed on the radar screen just above his left knee. He was closing on the first, in fact, when the first explosion tore the sky apart just in front of him.

"Holy shit!" he called, as the fireball blossomed a few hundred yards away. He pulled hard on the stick, banking away as the invisible force field buffeted the plane. A few seconds later and the explosion might have taken him out. At first, in fact, he had taken it for enemy fire and was calculating his response as he spiraled skyward, automatically locked in evasive mode.

As he came out of a roll, already three miles up, he caught sight of the mushroom cloud that rose high above the water below and realized what had happened. He checked the radar display at his knee again and confirmed his suspicions. Where two blips had appeared only moments before, only one now displayed. And that craft appeared to be turning in a wide arc, heading back the way it had come.

The pilot leveled off the F-16 and pressed the button that opened his secure line. It took less than a minute to describe the situation and to receive his orders. Before the Cuban vessel had quite completed its turn, the pilot of the F-16 had activated the other cockpit screen, the four-by-four square that glowed just above his right knee like the readout of a miniature arcade game. The two AGM Mavericks that the F-16 carried were G class, containing chips and circuitry that allowed them to make target entry just at waterline.

And they would be so instructed in this case, the pilot thought. He made the proper entries on his keypad to arm the missiles, and then the F-16 dove.

Zeneas was already out of the command cabin and moving along the rail toward the ship's stern, when he noticed a young seaman bursting through the opposite door of the compartment, shouting something at the cutter's still-glowering captain, waving a scrap of paper torn from a printer and jabbing frantically toward the sky.

Zeneas turned to glance into the inky darkness and saw nothing at first. The smoky haze that had lingered following the explosion of the *Bellísima* had begun to dissipate, though, and gradually the sight took shape: At first it was a tiny wedge of darkness against the slightly lighter backdrop of sky, but it was growing larger at an alarming rate, doubling and redoubling its size by the instant.

A jet, he realized, the noise of its engines still yet to catch up with its incredibly expanding shadow. Americans, he thought next, and felt a smile of satisfaction cross his features. A bit too late for the cavalry's charge, wasn't it?

He might have made some gesture of insult, in fact, if he'd thought the pilot could see it. And that is when he saw the burst of white smoke bloom at one wingtip of the approaching jet, followed in the next moment by another.

Something lurched inside Zeneas's chest, his body registering the truth of what was to come even before his mind could comprehend. He turned toward the command bridge, as the jet soared on past the cutter, banking up and away even as the thundering roar of its engines washed over him.

"We are in Cuban waters . . . " he cried, hearing indignation and outrage in his voice. It could not happen, he was thinking. It would not be countenanced by the regime . . .

His hand had just fallen upon the lever that would open the door to the bridge compartment when he felt the strange sensation: exhilaration at first, a sense of being propelled through an open portal to somewhere at amazing speed. There was heat, too—one searing jolt of it—along with a brilliant flash of light that also brought with it the agony.

Melting, he thought. *What it means to melt . . .*

And then there was one more pillar of flame leaping up toward the nighttime sky, and finally, there was nothing at all.

42.

The Florida Straits
Dawn

Bits of wreckage, little of it recognizable, littered the swells, which were moderate this day—no more than six to eight feet—and still gray in the early light. There were bits of styrofoam and chunks of wood and some of fiberglass, along with an occasional plastic jug or bottle and scrap of cloth mixed in with clots of seaweed and bits of matter too vague to be distinguished.

There was no evidence really that any of it had been part of any boat destroyed. It could all have simply been swept out to sea along with the normal, steady exodus of trash from Havana Harbor.

The last was the idle thought that crossed Deal's mind as he dug his tiny paddle into the gray water, trying to keep the nose of the raft pointed into the waves. His old man held a paddle, too, but he was making no normal use of it. He held the thing upside down, in fact, and was tracing his finger along the flat surface of its business end as if a message had been printed there.

"You say this fellow you're talking about"—the old man broke off and glanced up at Deal—"this Barton Deal . . ."

"That's you," Deal said, digging his paddle deep. "*You're* Barton Deal."

"Whoever he is," the old man said with a dismissive wave. "This fellow pretended to kill himself and then ran off to Cuba, never even told his family?"

"He never did," Deal said. He tried to meet the old man's gaze, but those eyes were locked somewhere on another place.

The old man snorted. "Why would a man do such a thing?" he said, disbelief evident in his tone.

"I don't know," Deal said. "I've been hoping you might tell me."

The old man glanced at him. "How the hell would *I* know?"

Deal stared back. Not a glimmer in those steely eyes. "You could help with the paddling, at least," he said. "For all we know, we'll wash right back to Cuba."

The old man snorted again. "You don't know anything, do you? This here is the Gulf Stream, boy. All we have to do is stay afloat. We'll end up in Europe one day."

"You seem awfully confident."

"I've read what the big fellow says, that's all."

"What big fellow?"

The old man gave him a disgusted look, then consulted his paddle and began to recite, as if the words were printed in front of him: "*. . . this Stream has moved, as it moves, since before man, and* *that it has gone by the shoreline of that long, beautiful unhappy island since before Columbus sighted it . . ."*

He broke off there to command Deal's attention with a snap of his fingers. "That's Cuba we're talking about, you know."

Deal nodded. "I guessed as much."

"Only because I told you."

"Dad . . ."

The old man held up an imperious hand. "Just listen," he said. *". . . because that stream will flow, as it has flowed, after the Indians, after the Spaniards, after the British, after the Americans and after all the Cubans and all the systems of governments are all gone . . ."*

The old man was staring at him with an imploring look on his face now. "That's how we know we'll get to Europe, don't you see."

"I'm afraid I don't," Deal said. "Not without food and water."

"Food and water, my eye," the old man said, sweeping his arm out over the sea. "You're not paying attention . . ."

He was off again, then: *". . . the palm fronds of our victories, the worn lightbulbs of our discoveries and the empty condoms of our great loves float with no significance against one single, lasting thing—the stream."* The old man concluded with a dramatic flourish and sat quietly staring at him, waiting.

"That's amazing," Deal said, finally. His shoulders were aching and he longed simply to slide back and drift, though that would surely mean the end.

"It's better than that," the old man said. "It's Hemingway."

Deal shook his head, savoring the five seconds' respite as the raft slid down the side of a swell. "I mean, how you remember all that, and you don't even know your name."

"Who says I don't?" the old man demanded, his eyes flashing

sudden fury. "Who the hell are you to talk to me like that? I've bested many a better man than you, my boy."

With that, he snatched up the paddle by its handle and swung it without warning, the leading edge narrowly missing Deal's skull. He was positioning himself for another backhanded swipe when Deal let go of his own paddle and did the only thing he could.

He leaned forward, bracing himself with one hand, driving the heel of his other into the point of the old man's chin. His old man's eyes blinked once, then closed as if a switch had been thrown. In the next second, he had slumped over sideways in the raft.

Deal stared for a moment until he saw the rise and fall of his old man's chest begin. He shook his head, then picked up the paddle the old man had dropped. It was dawn now, the sun a slivered red thumbprint on the eastern horizon. He glanced at the flat face of the paddle, just to be sure, then gave his father another glance before he tossed the thing overboard and began to row again.

He could do this, he told himself, as the waves rose and fell before him. Thousands before him had. He would do it for as long as he possibly could.

43.

"YOU GOING to let us know exactly what happened?" Driscoll asked Vines.

He and Russell and the government agent had the flying bridge of the Coast Guard cutter to themselves, now that Vines's man had descended back to the communications room to monitor the progress of the search. There hadn't been much time to talk since the moment Vines had come to rush them from the reconnaissance center at the Interests Section. There had been an accident with the *Bellísima*, that's all he would say. A search was being mounted in the Florida Straits.

While it had still been dark, the three of them had been driven to a small fishing village just east of the city, where they'd boarded what looked like a smaller version of Fuentes's yacht, piloted by a crew that seemed as Cuban as it was possible to get. Inside an hour, they'd rendezvoused with the Coast Guard cutter and transferred on board.

Now, it was well past dawn and half a dozen ships were out in the Straits, or so they'd just been informed, and a pair of reconnaissance planes had been diverted from their normal drug-intercept surveillance to join the search. Still, there were hundreds of square miles of featureless water to cover. Every day drug runners in boats the size of freight cars found their way to Florida undetected. What were the chances of finding two men adrift and bobbing in these waves? For that matter, what were the chances that they had survived the sinking of the *Bellísima* to begin with?

"It's a pretty simple story," Vines said without taking his binoculars from his eyes. "There were two ships out here—the one we had our eye on and a Cuban naval vessel following it." He turned and dropped the binoculars, staring at the two of them bleakly. "First, the *Bellísima* disappeared." He raised an eyebrow. "Now the Cuban vessel's gone as well."

"You can do better than that," Driscoll said.

"Not officially I can't," Vines said.

"I don't give a crap about official," Russell Straight said, staring past Driscoll.

"Hold on," Driscoll said, holding Russell off. He turned back to Vines.

"Are you saying the Cubans sank the boat that Deal was on?"

Vines stared back at him, his expression glum.

"And then something happened to this Cuban boat, too?"

Vines lifted his hands in a helpless gesture. "I can't tell you how it all played out. All I can say is that the *Bellísima* is missing."

"Fucking-A," Russell muttered, still struggling in Driscoll's grip.

"That's not going to do much good," Driscoll said.

Vines nodded, then undraped the binoculars from his neck. "He's right," the agent said, thrusting the glasses toward Russell. "Why not try doing something worthwhile."

44.

DEAL HAD no idea how long the sun had been up, but it seemed like a long time. Complicating it all was the fact of his vision. Whenever he tried to read his watch, the numbers pulsed and waved in a way that made figuring time impossible. He had discovered himself unbuttoning his shirt, however, and had forced himself to stop, remembering that undressing yourself was what happened to people who became delirious with thirst.

Counterproductive to strip down, actually. The more skin exposed to the sun, the quicker the cooking. Then again, he thought, maybe it would be best. Maybe his old man had the right idea. He had yet to reawaken after the blow that had sent him under.

Good going, Deal. Put your old man in a coma. Now die.

He noticed his hands fumbling automatically with the buttons of his shirt. Who cares, really. Strip down, maybe go for a swim.

He found himself thinking of Angelica, then. Wasn't that her name? She'd undressed him and that had gone quite well, if deliriously.

A voice from another country suggested that he might never see that woman again if he let this tiny boat founder. Once in the water without vests, they'd be sunk.

A good one, Deal. Sunk. Har-de-har-har.

He saw other faces swim past his hard-to-focus eyes. There was Janice, of course, and Mrs. Suarez, and the one that stopped him cold for a moment.

Dear Isabel. How lonely he would be swimming in the deep without her. How tired he was, though. How sorry he felt that Daddy could not explain.

There was Daddy lying at his feet, in fact. That man had not bothered to do any explaining of his own, either.

Oh my, Deal thought. How hard this life had been.

It was time to rest. He could not deny it. He brought his paddle to his breast and lay back. His head struck the survival box, and he reached to move it aside.

There was a flare pistol inside, which he'd meant to use at a time when it might do some good.

His shirt had somehow come off, he noted. Still, he'd fire the pistol.

He cocked it and held it firmly in both hands and believed it to be pointing skyward when he fired. There was a popping sound, and a recoil, and a puff of smoke up high somewhere, but not the kind of fireworks you'd see if it were night. Oh well.

He was comfortable there on the cushiony floor of the boat,

the water slipping under him like silk, now, and splashing over him as well. He couldn't help but close his eyes.

He thought he felt the paddle being lifted from his chest. He thought he saw an old man rise grimly above him, digging into the water for all he was worth, but visions are a dime a dozen when you're around the bend.

He wasn't sure how long it took until the violent wind began to press down upon him and the water came alive with sudden waves. It was the mark of the end, though; he understood that much.

He saw something huge and dark and sharp-winged sinking down upon him, until it had blotted out the very sun. The angel that comes, he thought.

So sorry, Isabel. So sorry, old man. So sorry, Angelica and everyone. So long.

45.

". . . HE NO LONGER *dreamed of storms, nor of women, nor of great occurrences, nor of great fish, nor fights, nor contests of strength, nor of his wife . . ."*

The words drifted down to Deal in a halting monotone, the voice familiar but otherworldly, as seemed only befitting. He was floating along somewhere, high up and wherever it is you go, wrapped in a giant cotton cloud, a vague light hovering above his eyes, a sense of peace and well-being pervading all. It was only right, he thought, after all the goddamned struggle his life had been.

"He only dreamed of places now," the voice continued, *"and of the lions on the beach. They played like young cats in the dusk and he loved them as he loved the boy."*

It was a very familiar voice, he realized, and the words were not so much being spoken as read aloud. Truly he had died and gone somewhere else, but what kind of afterworld was it that featured Russell Straight reciting the works of Hemingway?

"Are you waking up?" He heard another voice then, this one much closer by. Another man he'd come to trust in that other realm, he was thinking. "It's about damn time, I'd say."

Deal felt his eyes come open. He lay quietly, seeing nothing but whiteness hovering above him. A skyscape as blank as a popcorn-finish ceiling, he thought, another odd feature of the afterworld.

But that is exactly what he was staring at, he realized. The popcorned ceiling of a cool and dimly lit institutional room.

Furthermore, no angels hovering there. Just the face of beefy ex-detective Vernon Driscoll peering down at him in concern.

"Welcome back," Driscoll was saying. "You been out the best part of a day, my man."

Deal blinked as Driscoll's face wavered in and out of focus. He tried to speak, but his tongue felt far too thick.

His head lolled back on his pillow and he found himself staring now at a silver pole with a hook that held a plastic fluid sack. He traced the plastic tube that ran from the bottom of the bag down to the rail of a hospital bed, and then to an arm that lay on a mattress. He realized finally that the flesh the tubing was fastened to was his own.

Driscoll was nodding as he turned back. "They spotted you just in time. You two wouldn't have made it another day out there. Kind of gives you a new appreciation of what all the rafters go through, doesn't it?"

Deal worked his tongue at his swollen lips. "Two?" he managed. It sounded as if someone with a boozer's ruined foghorn voice was speaking.

"Yeah," the ex-cop said, nodding. "He made it. He's in the next room, still unconscious, though. That's Russell over there reading to him. The nurses said it might help bring him around." Driscoll pointed over his shoulder with his thumb. Russell's recitation had quieted, but the cadences still rumbled though the wall.

Deal had spotted a water pitcher by this time—a blue plastic obelisk flanked by a couple of matching glasses on a nearby table. He pointed, and Driscoll reached to pour for him.

Deal drank the water greedily, spilling some of the cold liquid down his cheeks and neck. "Better take it easy, pards," Driscoll began. "Maybe I ought to get a nurse in here."

Driscoll's hand was headed for the call button, but Deal caught him by the sleeve. Deal used the strength in the big man's arm to pull himself up to a sitting position. He waited for the walls about him to stop their pulsing, then fought his gaze into focus on Driscoll. He had another hit of the water, then willed his unwieldy tongue into action.

"Help me up," he said to Driscoll, swinging his legs out over the side of the bed.

"Hey . . ." Driscoll began, but stopped when Deal held up his hand.

"I'm all right," he said, his voice croaking.

"Yeah, sure you are," Driscoll said.

"I want to see the old man," Deal said. He had his feet on the cool tiles of the floor now.

"There's plenty of time for that . . ."

Deal yanked the IV out of his arm and reached for Driscoll. *"Now,"* he said.

Driscoll glanced down at the wad of shirt Deal was holding in his fist. Deal unclenched the fabric.

"Come on, Vernon," Deal managed, "help me out here."

Driscoll hesitated for a second, then muttered a curse. He hooked his arm about Deal's shoulders and heaved him up from the bed, then waited as Deal got his footing steady.

"Okay," Deal said. "Let's go."

Inside the next room, Russell Straight sat in an uncomfortable-looking gray-metal chair at the bedside of the old man, tracing his finger along the page of a paperback book as he read. When he heard the commotion at the door, he glanced up.

"What the hell?" he said. He rose from his chair, his finger bookmarking his page. He took a step toward Deal and Driscoll, a smile slowly erasing the surprise on his coppered features. "We thought you were history there for a while."

Deal nodded, reaching to clasp Russell's outstretched hand. "Me, too," he said. He untangled himself from Driscoll's grasp and moved on toward the silent figure in the hospital bed.

"How's he doing?" he said. He'd reached the bedside now and stood steadying himself with a hand on one of the rails.

"The doc says all his vital signs check out okay," Russell's voice came from over Deal's shoulder. "He just doesn't seem to want to wake up."

Deal stared down at the old man's grizzled face. "He was awake out there on the raft. He kept us going after I folded up."

"Is that so?"

Deal turned to see the doubtful expression on Driscoll's face. "I caved in," Deal said. "Passed out. I looked up right before the helicopter found us—he was at the controls."

Driscoll shrugged. "Whatever happened, you made it."

True enough, Deal thought. Why argue the point? He turned, staring down at his father's sleeping face. Even if he'd imagined that his old man had taken over the paddling, what did it matter? That was nothing compared to the fact that he lay here before him now.

"By the way," Driscoll was saying, "we had a hell of a time getting hold of Janice and Isabel. They were all in some smoke lodge on top of a frigging mountain in New Mexico. They had to send an Indian hiking in on foot to tell them. They should be in Key West sometime this evening."

Deal nodded and gave Driscoll a grateful smile. He'd get to see his daughter again after all.

"Janice was pretty upset when she heard about it," Driscoll continued, "what with all the fuss in the papers and everything."

Deal stared at him, uncomprehending. "Papers?"

"Man, you don't know what kind of fuss you caused," Russell said. "You're the biggest thing since the Cubans went after Brothers to the Rescue."

"What are you talking about?"

"The Cuban boat that blew you out of the water, that's what I'm talking about. Exploded and sunk out there in the Straits, all hands missing, including the head of Cuban State Security, some guy named Zeneas. The Cubans claim one of our fighters did it."

Deal stared at him. "Did we?"

Russell shrugged. "Ask Vines, if you can find him."

"So far, your name's been kept out of it, on both sides," Driscoll said. "The Cubans claim it was an unprovoked attack on one of their ships that was in protected waters."

"What do we say?"

"Nothing, officially," Driscoll said. "So far as the U.S. is concerned, the Cuban boat went down in international waters, there must have been some kind of accident on board. There's been no mention of Fuentes, the *Bellísima,* any of that business."

"How long do you figure that's going to last?"

Driscoll gave his all-purpose shrug. "For as long *you* want, I'm guessing. The Cubans have no motivation to let it be known what their ship was doing out there that night, and we sure as hell don't, either."

Deal stared back, letting it all sink in.

"I just wish I'd been there to see that Cuban boat go down," Russell said.

"It was a bright light in the sky," Deal said.

"I'll bet," Driscoll said, giving him a look. "Of course, nobody knew at the time that you'd made it."

Deal gave him a look. "I wasn't so sure we had."

"Hey, I almost forgot," Russell said. "The woman who helped you get your old man out . . . she met us at the dock just after you took off with Fuentes. She gave me something for you."

Deal turned to find Russell digging in his pants pocket. "Here," he said, extending his hand. "She said you'd want this."

Deal stared down at the gold signet ring in Russell's open palm. A hundred images seemed to explode inside his head simultaneously, accompanied by an array of emotions that seemed just as diverse and bewildering. Resentment. Anger. Most of all the ache of loss.

"Yes," he heard himself saying. He reached to take the ring from Russell and hefted it for a moment in his own palm. As a child, he'd sometimes begged his father to let him hold the ring, had been amazed by its density, by its *is*-ness that exuded his father's very being.

The sort of thing that matters to children, he thought. As if you could hold the whole of a person you loved cupped inside your hand.

"It's his, you know." He nodded at the sleeping form before them, then reached for his father's hand. The ring slipped easily onto the old man's finger, Deal noted, a fact that gave him little comfort.

"Hard to believe he's back," Driscoll said at his shoulder.

"It is," Deal said. He turned after a moment and gave Driscoll a speculative look. "I don't suppose you know anything about that night he disappeared, how he made it out of the country and all that?"

Driscoll's face registered surprise. "You're kidding, I hope."

"I'm asking, that's all. Someone in the department had to have been in on it."

"Well, it wasn't me, buddy boy."

"There was something else I heard mentioned, too," Deal said. "A pot of money he left behind, supposed to tide my mother and me over."

Driscoll stared back at him. "Maybe whoever it was who helped your old man out of the country misplaced it."

"Anything is possible," Deal said. "It remains a mystery, though."

Driscoll nodded. "It does indeed." He pointed at something over Deal's shoulder. "Maybe the old boy can help us out with it."

Deal turned, realized with a start that the old man's eyes were open. He felt the slightest pressure at his hand and glanced down to see his father's fingers clasping his own.

"How about it, old man?" he found himself saying. "Are you coming back to join us, then?"

The old man blinked. "I thought I heard someone telling a story," he said. He glanced dazedly around the room, at Driscoll and Russell, then back at Deal. "I like a good story," his old man said at last. "Why don't we hear some more?"